# END STREET VOLUME 3

RJ SCOTT

AMBER KELL

Love Lane Books

# End Street Volume 3

**Including: The Case of the Purple Pearl & The Case of the Guilty Ghost**

Copyright ©2013-2015, 2024 Amber Kell, Copyright ©2013-2015, 2024 RJ Scott

Cover design by Meredith Russell

ISBN: 9781785645662

*For everyone who loves End Street, and always for our families.*

# THE CASE OF THE

*Purple Pearl*

# Chapter One

"WHAT ARE YOU DOING?"

Sam sighed. This was the fifth time today their visiting gargoyle had asked him that. Three weeks had passed since it had decided to stay at the house and wait for Sam to find it a master. And those three weeks had lasted a very long time.

"Taxes," Sam muttered. The same answer he'd given every single time he'd been asked.

"I don't like math," the little gargoyle said. He waddled across Sam's desk, leaving small muddy footprints on a neatly filled-in form. Sam couldn't even muster the energy to get angry.

"Are you going to tell me your name yet?" Sam asked. He placed his pen on the desk and leaned back with a stretch, eying the small gargoyle against the hulking monstrosity that sat immobile on the corner of his desk. They were so dissimilar, in size and expression.

"You know I can only tell my master."

"I can't keep calling you the little gargoyle. I'm going to have to give you a name."

The little gargoyle turned in a circle to face Sam, then

squatted into a pose with his mouth open in a snarl. It looked pretty mean, and Sam edged back.

"What's wrong?" he asked.

The gargoyle's expression changed back to the one he usually had; that of a dopey baby.

"Nothing, I was just giving you my fierce face so you can give me the right name. I'm not having you calling me Sunshine or Cutie. I want something strong like Zephariel Angel of Vengeance."

Sam couldn't help the snort of laughter, then immediately felt guilty when the gargoyle's expression fell. "Sorry," he apologized. "It's just, uhm, that name is taken. How about Leo, like a lion, a brave, strong lion."

The gargoyle tilted his head in contemplation, then nodded. "Leo, I like Leo. I'm done with you now. You already have a gargoyle. I'm going to find my true master."

That decided, he jumped down off the desk and waddled over to the door, sidestepping awkwardly when Smudge slunk in with intent in every step. In a leap, Smudge was up on the desk, sitting right on the tax forms and staring straight into Sam's face.

"*What are you doing?*" Smudge asked telepathically.

"Taxes," Sam answered. He didn't add a sigh this time.

"*You should be tracking down what kind of other your uncle's pet gargoyle is.*"

Leo, the newly named visiting gargoyle, had declared that the old paperweight on Sam's desk that looked like a gargoyle, walked like a gargoyle, and was stone like a gargoyle, wasn't actually a gargoyle at all, but *other.*

"Where do you suggest I start? And why can't you tell what it is, oh powerful familiar." Sam couldn't help the sarcasm. Smudge was capable of putting souls back in bodies and using heavy magic, but he couldn't track down what kind of paranormal had been transformed into an ancient crumbling gargoyle paperweight?

"*I'll forget you said that,*" Smudge said condescendingly. "*I've been busy.*"

"With what?" Sam asked. Privately he thought Smudge spent too much time cleaning himself with his paws up in the air and his tongue—

"*I can hear you,*" Smudge warned. "*And who else do you think can keep your attic spider infestation at bay?*"

Sam shuddered. He didn't like small spiders at best, let alone the giant ones Smudge had suggested lived only a few floors up. "Good work," Sam praised. "And as to our paperweight friend here—" Sam tapped the solid stone *thing* on the head with a stapler. "—I've put out a request to everyone I know as to who may be missing someone. I used the ParaGoogle to see if anyone knows anything. Not sure what else I can do at this stage."

Smudge gave a feline version of a huff, deliberately washed himself on the desk for a good five minutes, then disappeared out of the room. Sam shook off the fur that had fallen on his paperwork. This needed to be done and, unless he finished it soon, he'd have the authorities fining him all over the place.

A knock on his office door jerked Sam from his sad contemplation of the bills he had to pay. Although he'd earned some money recently and he owned the building where he worked and lived, the flow of money going out far exceeded the money rushing into his pockets.

Taxes were a bitch.

"Come in!" he shouted.

Sam lifted an eyebrow at the sight of the dark-haired man entering his office. The strangest part of his visitor was his apparent ordinariness. The man's eyes didn't glow with vampire ire, he didn't growl with pent-up werewolf angst, and his average height and weight could only be explained one way. Human. He must be lost.

"Sorry, I knocked on the front door but no one answered. I hope you don't mind me letting myself in." The man indicated the entrance with a vague wave.

"No. Of course not." Sam would have to learn to either lock his outer door or get an alarm of some kind. The doorbell had stopped working a few days ago, and Sam suspected their water heater might be ready to explode at any moment. Bob swore it would be fine, but it gurgled at Sam the last time he went to the basement to get the laundry. He might have to give in and hire a handyman. Neither he nor Bob were very useful around the house.

"I'm Abbott Williams. I heard you were a detective." The man held up a flyer as if that explained his presence.

Sam stood to shake hands. "I'm Sam Enderson. Nice to meet you. Yes, I am a detective." He accepted the yellow paper Abbott handed over. It listed Sam's detective agency, their location on a little map, and little else. It did have a nice picture of the building, though. "I don't remember having any flyers printed up."

Abbott shrugged. "I found it at the bar down the street. Anyway, I need you to follow my boyfriend around. I think he's cheating on me. Are you interested in the job or not?"

Sam tossed the flyer on his desk to study later. Bob probably made them and forgot to tell Sam about it. "Break up with him. That's what I did."

"Some guy cheated on you?" Abbott made it sound as if he couldn't imagine such a thing happening.

"Yep. But I got over it." At least that's what Sam kept telling himself whenever he thought of his ex's betrayal. Bob usually pulled him out of the bad memories with a blowjob. Worked every time.

The young man's mouth tightened in annoyance. "I can't just break up with him."

"Why not? If you really suspect he's cheating on you, he probably is." Sam knew from his own experience that glossing over problems in a relationship didn't improve the situation. "You're better off without him."

"I don't want to be without him. I love him."

"If he loved you back he wouldn't cheat," Sam said flatly. He'd hate to be the one who had to tell Abbott he'd been right about his boyfriend.

"I can pay," Abbott insisted. He pulled a wad of cash out of his pocket and tossed it on the desk. "I don't want you to do anything else. I want to know the truth. Just find out if he's cheating. After that, I can decide what to do."

The man's desperate words struck a chord with Sam. Of course, so did Abbott's nice crinkly stack of bills. "Have a seat and tell me all about this boyfriend of yours."

What could it hurt to do a little surveillance? After all, hadn't Sam gotten into this business to help people? Surely hunting down one human and taking some pictures would be way easier than the other stuff he was always tangled up in. Bob should be happy that Sam finally got a non-supernatural case. At least this time no one would be trying to set him on fire.

Once he'd settled in the chair opposite Sam, Abbott handed over a photo. "This is Greg."

Sam took the picture Abbott handed over. A dark-haired man with green eyes looked back at him.

"He's cute."

"I know," Abbott said.

"Okay," Sam began. "I'll take the case, but the usual

proviso is that if I find something you don't like, the End Street Detective Agency can't be held responsible."

Abbott nodded. "I understand."

Sam pushed across the requisite forms and disclaimers, which Abbott signed. They shook hands, and then Abbott gave some extra details about places and dates and where Sam might find the philandering boyfriend before he left.

Sam counted the money; easily enough to cover the bills for the next two weeks.

A quick, easy job for good money.

Now *this* was what being a private detective was all about.

## Chapter Two

BOB STARED AT SAM AS IF HE'D TURNED GREEN AND GROWN two extra heads.

"You took a cheating partner case, the kind of case which you despise and once likened to a devil's ass, *just* because the client is human?"

Sam rolled his eyes. Dealing with his vampire boyfriend sometimes took more work than anything else in his life. Bob tended to dislike any decision Sam made without him.

"It's a job, and besides, the guy he's looking for doesn't look human."

"A job that sends you to a questionable location," Bob argued, ignoring Sam's statement. He folded his arms across his chest and glared down at Sam.

"If you're scared you don't have to go with me," Sam said.

Bob growled. "If I hadn't come home in time you would've been out there on your own."

"I would've been fine." It wasn't as if Sam couldn't take care of himself. He might not know how to use them most of the time, but he did have magical abilities.

"Don't ever take a case without me again."

Sam sighed. Bob's earnest expression cut him deep. He could ignore the vampire when he became bossy, but the endearing concern in Bob's eyes twisted the guilt-formed knife in Sam's chest.

"I'm not completely helpless, and I'm not going to ask permission. I'm a grown man."

"A grown man who could be heading into a setup." Bob slid a strand of Sam's hair back behind his ear.

"What are you talking about?" Had he missed a chunk of conversation somewhere? He thought they were discussing his recklessness in taking a case without Bob's approval. Now they were talking possible double-dealings. Had Bob been watching Sam's old detective movies again?

"You have made some enemies, Sam. The sirens alone would love to get their hands on you. You can't assume everyone is going to tell you the truth."

"He wasn't lying." Sam didn't know how, but he knew Abbott had been sincere. "Let's go and find his boyfriend."

"Where'd you get the camera?" Bob asked when Sam pulled it out of the camera bag on his shoulder.

"I found it in the file room closet. I'm hoping it works. I don't think my smartphone will zoom in enough to get a good photo in this light."

"Does that one still use film?" Bob frowned at the camera.

"No. It's not that old. It's digital." Sam didn't know why but he'd felt compelled to bring the camera with him. His old camera had died a few months ago, and he hadn't replaced it. Finding this one in the file room closet had seemed fortuitous.

"Take a picture of me." Bob stood up straight and struck a pose.

"Why?"

"To test if it's working. Besides, then you'd have a picture of me." Sam didn't ask if cameras worked on vampires. Bob tended to take offense when Sam asked innocent questions like that. As if Sam should have some deeper knowledge of vampires *just* because he was mated to one.

Sam shrugged. He took off the lens cap then shot a picture of Bob. He checked the viewfinder for the picture and froze as he stared at the image. "That's weird."

"What is it?" Bob asked, wrapping an arm around Sam. He peeked over Sam's shoulder to get a look.

"Somehow I got in the picture." Sam showed the camera screen to Bob. It revealed a misty outline of Sam standing beside Bob.

Bob took the camera. "Let me test something."

Before he could refuse, Bob took a picture of Sam. He waited as his lover examined the screen.

"Well?"

Bob shrugged. "I think there's something weird with this camera. Maybe it's enchanted."

He turned the camera, and Sam saw Bob standing beside Sam, again in a misty shape.

"Huh. What do you think it means?"

Bob handed back the camera. "I don't know. It could be a soul camera."

"It took my soul?" Sam gasped. He should've known better than to touch his dead uncle's things. Nothing he'd known about his uncle had turned out to be true.

"No. It shows a person's soul mate. That would make sense, since it showed us each other," Bob concluded, with a smug expression.

"Hmm." Sam refused to support such a stupid theory. "I'll take some more pictures later and see what happens."

Bob rolled his eyes. "Don't try to overthink this. We were meant to be together; the camera proves it."

"Yes, but it won't help me with my current case. Abbott isn't going to understand if I send him pictures with some shadowy shape next to his boyfriend. How am I going to explain that?"

Bob pulled a small digital camera from his pocket. "We can use this one."

"Always prepared, aren't you?"

"I try. I wouldn't want you to blow your first human case."

Sam didn't say anything. He hated that Bob had to constantly save him from his mistakes.

"It's not like that, my love." Bob kissed Sam's cheek. "Consider me one of those essential accessories."

"Like a Swiss Army knife?"

"Yep, you should never leave home without me."

Sam raised an eyebrow. "I think that's a credit card ad."

Bob shrugged. "It's still true."

THEY WALKED to where Abbot had said Greg hung out after work. It turned out the café was only a few blocks from the detective agency. True to Abbot's statement, Greg was meeting a man at the café down the road from where he worked.

"Shh." Sam spied the man in Abbott's picture. Greg. "There he is."

A man with strawberry-blond hair stood way too close to Abbott's boyfriend. They paused outside the café to kiss. Sam watched the kiss with clinical detachment. Greg was attempting to clutch the blond but was being held at arm's length as he tried for a close embrace.

The blond looked around him, along the empty street, and Sam saw his hands began to glow.

"What is he doing?"

"Absorbing Greg's energy," Bob answered.

"He can't do that!" Sam stepped forward to interfere.

"No." Bob clamped a hand on Sam's shoulder. "We don't know what he is. He could be dangerous."

"So we let him suck the other guy dry? What if he's an incubus?"

"He's not." Bob's firm grip prevented Sam from running to help. With his other hand, he offered Sam the small digital camera. "Quick, take a picture."

Sam's hands shook as he lifted his uncle's large camera instead. Lining up the shot, he took a photo of the blond. Sam glanced at the result. "Oh, wow. Wait, this doesn't make any sense." He shook the camera like that was going to change what he saw on the screen. When he peered at the image again he realized shaking it hadn't cleared up one single thing.

"What?" Bob glanced at the camera's screen and for once appeared to have nothing to say.

Sam didn't know why but if Bob's theory about soul mates was right, the mysterious blond belonged to someone no one would expect. The gargoyle that sat on Sam's desk.

## Chapter Three

BOB FOLLOWED SAM INTO THE OFFICE AND WATCHED AS SAM poked the gargoyle sitting on the desk with his keys.

"He doesn't like to be poked," Bob offered helpfully. He'd seen Sam's expression when he'd looked at the photo, and it wasn't one he understood.

"How can a stone creature be the soul mate of some emotion-sucking incubus," Sam said as he poked at the gargoyle again. "Sometimes I don't get this whole world." He sounded so confused that Bob's protective nature surged forward.

He moved behind Sam then wrapped his arms around Sam's waist and pulled him close. "I don't understand this any more than you do," he began carefully.

"It's all bullshit," Sam snapped and wrenched himself out of Bob's hold. "All I wanted was money, so this heap-of-shit building doesn't fall down around our ears. I thought a human case would be safe, but all I got was a mess of something I don't know if I want anything to do with."

"Baby—"

"Don't do that," Sam interrupted, setting down his keys. "Don't tell me it's nothing to worry about or that it's okay."

"I wasn't—"

"And don't tell me a soul camera matching this blond and the gargoyle is a good case for us." Sam picked up a pen and tapped the gargoyle on the head. "Wake up," he ordered loudly. "Freaking paranormals and their problems. Always fucking with human lives."

Sam's sharp words cut Bob deeply. He knew Sam had issues with the world he'd been thrust into, but Bob didn't know Sam still held so much anger inside. He saw Sam turn to him with guilt in his eyes. "Sorry," he said. "I didn't mean you."

Bob wanted to laugh it off, sweep Sam off his feet and take him to bed, but hurt and self-pity swamped him. "It's okay, I know how you feel about paranormals." His calves hit the sofa when he stepped back. He sat down in an uncoordinated tangle of limbs right on top of Smudge, who had been lazing on the cushions. Smudge yowled, and Bob considered the moment complete when Smudge climbed him using his claws and hissed in Bob's face before leaving the room.

"Bob, I'm sorry." Sam dropped inelegantly to a crouch so he could be at Bob's level. "I wish sometimes a case could be straightforward. Just once."

Bob looked into Sam's soft brown eyes, and love washed over him. He didn't include Bob in his condemnation of the general paranormal population, nor Danjal, or Hartman, or come to think of it, one angel and some dragons; any of the people they'd met and come to know.

*I'll get a job and bring in some money, if we need more than what's in my bank account,* Bob thought.

Sam stared right at him, and then Bob saw the corners of

Sam's mouth twitch, and before he knew it, Sam was laughing. "As what?" he said with a laugh. "Freelance scaring services."

Bob liked it when Sam laughed normally, but this laugh had an edge of hysteria. Sam couldn't know that Bob had held some high-level jobs in his life. He'd been the parliament liaison for the coven he was no longer a member of, and he'd been a senator in the vampire parliament itself for over fifty years. He'd never shared that old part of his life with Sam. He couldn't. There were too many secrets that he shielded in his thoughts, so Sam would never know.

"I don't know," Bob finally said, not able to keep the hurt from his voice. "Something I can do while watching you," he added. He couldn't accept a job that would take him away from Sam.

Sam stopped laughing as suddenly as he'd started. He crawled onto the couch to straddle Bob's lap. His expression was serious as he spoke. "I'm sorry, Bob, I think the last few months have messed with my head." He snuggled into Bob's hold and, in that instant, the balance was restored. For a second everything had been far too serious for Bob's liking. He'd been too close to talking about his past and putting Sam in danger for no reason.

"I'm sorry, too," Bob offered. He wasn't entirely sure what he was sorry for, but whenever they argued both always apologized. Anything that made Sam happy was worth a few words to restore the peace between them.

Sam sighed against him. "Nothing for you to be sorry about." They snuggled close and exchanged kisses and only stopped when there was a knock on the office door followed by someone entering. Bob looked over Sam's shoulder. Abbott Williams stood in the doorway, waiting to be acknowledged. He looked from Bob and Sam to the ceiling, then the floor as if embarrassed to have caught them making out.

"I got your text," Abbot said.

Sam wriggled off Bob's lap then brushed himself down.

"Your suspicions were right." Sam showed Abbott the photo on the camera that showed the illicit meeting in the best light. The gargoyle was a hazy image behind the couple.

"What's that?" Abbott pointed to the gargoyle.

Sam shrugged. "A temporary art installment."

"Oh." Right in front of them Abbott crumpled into tears, and Bob leaped to his feet to guide Abbott to the sofa. Sam passed over a box of tissues and waited along with Bob for Abbott to speak.

"I knew it." Abbott sniffed. He blew his nose and pushed himself shakily to stand. Visibly pulling himself together, he pocketed the used tissue and nodded at Sam and Bob. "Thank you, send me a bill for any outside expenses," he said. Without another word, he left.

"Poor guy," Bob offered.

Sam huffed a laugh. "He's better off out of a relationship where he can't trust his lover."

Guilt hit Bob low in the stomach. Sam frowned as if he sensed Bob's emotions through their connection, but didn't comment. Bob forced a smile onto his face. "Do we have enough money to get the boiler fixed?"

Sam opened the small safe in the wall. He pulled out an envelope and counted the money inside. "Yes, and just in time. I swear that freaking boiler was in full meltdown mode this morning."

"It's never really recovered from the pipe damage after the dragon-siren battle."

Sam sat back in his chair. "We should bill the dragons."

Bob imagined a dragon paying any kind of account.

"Good luck with that," he muttered. "You'd have better luck collecting money from sirens."

Smudge walked back into the room and jumped onto Sam's desk He rubbed himself against Sam's arm, spreading his scent.

The noise of stone against stone broke the quiet scene. "Who's that?" a gravelly voice asked.

The gargoyle moved in shaky groaning increments to stand upright to its full twenty inches or so. He was looking down at the soul camera that lay screen up on the desk.

"Now you come out," Sam said. "You realize I poked you three times."

The gargoyle normally snarked back. He wasn't known for his ability to say anything much in the way of *nice*. Bob didn't like gargoyles unless they were inanimate and on the walls of a church. The lack of expression on the gargoyle's face as it silently stared at the camera was freaky.

"Why do you have… is that…" In a sudden motion, the gargoyle crouched back into its stone shape and stilled.

"What the hell?" Sam poked it again with the same pen as before. No movement, none at all. "Is it just me or did he looked shocked."

"He doesn't have expressions," Bob offered in support of why he hadn't noticed.

Sam looked up at him disbelieving. "Yes he does, didn't you see…" He trailed off. "Don't tell me, I'm the only one that saw the shock and grief on the gargoyle's face."

Bob shrugged. "All I saw was stone and lidless eyes." He shuddered. He hated those lidless eyes.

One more poke and Sam dropped the pen on the table. He returned to idly scratching Smudge behind his ears. Smudge purred, and Bob knew, given half a chance at having Sam scratching his ears, he'd probably be purring as well.

"Let's have a closer look at this." Sam rummaged one-handed in his drawer and pulled out a couple of cables. Examining them, he finally found one that slotted into his uncle's camera then he pushed the other end into the ancient computer on his desk.

As the PC whirred and spluttered to life, Bob leaned over and pressed a kiss to Sam's lips. "I love you," he said.

Sam answered with a kiss of his own, and with Smudge twisting between them trying to find a comfy spot to park his furry butt, Bob kissed Sam with the same intensity as he had the first time.


SAM WAS SO sorry he'd lost it with his whole "paranormals are bad" speech. He didn't mean it anymore, not since he'd fallen in love with Bob, but he still couldn't fully embrace the fact that he may have something inside him he couldn't explain.

Lately, he could swear Bob had blocked their mental connection. Sam constantly wanted peace where he could think what he wanted without Bob hearing, but, before, Bob never stopped Sam from hearing everything he thought. Everything, from what they were having for dinner to Bob's protracted thoughts about which black pants he was going to wear when he got dressed. But for the past few weeks the thought stream had slowed to a trickle. Why would Bob block him? And why did Sam feel this overwhelming sensation of guilt from Bob?

His bracelet knocked against the calculator on his desk with the clear ring of crystal and the deeper thud of gold. The weight of the jewelry reminded him of the path he and Bob had traveled so far. Bob wouldn't block him. Bob loved him.

*I've never loved anyone as I love you*, Sam thought.

Bob pulled back with a grin on his face and opened his mouth to say something, but Sam held up a finger. Out of the corner of his eye he had caught sight of the photo rendering on the computer monitor.

"Look," he said, and pointed at the screen. Bob moved around to stand next to him and peered over his shoulder at the image forming line by line. "Look at the blond's face."

Sam knew exactly what he was looking at. Superimposed over the blond man's utterly perfect features was a pattern he recognized. It wasn't ingrained into the skin, merely a suggestion, an overlay similar to the image of the gargoyle. The shapes were like the ones he'd seen on only three people before. The fae triplets. His first case at the agency—twins looking for their missing third. The markings and tattoos on the man's right cheek, silver threading through his hair, and a pronounced widow's peak were all similar to the triplets'. The only difference was that this fae had long hair, and the triplets had short hair.

"You have got to be kidding me," Sam said, startled. "I thought fae kept to themselves and didn't interact with humans because of some unknown horrific complication." He air quoted the word complication, much to Smudge's dismay as the cat hissed at the loss of the scratching fingers.

Bob sighed. "This can't be a good thing. Our gargoyle's soul mate is fae."

Sam joined in with a sigh of his own. He didn't have anything against fae as such, they were a peaceful race unless provoked, but a gargoyle and a fae? That sounded like the kind of provocation the fae needed to come visiting and cause Sam trouble.

*Great.*

## Chapter Four

IDRIS MANAGED TO GIVE THE LATEST GUARDS THE SLIP. HE was used to it by now. He'd been on the run from expectations and rules for almost three years. He'd thought his last fake death had been enough to remove him from the fae radar. Something had given him away, and he would bet his life on it being Greg. That had been his last defense: hide among the humans and grow stronger from their freely given love, preferably during sex. The last one, Greg, had been soft and caring and doted on Idris to the point of obsession. He'd miss him.

Idris slipped into his apartment on Fifth Street near the para shelters and shut the door behind him. As soon as he was inside he dropped the glamor that hid his true appearance from the rest of the world. Not his features, not his nose, or his silver eyes, but the tattoos and lines that marked him as fae had to remain unseen. One wrong glance from a paranormal with the sight and he would be found out. He peered at his reflection in the mirror by the front door and sighed at how pale he looked. He hadn't actually topped up his emotions since Greg, and that had been two days ago.

*You wouldn't have this issue if you could find your fated lover*. He could almost picture his mother as she threw these words at him the last time he'd been found and unceremoniously carted home. He'd had to use every single ounce of his powers to get away that time, and here he was, three years later, on the run like a criminal and no closer to finding his lover than he had been when he'd reached maturity at eighteen.

Crossing to the small kitchen, he poured a glass of water and almost dropped the glass when there was a knock at the door. Frantic, he looked toward the window. He could get out that way if he didn't mind a two-story jump. There was no way he could use magic; he was growing too weak. He had used the remnants of his power to hide his distinctive marks from the public. In fact, it was hard enough to raise the glamor to hide his features should he have to open the door.

Drawing back his shoulders, Idris decided he might as well face whoever was at the door. He checked through the peephole. He didn't recognize the man on the other side, although upon opening the door he certainly felt the punch to his nose and the accompanying crunch.

This was no fae guard. This was a human.

"You bastard," the man shouted as he pushed Idris back into the room. "I loved him, and you took him." Another punch. Idris was too startled to duck, although he did manage to turn a little, so the punch hit his cheek rather than his nose again.

"Who?" Idris managed to get out before the visitor tackled him to the floor and straddled him, punching randomly at Idris's chest and stomach.

"Greg. My boyfriend. The only man I ever loved, and you took him."

Hell. Idris was usually so careful, always checking to see

if a man was free, but recently he'd grown desperate, as the time between refilling his magic grew longer and longer.

"I'm sorry," he shouted as he gripped the man's fists and attempted to twist the larger man away from him.

"He called me, told me he'd fallen in love. I trusted him." Tears flowed freely from the man's eyes. Idris absorbed the stranger's passion. The emotional energy refreshed him enough so he could flip their positions and pin his attacker to the floor. He glanced at the door, and with a thought he closed it. He didn't want witnesses to this or to what happened next.

"What is your name?" Idris asked gently.

"Abbott," the man said brokenly.

Idris pushed a little of his calming magic toward Abbott and watched as Abbott began to relax. Bit by bit, Abbott settled, and finally Idris released his hold. He sniffed back the blood in his nose and wiped the remainder on his sleeve. Slowly, he backed away from Abbott, then stood. He extended a hand. Abbott looked confused. Like he couldn't remember why he was even there. He took the hand, and Idris helped him to stand upright before making a show of brushing the man down. He couldn't, in all conscience, take more emotional energy from Abbott, but he'd received enough of a boost from Abbott's anger and passion that he felt stronger.

He could leave it at that, suggest that Abbott go home, but guilt suffused him, and he knew instinctively what he had to do. Gently he pressed his hand to Abbott's forehead.

"You need to find Greg. Okay?"

"Find Greg," Abbott repeated.

"Find Greg, hold his hand, and tell him you love him." He made sure the right spells were in Abbott's blood so that they only worked on Greg. Luckily he had the essence of Greg inside him. Otherwise this wouldn't work at all.

"Hold his hand. Love him," Abbott repeated with the ghost of a smile on his lips.

Abbott's eyes were glassy as the last vestiges of Idris's energy filtered from him and into Abbott.

"When you touch him, he won't remember me, you won't remember me, you will just remember love."

"Touch. Remember. Love."

"Go now. Find Greg, tell him what I said."

Abbott shook his head a little but left without another word. Idris shut the door behind him. How had a human found his home so easily when he'd been able to avoid palace guards? He slumped on the sofa and lowered the glamor hiding his face. Sleep began to pull him under. He was going to have to go home soon, just to be able to stop running. Then he'd have to face whatever marriage arrangement his mother had made.

Politically sound, it would be a marriage of fae clans, certainly not love.

He was the son of the fae queen, a prince with centuries of responsibility ahead of him, but all he wanted was love.

Just to find the one.

He'd thought he'd found him, but that had ended in betrayal and the death of the man he'd loved.

Why was this so hard?

## Chapter Five

SAM MOVED UNCOMFORTABLY IN HIS EASY CHAIR. IT WASN'T the seat with the fluffed up pillows that caused his discomfort. No, it was more the unease created by the two guards, with blades out, standing between him and Bob, and staring down at Sam like he was a brain in a specimen jar.

*"You didn't tell me it was going to be like this,"* he thought.

*"It's like they think I'm going to do something."*

Bob peered around the guards. They weren't staring at the big scary vampire, but at Sam. Bob didn't seem at all fazed by their behavior.

*"There's magic in the palace to stop vampires causing trouble,"* Bob replied. *"Come to think of it, there's magic stopping any paranormal violence or incursion. I guess humans don't visit the palace often."*

*"Not helping,"* Sam sent back. *"What can one human do against the fae and all these sharp blades? And whose idea was it to come here anyway?"*

*"Yours, my love."* Bob chuckled, and the guard nearest him checked him out sharply.

*"Stop upsetting the soldiers before they stab you,"* Sam suggested. He wished he could chuckle about this, or find it funny by any stretch of the imagination, but it was so not happening today. He'd woken this morning with no cases on his desk and the bright idea of checking in with the fae triad to see if they recognized the blond guy in the photo.

He'd cropped the human out of the picture, and the gargoyle, so all that remained was the fae in an odd position, leaning to the left. When the photo printed, it didn't show the marks on his face. The blond man was nothing more than an exceptionally pretty guy splitting up a couple with emotion-sucking kisses. Nothing unusual there, Sam told himself.

The soft slide of material on marble had Sam checking out the sound and rising to stand when the triplet fae approached. They inclined their heads in absolute synchronicity, first at Sam then, very deliberately, at Bob.

"You can leave," one of them said to the guards.

The guards didn't argue and strode away into the shadows of the wide hallway.

One of the triad spoke, although Sam couldn't tell which. "You wanted to see us, Sam Enderson?"

"And also you, Bob-the-Vampire?" The way they added Bob's title was funny. Sam chanced a look at Bob, but Bob didn't appear amused. He looked deadly serious and utterly focused. Sam made a small bow to the three fae and he sensed, rather than saw, Bob doing the same thing.

"We're working a case," Sam lied.

*"It's not really a case, is it?"* Bob commented.

*"Shhh. Let me deal with this,"* Sam replied. He continued talking to the fae. "This case concerns a man, and we think you may know him, or know of him." Sam held out the photo and turned it around so the three fae could look at the candid shot.

What happened next kind of surprised him.

Well, in hindsight he shouldn't have been surprised at all.

He woke up in a cell.


DARK IRON BARS covered one side of the cell from solid rock to solid rock, and there was nothing in the way of a window at all. Ambient light issued from shards of crystal in the wall and as he watched the brightness flicker, he acknowledged that his head hurt. Not *just* a headache, but an overwhelming band of agony that pressed on his temples. He moaned and shuffled on the hard place where he lay, then stopped moving when his forehead brushed material. He blinked up at Bob's face peering down at him. There were tears in Bob's beautiful amber and gold-flecked eyes. Sam had never seen his vampire lover cry before.

"Wha'appenss?" Sam slurred.

Bob touched a cool hand to his forehead. Sam realized he was cushioning his head on Bob's lap. The sense of being held was comforting, the pain knifing behind his eyes, not so much.

"I don't know," Bob answered softly. Those simple words made Sam wince. "Last I recall the triad looked at the photo, and the next minute we're in here." Bob sighed and continued the soothing massage on Sam's temples. The effect was instantaneous, the pressure just enough to help the headache dissipate a little at a time. Sam lifted a hand to press against his eyelids and smacked himself in the eye. Startled, he realized why. He was missing the weight of the bracelet.

"My charm bracelet," he said. "They took it? How could they do that?"

Bob shook his head. "I wish I knew." His voice was low,

but Sam could hear something in the tone of it. Something Bob wasn't telling him?

"Bob?"

"I'm sorry you're in here," Bob offered. "I should never have become involved in your life. If I'd not walked into your home that first day, you wouldn't be here."

"No," Sam interrupted before Bob could say something he couldn't take back. He lifted his hand higher and laced his fingers with Bob's. "I love you; I wouldn't have it any other way." He squeezed Bob's fingers and was rewarded with a smile. "We'll get out," Sam added. "We always do."

"You don't understand, Sam," Bob began shakily. "I can't help you this time. No one gets out of the fae queen's dungeons alive. Not even you."

## Chapter Six

SAM LAY IN THE CELL, THE COT HE RESTED ON TOO HARD AND a far cry from the comfortable bed he shared with Bob. His lover had retreated to the far side of the cell and seemed to have fallen into some sort of funk, blaming himself for their situation. How it could be Bob's fault when the entire situation had been Sam's idea, he didn't know.

"Bob?"

"Yeah, babe?"

"Why do you think this is your fault?"

"Because if I didn't come see you, you would've stuck with only doing human cases. It's because I dragged you into our world that you are going to rot in the queen's dungeon."

"It isn't like you to be so melodramatic. Isn't that my job?"

"I'm so sorry," Bob reiterated.

Sam sighed. "This is going to be a long incarceration if you can't think of something else to say."

"It's not going to be that long. Usually, prisoners of the queen's court die of neglect."

"You really need to work on your prison pep talk," Sam said.

*"Ready to leave, Sam?"*

Smudge's voice echoed in Sam's head seconds before he spotted a pair of bright cat eyes.

"Hey, Smudge. I don't know. I mean, this is such an awesome hotel." Sam swallowed back the sob of relief building in his throat. Bob's depressing behavior had brought him down lower than he'd expected. His vampire lover usually had a more optimistic spirit.

"How are you going to get us out of here, Smudge?" Bob asked, his tone flat.

*"I'm Sam's familiar. I can manipulate his place in the universe."* Smudge replied like it was the most normal thing possible. After all, couldn't everyone do that?

"Me? Just me?" Sam looked straight at Bob, who wouldn't meet his gaze. "Hell, no. I'm not leaving Bob."

*"I can only carry you because of the spell's blocking magic. I am not bonded to your mate."*

"Shouldn't you be bonded through me?" Sam didn't like the slippery paranormal world where people were often sacrificed for another without rhyme or reason.

*"Familiars don't work that way. We only truly bond with one. You are my one."*

Sam sat back on the bed. "I'm not going."

Bob stood from where he crouched and leaned over Sam. "You are going," he said. His tone was dead, final, and Sam cringed a little. There was no expression in Bob's eyes, nothing at all.

"You can't make me leave you," Sam snapped.

Bob stepped back and punched the stone wall where he'd been leaning. A piece broke off. Bob picked it up and showed it to Sam. The shard was sharp and dangerous-looking. He held the blade to his chest.

"I can," he said.

"Bob."

"If you don't go with Smudge I will kill myself here and now."

Sam stepped forward. "It's not wood," he said. He sounded stupid even to his own ears. He should be grappling for the stone shard, not thinking everything was going to be okay based on supernatural stories he'd read as a child.

"Any sharp object…," Bob said.

Sam stepped closer, but Bob moved back until he was against the wall. "Bob, no, there has to be another way."

"Go with Smudge."

Sam shook his head. "No." Bob lifted one hand and closed his eyes. Sam lunged. The blade slipped, slicing through Bob's jacket, but thankfully not through his chest. Sam grappled for a moment, clutching Bob's hand and attempting to force the weapon from his hand. The stone sliced into Sam's hand. His grip began to falter from the slickness of his bloody palm. Bob's fangs extended and he seemed to break in front of Sam's face, stumbling to his knees.

"*Stop!*" Smudge shouted, and an unseen force separated Sam and Bob, flinging them to opposite sides of the cell.

Sam lay where he was for a moment, looking at his hand and the blood that pooled in his palm. As he watched, the cut quickly healed until all that was left was the blood. He wiped it on his pants then drew his knees up, circling them with his arms.

"Don't leave me," he implored. "Ever."

The thought of a life without Bob, of a single moment

without the other half of him not being there? He couldn't begin to imagine such a cold place.

"I'm sorry," Bob said. "I want you to go. I want you to be safe." He was crying again. "You have to be safe."

Smudge moved between them. "*Both of you will be silent. I will take Sam home, and then we will work out a way of getting you out of here, Bob.*"

Sam crawled over to Bob and sat right next to him, gripping his arm. "I'm not leaving you." Defying his familiar was okay, right? Smudge wasn't the boss of him. What if they returned to the agency and they couldn't figure how to get Bob out? What happened then?

A flash of light blinded Sam, and he blinked to get his eyesight back to normal.

"I can help." Sam watched in astonishment as the gargoyle from his desk flapped into the cell, seemingly from the ceiling, and landed on the floor beside Sam. How the hell did he get into the fae queen's cell? Was it only his imagination or did the gargoyle look bigger, his face elongated, his wingspan wider?

"How did you get in here?" Bob asked.

The gargoyle's face twisted with emotion and Sam wondered if Bob could see the change in expression. He glanced at Bob, who was staring open-mouthed. At least he'd stopped crying.

"It's my fault you're here. I can get you out," the gargoyle said.

"How? What did you do?" Sam didn't know if he trusted the gargoyle. What did they really know about the creature?

"I'm fae," the gargoyle said, hunching his shoulders. "Between your familiar's magic and mine I can bust you both out of here."

Bob linked his fingers with Sam's into a firm grip. "How is a gargoyle part fae?" Bob asked.

Sam hadn't thought to ask that question. A gargoyle was most definitely not a fae, unless he'd missed something in his paranormal identification crash course. Instinct had him glancing at the door. He could sense someone coming closer.

"Smudge," he urged.

*"We have no time for tales,"* Smudge intoned. *"It is time to leave."*

Sam bit his lip. He was not leaving Bob in this prison.

Bob gripped Sam's upper arms. "Please go, Sam. If you're not here, they might let me go. I'm not as important to them."

"Why would they let you go? You were there for the photo too."

"But you are, by far, more interesting. I'm *just* a vampire. You are special."

The sound of footsteps pulled their conversation to a halt. Suddenly whatever Sam wanted to do, it was too late.

*"My magic is being blocked,"* Smudge said. Stone scratching on stone indicated the gargoyle had moved into the shadows, but Smudge didn't budge from Sam's side.

Sam stood up to confront the newcomer; Bob came to stand beside him. The reassurance of Bob next to him was enough for Sam to face anyone. He weaved his fingers through Bob's.

"*I love you*," he thought.

"*I love you too,*" Bob replied.

"*Shhhhhh,*" Smudge snapped in an irritated fashion. *"I can't think."*

Smudge twined between Sam's legs, rubbing and purring. Sam wondered if he were channeling a real cat to give Sam some comfort.

The door swung open, revealing one of the guards they'd seen outside the throne room.

"The queen has commanded your presence, human hybrid," the guard said, gesturing to Sam.

Hybrid? Well, that was a new one. Sam didn't argue. With a squeeze of Bob's hand, he stepped forward. Only to be pushed aside violently as the gargoyle scurried past him, remarkably quick for a stone thing. He threw himself at the guard.

"I won't let them kill you, Sam!" Gargoyle shouted when he moved. As the two clashed, the bright flash of their combined magic threw the guard back into the corridor and left the gargoyle sprawled in an ungainly mess of stone limbs on the floor. Magic crackled like a curtain across the door, encasing the entire room.

*"Now we are trapped,"* Smudge grumbled.

The gargoyle writhed and screamed, the sound echoing through the chamber. Sam resisted the urge to cover his ears. "Gargoyle," he shouted. He ran over to the creature convulsing on the floor and fell to his knees beside him. The gargoyle shook and screamed until Sam worried about its health. Could you actually kill a creature made of stone? Would he shatter and break apart like a boulder?

Sam shuffled closer. His hands shook and began to glow. A white light engulfed his fingers as they crackled with energy. Helplessly he looked from Bob to Smudge. "What do I do?"

*"Touch him,"* Smudge said.

Despite doubting the wisdom of listening to a powerful familiar, Sam gave in and did what Smudge said. He took a deep breath and pressed his light-filled hands against the gargoyle's chest.

The gargoyle stilled. The convulsions stopped, but the creature didn't open his eyes.

"What now?" Sam asked the familiar. "Nothing's happening."

*"Have patience."*

Sam watched as the white glow bled from his hands and coat both him and the gargoyle from head to foot until they were engulfed in bright magic. The scent of ozone filled the air, and Sam's breathing quickened. He felt powerful, strong, almost invincible.

The gargoyle gasped and arched into Sam's touch. The glowing changed to a pulsing rhythm, like a heartbeat shining across them.

*"Keep touching him. No matter what, don't let go."* Smudge commanded.

Sam's hands burned. The pain was incredible, and he wanted to let go. Blisters formed on his palms, but he kept his hands against the gargoyle's chest.

The flesh beneath his fingers turned pliant. Rough, stony hide changed to soft, smooth skin. The gargoyle's body stretched and reshaped until he was longer than Sam was tall, and dark patterns swirled to form a shirt and pants. When the glow finally receded, Sam toppled to the floor. His hands ached, but the pain had ceased. He turned them to check for damage, but all he could see was smooth unblemished skin. Bob kneeled beside him, his expression concerned.

"I'm fine, Bob. You don't need to worry." He'd set his own hands on fire before he admitted how much he appreciated his lover's attention.

*"When will you remember I can read your mind?"* Bob's voice slid through Sam's head.

Sam blushed. He tended to push out of his mind anything

he didn't want to remember. Bob reading his thoughts was one of them.

*"But then I wouldn't know you enjoyed my attention."* Bob flashed his sharp teeth in a wicked smile.

Sam rolled his eyes. Now that the pain had faded he took a good look at his gargoyle, or ex-gargoyle, as the case may be. Dark hair tumbled across a pale face. His flawless features would've made a model weep with envy and maybe stab him in the back. The only flaw was a silvery mark on one cheek.

"Wow, Gargoyle de-spells nice," Bob muttered.

"What happened?" Sam gasped, his throat dry and parched, like he had screamed along with the gargoyle.

"You broke my curse? How could you do that? Only the pearl can…," a deep, gravelly voice had Sam checking everywhere until he realized it was the gargoyle who had spoken. He rolled to stand. Bob helped him, and residual static sparked between them.

*"It is only temporary. He will turn back in a few days. You need to break the curse for this to be permanent,"* Smudge suggested.

"What happened to you?" Bob asked. He reached out and touched the gargoyle beside Sam, carefully checking his vitals.

"When did you become a doctor?" Sam tried to calm his irritation over Bob touching another man.

Bob's mouth twitched, but he didn't say anything. Sam pressed his lips together to stop any more petty words from escaping. He hoped his thoughts shouted his displeasure at the vampire.

"I was cursed," Gargoyle offered. Sam wished he could think of this gorgeous man in front of him in any other way than *gargoyle*. That description didn't match anymore.

"Cursed with a spell?" Sam prompted when the gargoyle said nothing else.

Finally, the gargoyle spoke. "I was cursed after I fell in love with a fae prince. The Queen, his mother, didn't approve of me." He leaned back against the wall but quickly moved away when the walls lit up, the magic responding to his touch.

"She cast a spell on you?" Sam asked.

He shrugged. "I can't say for sure, but after magic turned me into an ugly stone gargoyle, I couldn't face my beautiful Prince. He deserved better."

"You don't think he would've still loved you?" Sam asked. He glanced at Bob, and for a second allowed himself to imagine the world without his vampire lover. Hell, it wasn't a life worth contemplating.

Bob snorted at Sam's words. "You don't understand the fae. Everything is based on beauty and bloodlines. A fae with no royal blood would be treated poorly at court whether he was married to the prince or not."

The gargoyle nodded his agreement.

"Oh." Sam didn't know what to say. "But if it's a curse can't it be reversed?"

The gargoyle laughed, a loud grinding sound like boulders rolling down a hill. "You've given me a couple of days of being me again, at the most. Now that you've turned me almost human I have a limited time. It's my understanding that once I turn back to stone I will stay that way. The only thing that will turn me back into a proper fae is a purple sea pearl and the only one in existence belongs to the sirens."

"Of course it does." Sam sighed. "It would be too much to hope it belonged to the fluffy bunny brigade or the flappy butterflies group."

Bob's mouth flattened into a straight line. "No chance at all."

"Wow." Sam filed that information for later and turned his attention to the matter at hand. "We can't keep calling you Gargoyle. What's your real name?" he asked.

"My name is Halstein, but you can call me Hal."

Sam arched an eyebrow as he regarded the fae. "You're a fae called Hal?"

"Halstein is a Norse name; it comes from the Norse words for rock and stone. Which is why the spell the queen used turned me into a Gargoyle," Hal explained. "Or at least I think it was her way of playing a cruel joke."

"It's an odd name for a fae," Bob said.

"Says Bob-the-Vampire," Hal snapped.

Bob shrugged. "Just saying."

The guard stirred outside the cell, groaning, he pushed himself to stand. He stared into the cell with a mixture of horror and amazement on his face. If Sam could read his mind, he'd probably see a lot of curse words tumbling through the guard's head. The guard disappeared momentarily then returned with five other big, strong guards. Evidently a human, a vamp, a cat, and a guy who looked like he'd be knocked down by a feather, needed six fae guards.

The original guard snapped his fingers. Magic curled around his hands and traveled up the blade he was holding. Sam was impressed. Or rather he'd have been impressed if he wasn't feeling ever so slightly freaking scared.

"You three will come with me."

*Three? So, the guard has discounted Smudge then?*

*"Interesting,"* Bob thought.

Sam agreed. Could they not sense that Smudge was his magical companion?

"Why?" Bob stepped in front of Sam, blocking him with his body.

"The queen requested Sam's presence, but I'm certain she'll want to see this." The guard's wide eyes took in Hal's appearance, and he pointed directly at him. "Come on out, please. Singly."

*"We should do what he says."* Smudge flicked his tail against Sam's calf.

Bob looked over his shoulder at the cat. He shrugged then headed out of the cell; the rest of them followed. Sam wasn't leaving Bob, Smudge wasn't leaving Sam, and their gargoyle had become a fae named Hal. Not much they *could* do except follow the guards.

## Chapter Seven

THE LONG TREK UP THE SPIRAL STAIRCASE HAD SAM wondering how far below ground they had been trapped. He had plenty of time to decide he was never going to take a human case again. It was his wish to take on a non-paranormal client that got them into this mess. Sure, the paranormal cases often threatened his life, but none of them had resulted in potential lifelong imprisonment. He thought he preferred death to prison or some hideous curse where he was turned into stone.

Hal faltered every so often. Evidently uncurling from his stone shell had taken a toll on his body. Gasping for air, the ex-gargoyle depended on the wall to hold him up as he climbed. Sam slowed his pace so Hal could keep up and not get a fae sword jabbed in his back to hurry him along. The guard's enchanted blade lit the way, and the one time Bob stepped out of line a crackle of energy spat from it and circled his wrists in sparking bonds.

When they reached a pair of double doors, the small group came to a halt. They were faced with more guards in front of the doors of ornately carved wood and precious stones—an entire phalanx of them.

"The queen requested their presence," their guard said.

"She requested the human hybrid, not the rest of them," one of the door guards replied.

"She'll want to see him." He pointed to Hal, who stood in the shadows until two guards hustled him closer to the light.

"Why?"

"Because he was a gargoyle until about ten minutes ago." The words weren't particularly sensational, but each guard at the queen's door stared at Hal as if he'd grown a second head instead of merely transforming from stone to flesh. Sam heard whispers from the far right.

"It can't be."

"Is it really him?"

"I heard rumors…"

"But it's impossible."

The speaker for the door guards eyed Hal with a wide-eyed expression as if expecting him to change back at any second. "How did he get into the prison?" he asked, showing no sign of letting them inside.

"I don't know." Their guard turned to look at them, clearly looking for an explanation of how Hal got into the place. Like Sam knew.

"Can we get this over with?" Sam asked. He was beginning to think the guards would talk forever, and he'd die of old age outside the queen's chambers.

Bob laughed.

"Something funny, vampire?" their guard asked.

Bob shook his head. "Nope. If you two are done chatting and exchanging gossip can we go inside now, or did you plan to keep the queen waiting?"

A guard who hadn't spoken yet yanked open the door. At least one of them was using his common sense.

Sam nudged Bob with his elbow. "*Stop adding oil to the fire.*"

The last thing they needed was for the vampire's bravado to anger the fae queen.

"*Catch.*" Sam only had a second to process the command before his arms were filled with his black familiar.

Sam grunted. "I think we need to cut back on the fish." A pinprick of claws had Sam recanting. "Sorry." Smudge purred but didn't speak.

Sam carried his familiar into the chambers with him. He had long since abandoned the idea he could get the cat to do anything he wished. If Smudge wanted to be carried, Sam would carry him. The familiar never did anything without a good reason. Smudge didn't give in to flights of fancy.

The queen sat upon an elaborate gold throne that shone beneath the chandeliers. She had the same ethereal glow Sam noticed with all the fae, even Hal. But there was something brittle about her. Her cold, expressionless face had the now familiar line of silvery tattoos covering one side. Sam examined her markings. They were different to the triplets' marks and Hal's. Was there an encyclopedia of fae symbols somewhere explaining to an outsider what they all meant?

"I see we finally meet the great savior of all fae, the human hybrid Sam Enderson."

"Just Sam is fine," Sam said as respectfully as he could manage.

The queen dismissed his words with a wave of her hand. "My nephews have told me much about you." The queen's voice chilled Sam's blood like icicles across his skin. He hugged Smudge closer, never more thankful for his familiar's warmth.

For the first time, he spotted the trio standing off to the side. Ah, so the triad were nephews to the ice queen.

"Then you have me at an advantage… Your Majesty," he added with a slight inclination of his head. He wanted to say something snappy like they never mentioned her, but he didn't want to push his luck.

The trio watched Sam with the same intensity they always did. One of them stepped forward with Sam's charm bracelet in his hand. Smudge climbed Sam's chest then resettled around Sam's neck, claws digging in.

Sam held out his wrist when the fae didn't immediately hand it over. "Why did you take it?" he asked carefully. "More importantly, how did you take it."

"We added more protections." The fae cast a sly look at the Queen beneath his lashes before he snapped the bracelet around Sam's wrist. "And, it's fae magic we can work with."

"Thanks." Sam had never been more grateful for the comforting weight than he was now. He didn't like having the magic around his wrist, but he needed the markers from people who owed him and could get Bob out of there in an emergency.

*"And you,"* Bob admonished him.

The triad fae leaned forward and whispered in Sam's ear. "We knew if we grabbed you and put you in the cells you'd attract your friends."

Smudge swiped at the fae, who deftly avoided Smudge's claws before walking backward to join his brothers.

The queen sat silently. The guards didn't move, and Sam was slap bang in the middle of an awkward silence. Great.

"How did you lose the prince?" Hal shouted from behind him. Sam was torn between being relieved at the interruption and worried that Hal would be struck down dead where he stood.

The triad fae tilted their heads in unison. "How did you know we lost him?" they asked in a synchronized voice.

Hal stepped forward to stand next to Sam, his steps more certain like he was shaking off the spell of stone and finding his feet. "Because he's not sitting like a proper puppy beside the queen bitch," Hal snarled.

Electricity crackled between the queen's fingers. "It is not your place to talk, commoner." The queen spat the words. Sam sensed she was waiting for Hal to do something further so she could smite him with some great fae magic.

Hal didn't stop. "I've already had the love of my life torn from me and spent decades as a stone desk weight. Anything else would probably be a step up." Sarcasm dripped from his lips. Did he want to die?

*"Without Idris, I am nothing."* Hal's thoughts poured into Sam's mind like a gurgling stream. He could hear Hal's internal conversation as clearly as he could hear Bob's. Sam stared at Hal in horror. Hal really did want to die.

The queen lifted her hand. Sam grabbed Hal's shoulder, clumsily holding Smudge still with one hand on his familiar's furry butt. A wave of energy washed over him, bright-white and sparkling like raindrops in the sunshine. A million rainbows filled the room and twisted in and around Hal and Sam. He heard Smudge purr in contentment before growling soft and low.

Energy ricocheted from the walls and floor, knocking guards to the floor, unconscious, before finally slamming into the queen. The royal didn't scream as the reds, oranges, blues, and greens pulsed around and into her. Instead she collapsed in her chair, eyes rolling back in her head.

Hal's mouth dropped open. "What did you do, Sam?"

"I don't know." Sam's tight voice was strangled with emotion.

*Is she dead?*

He looked around the room, cataloging who was still standing. Hal and Bob stood while Smudge jumped to the floor and began to lick his paws. Sam tore his gaze from his familiar to find the fae triad smiling at him with identical expressions of glee. "We knew it would work," they said in unison.

Each of the triad fell to his knees in front of Sam and pressed their foreheads to the floor before rising to their feet again in smooth, graceful movements.

"What did you do to me?" Sam shouted. He was filled with horror that somehow he had been used as a conduit to kill. Emotion boiled inside him and to his absolute shame tears dripped down his cheeks.

Bob was at his side immediately, hugging him close. "What did you do to him?" Bob shouted at the fae triad.

They looked confused, and then they began speaking sequentially like one long three-part sentence.

"Only began to make him what he was always meant to be."

"To join with his mate and be strong."

"A sorcerer. Our Great Mage. The holder of all secrets."

Sam buried his face against Bob's chest. The emotions inside him left him drained. He'd killed someone. He hadn't meant to. He wrenched himself free to face the triad again.

"I will never forgive you for this," he shouted at them. "Smudge, you have to do something. Get her back."

"Hey, it isn't your fault. You were only the conduit." Bob rubbed Sam's back.

Sam sank into his lover's touch for a moment before breaking away to run to the throne.

He dropped to his knees beside the queen, touching smooth cold skin and finding no pulse.

"There is always a new monarch. The queen is dead, long live the king," Hal intoned sadly. "Idris is the new king. We need to find him."

"Idris? Where is he?" Sam didn't look forward to explaining to her successor that he'd been the one to kill her. What did they do with the queen now? As if someone in fae heaven, or wherever they went, had heard his question, a blinding white light filled the room, and when Sam could focus again, the queen was gone.

The fae triad moved to stand near the throne.

"Now Idris can come home," they said as one.

Next to Sam, Hal seemed to crumple as if his strings had been cut. Sam immediately supported him. "Are you okay?" he asked quickly.

Hal nodded, his face pale. "Idris," he whispered, his face a mask of despair.

"What's wrong?" One of the fae triad moved to stand beside Hal and Sam. Close up Sam got a really good look at the silver tattoos on the fae's face. They pulsed with light. "Idris is coming home. Your mate is finally taking his rightful place, and you will be here at his side."

Hal bowed his head. Then lifted it and looked straight at Sam.

"Not when I turn back to stone."

Sam grasped Hal's hand tight. Suddenly he knew exactly what to say. The fae called him a Great Mage, a sorcerer. Well hell, he was neither of those, but Smudge was pretty powerful, and he had Bob at his side. Together they would find a way to fix this.

"We'll find this pearl you talked about, and we will lift this curse."

Sam knew he sounded convincing. He wished he felt that

way inside. How could they fix this mess? Sirens had a magic pearl, a purple one, that would destroy the curse. Only one small problem. He hated sirens.

And they kind of hated him back.

## Chapter Eight

IDRIS SMOOTHED A SHAKING HAND OVER HIS SILK TOP. HIS mother was dead. He had felt her heart stop. How had she died? Although he had longed for a time when she didn't control him, he hadn't anticipated her death for many more years to come. With her death, he was next in line for the throne. A throne he'd never wanted and certainly didn't need, but when had he gotten whatever he needed? His life was filled with moments of disappointment.

Was there a new enemy among them? Or someone he could call a friend?

He didn't know if it was safe to return to the castle. What if whoever killed his mother was waiting for him to appear? So many questions and no answers to them. He mentally ran a list of the people who might be safe to contact. It was a fairly short list.

The crackle of magic distracted him from his inner musings. Crap. He had to get out of there before whatever hunted him found its prey. His mother's death may have been the first part of a grander conspiracy to end the royal line, and he was too weak to fight back.

*I need to find someone to feed from, soon.*

He snatched the emergency bag he kept by the door, fully stocked with clothing, money, and food. Ever since the day he'd run from the palace, the day his lover, Halstein, had died, he'd been hunted by his mother's guards, and he'd stayed prepared.

A flashing light caught his attention as he ducked through the door.

*Crap.*

*Magic.*

*Don't look. Never look at the magic.*

He knew the rules; he knew them well. But that still didn't stop his curiosity from being piqued. Someone was coming, and he needed to know who to avoid capture. The magic wasn't strong, but it prickled on his skin. He wasn't staying around to argue. He tensed to run.

"Wait! Stop, Prince. We're here to take you home."

Despite the guard's words, Idris didn't slow. When had the castle ever been home? Not since the death of his lover had he wanted to be in that cold place. Some people came into your life and changed you, and for Idris, his low-ranking fae lover had been it for him. If only Hal's supposed death hadn't scarred him for life, Idris might have been able to find someone new.

"Please, Your Highness." Idris took the last of the steps in one go and ended up face-to-face with two shocked palace guards, neither of whom, evidently, had expected him to run. They didn't react fast enough. Idris used the wall to jump over them before somersaulting in the air and landing on his feet on the other side of them.

Before he could regain his lost momentum, magic snagged at his feet, and he sprawled in a very un-kingly way on the cold sidewalk. He shook free of the magic quick enough, and no one stopped him again. If anything, they stood there staring at him with entreaty in their expressions. Each of them offered their hands to help him to his feet.

He could have continued to run, but what would that have earned him in the end? Eventually, he'd have to face them, those people who had mocked him when Hal had left, and pitied him for bad judgment. More so when he never returned, missing, presumed dead.

Idris ignored their hands and clambered to stand on his own as he faced the guards. Tilting his chin up he adopted his most haughty expression. "What happened to my mother?"

He might as well get this part over with now. Once he found out who killed her he could decide what to do next.

"If you could come with us, Your Highness," one of the guards said in a gentle tone.

Idris stared at the guard and judged the honesty in the fae's words. Could this be a trap? Could he trust them not to turn on him in the end and kill him? There were people within the court who had wanted his mother dead, and would probably want him dead as well. Possibly his cousin triad who were next in line after him. They were kingmakers, the power behind the throne, and as much as they were the only ones who comforted him after Hal vanished, he never understood them and their freaky powers. To say he loved his cousins might be a stretch, but he respected them. If they didn't want him to be in power, he wouldn't be. To this day, he didn't know why they hadn't deposed his mother before now and taken the throne for themselves. It wasn't as if Idris would fight them for control.

Idris pushed aside all the conflicting thoughts in his head. "Who requested my presence?"

"Your cousins, and the hybrid Sam."

"Sam?" He didn't recognize that name and had no idea

who he might be. Maybe his mother had taken another lover while he was gone.

One of the other guards, his black jacket emblazoned with an insignia showing he was a high-ranking officer, stepped forward. "Sam is the one who killed her."

And therein lay the issue. Yes, Idris was next in line for the throne by birth, but he couldn't just step into the position. By fae law, Sam, as the victor of some battle Idris had no details of, could take the throne. The one who conquered the fae ruler could call on the ancient right to challenge the blood-family for the crown. It was one of their essential rules.

"And he wants the throne," Idris summed up. He was tempted to hand the whole damn mess over to Sam and hope to hell he did something about equality and fairness for all in the kingdom.

The officer shook his head. "You don't understand. He wants nothing to do with the kingdom. The throne is in flux if you don't return, Your Highness."

"Wait, he doesn't want the throne?" Idris had never heard of such a thing. Who didn't want to be king? Well, beside him. "Why did he kill the queen then?"

"Please. If you come with us, Your Highness, everything will be explained."

Idris thought it over for a long moment. There was nothing in the kingdom that he needed. They could rot for all he cared. None of this made sense, but a fae kingdom without a strong ruler would simply descend into chaos. Did he care? He could move away, have a life without looking over his shoulder. He could be truly free.

"Perhaps you'd like to meet the gargoyle?" One of the guards looked at him hopefully while the rest exchanged sly looks.

"Gargoyle?" When had they gotten a gargoyle? Maybe it

was one of Mother's new pets? Idris wasn't fond of the things, with their crabbiness and the way they turned to stone and stared at you.

"He came with the human hybrid, and is awfully interested in the royal line."

"And your mother needs to be laid to rest with the ancestors," another said.

Idris sighed. The guards were right, he should put his mother to rest if only to make sure he was really free. "Take me home." Idris might not have cared for his mother, but she deserved a proper burial.

The officer held out a hand. "We can use a portal," he said.

Idris shuddered. Teleportation had never been his strong skill. The magic needed to transport a body through time and space wasn't one he had in abundance. His magic went a different route. He could create an illusion, or cause a storm, or, on a particularly good day, charm the people and the animals around him. But he never had acquired the ability to move anything with his mind, much less himself.

"Fine," he finally agreed. The sooner he was back at the palace, the sooner this was over.

Two of the four guards grabbed his arms. Idris braced himself for the sense of displacement and nausea teleportation always caused. He'd heard that teleporting yourself eased those symptoms, but it wasn't something he'd ever know for sure.

They landed right in the middle of the queen's throne room, except now it would be the king's. Idris wasn't ready for that change.

He stared at the empty throne, and a familiar grief accompanied by panic swelled inside him. He shouldn't have come home. In this place was the last time he'd seen Hal.

"Idris!"

Idris spun about at the familiar voice, certain he'd been mistaken.

"Hal?" His voice cracked as he spoke his lover's name. He swallowed back the tears. He'd already shed too many for this one man. This had to be an illusion. Something conjured up by the human or the vampire who stood at the other side of the large hall. He blinked to clear his eyes but Hal, his Hal, was still there.

Hal rushed to his side, only coming to a halt when Idris showed no sign of opening his arms to greet him. "Idris?"

Tears filled Hal's beautiful green eyes. Unable to take the raw pain on his ex-lover's face, Idris wrapped Hal in his arms and held on tight. Only when they touched did he know for certain this was the same man he had loved with his whole heart. The same man who had abandoned him and their love.

## Chapter Nine

HAL PULLED AWAY AND SAW THE ANGER AS PLAIN AS anything on Idris's beautiful face. He wished like nothing else that he could take the pain away from him.

"I never wanted to leave you." He touched Idris's arm.

Idris stood silently as if in shock, then very deliberately he shrugged Hal's hand away.

Pain stabbed through him. All this time he'd wished for nothing more than to see Idris again. Even when trapped in stone and knowing it was impossible, he'd always hoped one day Idris would walk past the window, or come into the agency itself. Maybe he'd be looking for Hal.

"I thought you'd left me," Idris said brokenly. "I wished you were dead."

Hal stepped back. He'd always wondered what Idris had thought of Hal's disappearance. Now he knew. "You knew I didn't have any royal blood—"

"That didn't matter to me."

A cough interrupted them. "Uhm, maybe you should talk privately about this?" Sam said from behind them.

Hal looked over at Sam then to Idris. Deciding Sam was

right, he pressed a hand to Idris's chest. They disappeared from the throne room and ended up in the top room of the tallest tower in the fae kingdom.

When they'd fallen in love, this had been *their* spot; the one place that both men had hidden away so they could spend time together.

"Why here?" Idris asked.

"We needed privacy, and I have happy memories of this room." All times of day and night they'd managed to sneak away for stolen trysts.

"I need to...." Idris walked to the edge of the room then opened the window wide. He leaned out and inhaled deeply of the wintery air. Hal panicked a little and grabbed at Idris's jacket. Was the prince going to jump?

Idris shrugged him off again and rounded on him. With a finger stabbing the air between them, he reeled off a list of accusations. "You made a bargain to go on that quest with my mother, and then you disappeared. Why didn't you come back?"

"Idris—"

"You left me; you betrayed our love."

"Please—"

"And all because you thought taking on a quest was the only way to prove you were worthy. Loving me should've been enough."

Something snapped inside of Hal, and he shoved at Idris, sparks flying between them. "I wasn't good enough, we both know that, except I'm the only one brave enough to say so. People talked. Everyone told me you were toying with me because no prince could ever care for someone who worked in the palace kitchens."

"I loved you!" Idris shouted. The wind picked up outside the window. Gusts burst into the room, swirling around them.

"Idris, please, calm down." Hal's bones ached, his muscles stretching impossibly tight. Everything hurt. He knew he didn't have long in this form, and he had to make Idris understand.

If anything the wind grew louder, the rumble of thunder chasing up the mountain toward them.

"I woke up, and you were gone!" Idris shouted.

"You knew I went on the quest. I didn't abandon you."

"We agreed you didn't need to. What we had should've been enough."

Hal sighed. "How could you ever understand, Idris? You're a prince, and I'm nothing."

Lightning struck the tower. The smell of ozone stank up the air. If Idris didn't calm down soon, he'd take out the tower and the whole palace with it.

"That quest wasn't about us. You let my mother get under your skin. You didn't need to prove anything to me."

"I have regretted it every day since," Hal pleaded. "Please, Idris."

Idris folded his arms close to his body. "They said you'd turned tail and run, that you'd betrayed the quest and me."

"They lied."

The wind calmed a little. The tension that had crackled between them lessened. Idris slumped to the floor like his strings had been cut. Hal followed him down, crouching in front of him.

"Idris? Talk to me. You're so pale. Have you fed recently?"

Idris shook his head, glancing up at Hal. Hal's runes were stark against his translucent skin.

"I never wanted to," Idris said, his voice barely audible. "I only fed to survive one miserable day at a time without you. I haven't had a full meal since you left."

Hal's heart broke a little at the confession. He cradled Idris's face, then slowly leaned closer and closer still, until only a breath separated them. "Let me," Hal pleaded. "Let me provide for you."

They kissed. At first Idris hesitated, and Hal wanted to pull back, to explain how he loved Idris to the end of everything. Abruptly the connection snapped into place between them. Idris was an incubus of sorts. One of his more curious powers was the ability to recharge his magic through emotion. Somehow, he and Hal were combining their powers to make Idris stronger.

The kisses changed, became deeper, sexually charged. Hal whimpered as Idris gripped Hal's biceps and encouraged him to stand. Pressed back, one step, and then another, they only stopped when Hal was shoved against the stone wall by the window. The turbulent wind carried sheets of rain through the space, soaking them where they stood.

Hal was so hard, impossibly hard, but his muscles screamed at the movements, and he knew nothing would come of this. "We have to stop."

Idris broke the kiss, uncertainty in his expression. "Hal?"

Hal opened his mouth to say something, but all that came out was a gravelly cough. *Oh hell. Not now.*

Idris released his hold on Hal and stepped away. The lack of support sent Hal straight to the floor, and he groaned in pain. He sensed Idris watching, and then he was there at Hal's side, smoothing his hair.

"I took too much." Idris continued petting. "I'm so sorry."

"No, ill…," Hal muttered.

Idris passed his hands over Hal's body, muttering healing chants. Hal began to feel a little better. Cautiously he moved to sit. He didn't have much time.

"Idris, we need to talk."

## Chapter Ten

IDRIS SAT BACK ON HIS HEELS. HE'D NEVER FELT SO wretched and lonely in his life. He'd fed from Hal and for once his energy level was fully charged. But now Hal wasn't looking at him, and he wanted to talk. Idris's heart couldn't survive losing his lover twice.

"It's okay." He tried to put conviction into his voice but failed miserably. "I understand. It's been a long time, and I accept your choices."

"Idris, wait—"

"I won't stop you from leaving again."

"Idris, shut up!" Hal shouted.

Idris pressed his lips together to keep silent.

"Whatever you think of why I did it, I agreed to participate in a quest to prove my bravery. To show the queen, as your other suitors did, that I was worthy of her son."

"You didn't have to—"

"I know you think that, but if I wanted to be accepted by your mother I had to prove myself." Hal sighed heavily. "Look, in the middle of one of my trials I stumbled into a spell. I don't know for sure that the queen had anything to do with it, but she's the only one who knew the course the challenges would lead us through. It was a trap spell designed to keep someone wrapped in their own essence. "

"My mother sabotaged your trial?" Idris frowned.

"I don't know for sure." He didn't want to point fingers at a dead woman. Idris had enough bad memories of his mother.

"She told me that if you loved me you would fight through every item on the quest list to come home. But you never returned. You never walked through the door with your smile and all that love you had for me in your heart. She told me the quest would only kill a fated mate who cheated or betrayed their love. I knew we belonged together, so I thought…"

Tears dripped from Idris's eyes, but Hal didn't draw attention to them. Instead, he buried his face against Idris's neck and tightened his hold until the man in his arms could barely breathe.

"You thought I had betrayed you."

"Where have you been all this time?" The hurt in Idris's voice twisted Hal's heart.

Hal pulled away a little. "The spell was a curse. I couldn't return to you, not after what happened."

"What do you mean a curse? You look fine to me." Idris's sharp, accusing tone stabbed at Hal. He took another step back.

He turned to look out the window, too hurt to face Idris right now.

"The spell turned me into a gargoyle statue made of stone."

"Stone?" Idris said, horrified.

Hal nodded. "I was cursed to become a gargoyle. I turned to stone and was disposed of to a paranormal barter shop."

Idris slid a hand across Hal's back. "Oh my love, I thought you'd left me. But now you'll stay, won't you? We can be together again."

Hal held back his answer. That was all he wanted. The chance to see if their love was real. When he'd been cursed, his entire world crumbled but he still loved Idris. But none of that was possible. Evidently his lack of answer was a space that Idris could fill with his own assumptions.

"You're going to do it to me all over again, aren't you?" he said.

"No—"

"If you leave me this time, don't bother to come back." Idris removed his hand. Hal spun around and grabbed Idris's wrist.

"I will love you until the day I die."

"Then… what's stopping you from staying?"

"I don't have a choice," Hal began. "This change is temporary." He pushed back his jacket sleeve and held out his right arm to show Idris the gray and cracked skin. "I am changing back to stone every second I am here."

Idris felt his heart crack a little. He refused to believe their love couldn't overcome a curse.

"We'll fix this," he said. "There has to be a way to break the curse."

Hal shook his head. "Let's go back to Sam."

Idris recalled the human with the beautiful aura of magic. The same Sam who'd killed his mother. "What can he do?"

"Just, let's go back."

Idris nodded. "Okay." He'd wait to ask further questions until they were in front of Sam. He didn't want to make any more accusations to upset Hal.

In seconds, they were back in the throne room, and it seemed like no one had moved since they'd left.

"About time you came back," someone snapped.

Idris pulled his attention away from his lover to face the speaker. Who dared talk to him that way? The human from the corner. Was this Sam? "Who are you? What are you?" He had to blink a few times, the man's aura almost blinding him.

"I'm Sam. And Hal was actually *my* gargoyle."

"Hal is not *your* anything!" A new speaker growled. The vampire stepped up beside Sam to glare at them.

"And you are?" While Idris was gone, apparently his mother had filled the court with complete strangers. Strange, since she didn't think anyone but the fae were worth her time.

"Bob, Sam's mate." Bob's vampire incisors were quite impressive when he flashed them in his smile.

Idris doubted very many people got close to Sam and kept all their body parts. "He may be your gargoyle, but Hal is going to stay here with me until we figure out how to cure his curse."

He didn't want to make Sam his enemy, not when he didn't know what the man was capable of, and certainly not with Bob-the-Vampire snarling at him.

"We know *how* to break the curse," Hal said. He sounded defeated and hung his head.

Idris looked from him to Sam then back again. He frowned. "If you know how to cure it, why haven't you done it?"

Hal didn't answer. Instead, Bob stepped forward and placed a hand on Sam's arm. "We don't know how to get the pearl from the sirens," he explained.

Idris pressed fingers to his temples where a tension headache had already begun pulsing. "Pearl? What pearl?"

Sam chimed in. "The sirens' purple pearl. Apparently, it's the only pearl that can break the curse."

Idris nodded as if he understood everything he was being

told. He hadn't heard of a purple pearl, yet here was Hal, who he'd thought dead, standing next to this blinding-aura Sam who was discussing it like it was obvious.

"And you know this how?" he finally asked Sam.

"I told him," Hal said. "It took me a while, and it's only because Sam's uncle had an extensive library, but my research says only the sirens' purple pearl can break the curse."

Idris huffed. "Then it's simple. We get it from them." He wasn't going to tiptoe around the siren king. They were both monarchs, he wasn't afraid of a little water, and they could come to an agreement. Idris would do just about anything to have Hal back. It only then hit him that he was thinking of himself as a monarch. Hell, did that mean he'd accepted his new role? He couldn't think about that now.

"There's more to this curse breaking thing," Hal added quietly.

"Like what?"

"Like the fact that there has to be a personal sacrifice by someone to be able to touch the stone. Any paranormal other than a siren who touches it will die."

"Unless there is a sacrifice," Sam confirmed.

"Yes."

"What kind of sacrifice?"

"A lover's death." Hal murmured.

Idris couldn't help it. His first instinct was that he'd be happy to die if it meant Hal was safe and alive. Where did that thought come from?

"I have favors I can call in. Maybe we can find a way around this, but there's one more problem," Sam said.

"What's that?"

"Sirens hate me."

"Any particular reason?" Sam didn't strike him as a

particularly difficult person. He couldn't imagine how he could've made an enemy.

"I might have killed several sirens or at least been halfway responsible for their deaths." Sam's mouth turned down at the corners.

"How did you kill them?"

"Knife on some," Sam said, then turned to Bob. "Fire, but that was Danjal, who's a demon, not me really."

"And don't forget the bathroom incident," Bob suggested.

"Well, that was Mikhail and Jin." Sam waved a hand as if dismissing the event.

Idris didn't know how much more bad news he could handle in one day. First his mother died, and then he learned his lover was alive but cursed, and now the one thing that might cure Hal could be out of reach.

He addressed Sam first. He seemed the one everyone deferred to. "We don't have to tell him about your connection. If the siren king doesn't know you're involved, we don't have to mention it."

Sam raised an eyebrow at the triplets. "Wait, I thought the sirens had a queen?"

"There was a coup, and the queen was killed," Idris said. "The new king is a high ranking officer called Sturgeon."

"Oh that's bad," Sam said.

Idris sighed. "Worse than the bad we already had?"

"Way more. Sturgeon hates me."

Then Sam stiffened, his gaze focused over Idris's shoulder. Idris turned to find his cousins watching him.

"Welcome back, cousin." The triad approached Idris, then bowed slightly. They might not be kings but as a triad they had more combined power than any single fae. The hair on the back of his neck tingled with their magical energy. Idris tensed, suddenly overwhelmed. He couldn't do this. Not any of it. What was the point? He should give up now.

Idris jolted when his fingers were entwined with another's and gripped tight. Hal flashed him a slight smile before squaring off against the triad. He'd missed being one of an "us." Knowing at least one person was in his corner. He'd been alone for too long when a casual show of support almost had him sobbing. Hal holding his hand was familiar and soothing.

"Thank you, cousins." He could never tell them apart. As a child, he'd suspected they were three people with one soul split between them, and he'd wondered if they passed it around from one to another. He fought back the shiver of dread their presence always brought.

"The siren leader knows of Sam's connection to Hal. The sirens watch Sam most closely." Only one spoke out loud, but the other two mouthed the words silently in unison. It never failed to freak Idris out when they did that.

Idris turned his attention back to Sam. What was it about him that called the attention of the siren king? It couldn't just be Sam killing sirens. He certainly wasn't the only man to have done that in the past. Sirens were brutal fighters and often became embroiled in battles with the landlocked.

"What do you suggest we do?" he asked the triad. They would not have mentioned the problem if they didn't already have a solution. He'd learned long ago that his cousins were always at least five steps ahead of everyone else. No doubt that was why the queen was dead, and they appeared unharmed. He resisted the urge to hear the details of his mother's demise. Either they wouldn't tell him or the details would keep him up at night.

"Come with us, cousin, and we'll tell you our plan."

Keeping hold of Hal's hand, Idris followed. He didn't

comment when Sam, Bob, and a black shadow he determined was their cat came along. *He brought his cat?*

When they reached the hallway, Idris was suddenly overcome with feelings of utter hopelessness. How could any of this be happening? How could he save Hal?

At that moment, all he wanted was to have Hal on his own so they could talk without all the craziness.

Just talk. For a few minutes.

After all, if finding the pearl failed, Hal could turn back into stone.

## Chapter Eleven

WHEN IDRIS STOPPED DEAD IN HIS TRACKS, HAL NEARLY walked straight into him.

"What's wrong?" he asked.

Idris turned. The expression in his silver-eyed gaze had Hal's breath catching in his throat. So many years had passed since he'd been imprisoned in his stone form. He never thought he'd ever be able to touch Idris again, let alone talk to him. Emotion glowed in Idris's beautiful eyes as he shook his head.

"I need time," Idris whispered.

What did he mean? Time away from him? Hal's anxiety could be nothing more than the stone hardening his chest, but to see Idris looking so sad made Hal think maybe this was it. This was the moment when Idris said he didn't love him anymore.

"What do you mean?" Hal asked.

"I need time with you before we do anything else."

Relief flooded Hal. Idris wasn't abandoning him. He'd thought Idris meant time away from him.

"We only have a few days." The triplets spoke in unison. *Freaky*.

"As your king, I say we can take an hour," Idris argued.

The triad responded with a range of expressions. One sneered, another looked shocked, and the third looked scared. Was it possible they were capable of independent thought?

Idris tightened his grip on Hal's hand and led him away from the people surrounding them. Left, then right, over and over through a twist of corridors that Hal had no hope of recalling. They walked for ages. In all that time, Hal didn't speak. What was he going to say to Idris? What could he say?

Finally, they stopped outside a large carved oak door that Hal recognized from before he'd been cursed. Idris's suite of rooms. Before Hal could comment, Idris laid his hand on the wood and muttered words under his breath. The heavy door swung open with a creak. The scent of disuse hit Hal. Evidently no one had come to air out Idris's room. With a flick of his fingers, the moldy dusty smell disappeared, and the drapes opened to let in light. Another flick tidied the bed, swept the surfaces clean of dust, and brought the scent of lemons into the air. Hal inhaled deeply. This was the smell that reminded him of Idris. Every time Sam dusted his office he used a lemon furniture polish and Hal's heart had cracked a little more.

The door swung shut behind them. Hal watched Idris wander around the large suite, checking the various side rooms with cursory glances.

"I haven't been in here since…" Idris hesitated then started again. "Not since you left on that quest. The same morning I watched you leave."

"I didn't know you watched. You didn't say goodbye."

"I couldn't talk to you; I was so angry that you chose to do those stupid tasks when you already had my heart. It should have been enough when I told you I loved you." Idris pulled Hal close until he could rest his head on Idris's shoulder.

"She told me you laughed at me when you were alone with her," Hal whispered against Idris's warm skin.

Idris tightened his grip. "My mother?"

Hal huffed. "And that you thought I would fail."

"I'm sorry," Idris said. "I was terrified you wouldn't come back. I begged her to cancel the quest. She laughed, but she was right, I had thought you would fail."

Hal stiffened and attempted to pull away, but Idris held on tight.

"Don't you see how she set you up? I knew whatever trials were thrown at you, dragons or trolls, I knew she would always be there making sure you didn't come back. The day of the quest I was so angry, I wasn't going to watch you leave, but I did. From that window right there." Idris pointed to a window on the east wall. The prince would've had a good view of Hal leaving without easily being spotted from below.

"After I was cursed, I hoped you'd found someone else and were happy even if the idea of you with another man almost killed me." For the longest time, they simply stared into each other's eyes. Hal stumbled back when Idris lunged at him. Together they tumbled onto Idris's big bed.

"There's never been anyone but you. I love you. I'll always love you." With a wave of his hand, Idris had them both naked. Hal had never been so grateful for his lover's magic.

They fought for dominance, only because Hal wanted Idris to know how much he needed him, but it was Idris who pinned Hal to the bed. Victory gleamed in his eyes before he kissed Hal, a hard, claiming kiss. Hal's chest tightened again, and he felt his lungs empty of air. It was happening slowly, but every tiny molecule of him was turning back to stone. Soon, in a few days, maybe a little more, he would be stone again. He couldn't go back to that existence without feeling Idris in him and around him one last time. With a quick move, he twisted them, so he straddled Idris. The familiar prickling in his arms was another sign of the curse returning as it wound through Hal's body, pushing past any healing that Idris had managed to conjure. Desperation hit him.

Now. He needed to reconnect once more, and it had to be now. He couldn't ask Idris to search for the pearl. The legend said that both lovers needed to lay hands on the pearl to break a curse that entwined them. How could he ask Idris to force his way into the siren king's lands to meet certain death? Hal had to give in to the curse and return to his gargoyle state if only to save Idris.

"What are you thinking?" Idris asked.

"Nothing," Hal lied.

Idris either chose to believe the lie or he considered making love to be more important than Hal's fib.

"We'll talk," he said. "After."

With that, he tangled his fingers into Hal's long hair and tugged him down for a kiss. Hal was hard against Idris, and the kiss was so perfect and right. They moved against each other, Hal rubbing against him.

"So long," he murmured into another kiss.

"Too long," Idris answered. "I have been lost without you. I didn't have another lover that mattered, only humans from whom I could borrow energy. All the time you were gone. I had given up," he admitted. "I couldn't stand the thought of anyone taking your place."

"You had to find someone else. If I was dead, you

couldn't stop living," Hal said urgently. "I saw you with that guy in the photo."

"What photo?"

"You and a guy outside a café or something. You were holding him, and it looked to me like you were lovers."

Idris looked guilty. "I promise you he was nothing but energy to me" Idris's hollow tone tore at Hal's heart.

Hal groaned low in his throat at the desolate words. "I should never have left you."

Idris smiled up at him and with a click of his fingers a stoppered bottle of oil appeared in his hands.

"I want to make love with you," Idris said gently.

Hal knew this would be the last time. Nothing would make him send Idris under the ocean to the siren king's palace. Idris would find someone else to love eventually, and Hal would return to life on the corner of Sam's desk.

Idris rolled them over, oiled his fingers, and pressed against Hal, his mouth close to Hal's cock.

Closing his lips around the tip of Hal's cock, he sucked and licked and moved in tandem with his fingers pressing inside.

"Please," Hal begged. Idris moved them both higher on the bed. Sparks of magic flew around them, skating across Hal's skin, healing a few minute patches of stone here and there.

"I love you," Idris murmured as he pushed inside, his hands supporting Hal's legs.

"And I love you," Hal said back, his features a study in concentration.

They rocked together silently, Idris kissing away every single hurt. When he came deep inside Hal, Idris gripped his hips so hard he knew he'd leave bruises behind. Only when they separated did the reality of everything come back to Hal, and to Idris it seemed.

We need to go," Idris said. "I won't lose you." He pressed a final kiss to Hal's breastbone then rolled up and off the bed. In an instant, he was dressed, and Hal felt the thrum of magic through him as Idris dressed him also.

"We're not going anywhere," Hal said. He stood up and pulled back the shirtsleeve to expose the darkening skin, too rough to touch. Then he looked Idris directly in the eyes. "It's too fast; we're too late."

## Chapter Twelve

SAM SAT IN THE LUXURIOUS OFFICE OF THE DEAD QUEEN AND watched everyone walk around him with quick, cautious steps, as if they thought he would attack without provocation.

"What do you think they'd do if I yelled boo?" Sam asked.

Bob snorted. "Wet themselves. I've never seen a group of such wimp-ass fae in my life. They look like they are afraid of their shadows."

"They are afraid of Sam's power. As fae we can feel it," one of the triplets said.

Sam could never tell them apart and since they pretty much spoke together and stayed together there didn't appear to be a lot of need to separate them. They were always "the triplets" in Sam's head.

"I'm still mad at you three. You let me be imprisoned. The queen could've killed Bob." He didn't care so much about his safety, but his lover could've been harmed. He wouldn't forgive them anytime soon.

The trio all shook their heads. "To us you shine brighter

than the sun. Your power makes it hard to look at you sometimes."

"But I'm just...." He didn't bother to finish the sentence. He wasn't fooling anyone these days. "Maybe it's the gifts on the bracelet."

"The queen feared your power. Anyone with more magic than she had was considered a threat. Your magic is one of the reasons the siren king is trying to kill you. He wants you dead because he doesn't trust you. He won't leave any enemies behind him."

Bob wrapped his arm around Sam in silent support. For once, Sam leaned against the vampire and accepted his comfort.

"Maybe you can talk to him before you ask for the pearl," Bob suggested.

"You will need to have something he wants in exchange," the triplets said.

"What?" Sam straightened and gave the fae his complete attention. He had a feeling if he missed a single fact Hal would be a gargoyle forever.

"You'll have to ask him," one of the triplets said.

Bob growled. "If we go and ask him he'll have us killed before we get close to the pearl."

"No, you can talk to him through the magic pool. Mother used to talk that way all the time," Idris said, walking into the room.

Hal entered beside the fae prince, clutching his arm.

"What's wrong with your arm?"

"I'm turning back into a gargoyle," Hal said.

"Let me see." Sam stepped forward. He pushed up Hal's sleeve. Large patches of his flesh were beginning to turn gray. He was turning back into a gargoyle.

"Does it hurt?" Bob asked, looking over Sam's shoulder.

"Not really. It pinches as if my skin was gathering, but it doesn't hurt," Hal said, but Sam could see the fear in his eyes.

"How can we stop it?" Sam asked. For a second, panic overwhelmed him. What if he couldn't save the gargoyle? Hell, he wasn't sure he could get out of the room. The fae were a bit too fascinated with him.

"Stop it," Bob said. "You *can* do this."

His cold glare sliced through Sam's panic.

Sam took a deep breath then let it out. "What do I do?"

"You go to the queen's communication pool, and you talk to the siren king."

"You make it sound easy. Nothing is easy." The deeper Sam delved into the paranormal world; the stronger his powers became and the more complicated things turned out to be.

"I didn't say it was easy. I said it needed to be done." Bob wrapped his hands around Sam's shoulders and gave him a small shake. "Don't get negative now, Sam. Believe that we can beat this."

Could they?

Sam's confidence had taken a hit with Hal's quick regression to his gargoyle form. If Sam was so powerful, why couldn't he stop this from happening? He should be able to control Hal's transformation, but he didn't know where to start. Sam couldn't counteract curses from dead queens. Hell, he didn't know how to stop anything.

Bob shook him again. Not painfully, but like he was trying to discipline a recalcitrant puppy.

"Stop that," Sam snapped. If Bob kept shaking him, his brains would get scrambled.

"Then stop doubting yourself."

Sam sighed. "I'm trying. Sometimes I wonder why did I

ever leave the normal world. I should've pursued a different career. One that didn't make me deal with the paranormal."

"You don't want that because then you wouldn't have met me." Bob's slow fang-tipped smile melted Sam's panic.

"Good point." They might have problems, but he loved Bob. No matter how much he might argue with his mate, he wouldn't get rid of Bob for anything.

Sam walked over to the magic pool the fae used for communication. "I guess phones don't work underwater, huh."

"I guess not," Bob replied.

Idris stepped forward. "You have to put your hands here and here." He pointed to the slight indentations on the stone. "It will activate the pool. Concentrate on the siren king and he will appear."

Sam obeyed. A soft hum filled the air as if he had started a powerful machine. "I don't know if I like this." The pool vibrated beneath his hands.

"It'll be fine, my love." Despite his tender words, Bob looked as anxious as Sam felt.

In fact, no one in the room appeared completely happy. A quick glance around revealed the fae were all watching Sam as if worried he'd destroy their pool next.

"You called?"

Sam snapped his attention back to the water. Sturgeon looked up at him.

"Uh, hello." He winced. Not the best way to start a conversation with someone who hated his guts.

Sturgeon smiled, a sharp-toothed affair. "Hello, Sam Enderson. I want to thank you for getting rid of the fae queen. That bitch has been a thorn in our side for centuries. I guess you heard I'm in charge now."

"I guess congratulations are in order." Sam didn't offer them.

Sturgeon flipped a gold coin between his fingers as they talked. "Thank you. How is my favorite killer doing?"

Sam opened his mouth to deny the title, but perhaps from Sturgeon's viewpoint Sam was the bad guy. "I'm doing fine. I could use a favor."

Sturgeon's laughter wasn't pleasant. "You're an optimist, aren't you?"

"Am I?" Sam didn't feel too optimistic these days.

"You are if you think I'm going to do anything for you."

"I need your pearl." No point in trying to hide his goal.

"Which pearl?"

A whisper of dread flowed through Sam. His instincts flared. Sturgeon's eyes glowed, and Sam knew Sturgeon was stringing him along. "Your purple pearl." Was there more than one?

Sturgeon lost his smile. "And what do you want with the Pearl of Undoing?"

Damn, his chances just decreased. If the sirens named the damn thing, it must be important. "I'm trying to reverse a spell for a friend."

His experience with Sturgeon didn't make him want to share information.

"Always so noble," Sturgeon mocked. He ran one pointed nail across his lips. "I think it has to do with that ex-gargoyle hovering over your shoulder."

Sam turned to see Hal peering into the pool beside him. He sighed. Why didn't anyone ever stay where they were supposed to?

"Hal is turning back into a gargoyle. The death of the queen hasn't halted his curse. I want to stop it permanently, and for that we need your Pearl. What do you want in exchange?"

Idris hissed his disapproval.

Sam ignored him.

Sturgeon's eyes glowed with greed. "Finally, I have Sam Enderson at my mercy."

"What do you want, Sturgeon?"

"Your mate," Sturgeon said.

"No." Sam didn't even consider it. "I will come and destroy all your people before I let you have my mate for a second."

Sturgeon didn't appear upset with Sam's statement. He tapped his right index finger against his bottom lip. "Hmm, what do you have to offer me?"

Hal stepped forward. "I will owe you a debt."

The loud laughter came clearly across the connection. "What could you offer me, gargoyle?"

"He's my mate," Idris said.

Sturgeon leaned forward. "Now this is starting to get interesting. A fae king's favor would be valuable, but not as worthwhile as the fae queen's crown."

"You want my mother's crown?" Idris asked.

Sam couldn't tell if Idris was appalled or not. The fae king had a good poker face. It would serve him well in future negotiations.

"Yes, I hear it will bring the wearer good luck. I need good luck." The desperation on the king's face made Sam wonder if Sturgeon might not be enjoying his new position.

"I'll call you back." Sam lifted his hands and broke the connection.

"Why did you do that?" Hal asked, his mouth dropping open.

"Because I wanted to talk to Idris before we promised away his mother's jewelry."

"You can't," Idris said. He bit at his thumbnail, the only sign of his stress.

"Why not?"

"She lost it," Idris said.

"She didn't lose it, my king," the triplets said in unison.

"I really hate it when they do that," Bob whispered in Sam's ear.

Sam bit his lip to hold back his laughter. "What did she do with it?"

"She gave it to the troll king in exchange for some land," the triplets said.

"Do we know how to get it back?" Sam asked.

"We'll have to visit him and find out what he wants in exchange," Idris said, a resigned expression on his face.

"We can't just call?" Sam tapped the stones around the communication pool. There were too many kings and queens in his life. He needed to go on a royalty diet.

"It only works for water-based creatures and the troll king hides his palace. We will have to do a reveal spell to discover his home," Idris said.

"What if he won't give the crown up?" Sam asked. "If it brings good luck, he could've been enjoying its powers this entire time."

Idris's cold expression chilled Sam to the bone. "We will get it back one way or another."

Sam patted him on the back. "Let's try to do it with minimal bloodshed."

"I make no promises when it comes to Hal," Idris replied.

"Where would we find him?"

"Sam?"

"Yeah?" He turned to face Bob, who had a curious expression on his face. "What?"

"You already know him."

Sam thought for a moment. "I don't know any trolls. Except for Trawl. Wait, Trawl is the troll king? Shouldn't he live in a palace or something instead of under a slimy bridge?"

"Trolls don't think of rulers the same way as we do. They are more of a solitary race. Trawl is contacted if there are any problems with the trolls as a whole, or if anyone is systematically bothering them. Otherwise he's left alone."

"What makes him king then?"

"Birth. Trolls are a paternal society. His father was king, so he's king. No one else wants the job because it doesn't come with perks or power, so it continues to be passed down from father to son."

Sam wondered how trolls reproduced if they were so solitary but decided not to ask. His mind could only handle so much trauma in one day.

"Well, at least that is one bit of good news." Trawl liked Sam and might be more willing to negotiate a reasonable exchange for the crown. "Let's talk to a troll."

## Chapter Thirteen

SEVEN BRIDGES LATER AND BOB WAS STARTING TO WONDER IF they would ever find the elusive Trawl. He was in none of his usual spots and not even Sam attempting to call him while clutching his charm bracelet was helping. Idris and Hal accompanied them, much to the horror of the fae triplets, who appeared to want to shut Idris away in a box until all this was settled. Of course, that accounted for the ten guards who also followed them, at a discreet distance, of course, making for one big entourage.

Not since the first day he had set foot in the agency did he have such an incredible feeling of too many people being involved. He'd been selected for this mission, no, not a mission, more a pilgrimage, and he was happy to do it with just him and Sam. But no, somehow there were these extras that kept getting involved in Bob's prime concern—keeping Sam alive.

Hal had long since stopped being able to keep up a steady pace with them along the river out of the city. Closer inspection showed grayish scales forming on his exposed skin and he admitted he was feeling heavier.

A quietness had descended on the group. Hal and Idris had stopped whispering, the guards had ceased marching with heavy feet and the clatter of weapons, and Bob had concentrated so hard on blocking his thoughts from Sam that he realized he could no longer hear Sam in his head.

Sam stopped in the middle of the path, which had narrowed until it was only wide enough for one, and stared at Bob.

"What?" Bob asked. He glanced around him and moved a step forward as the others caught up with them. A quick order from Idris and the guards backed off, leaving Idris to help Hal sit on the nearest boulder.

"You're doing it again," Sam said pointedly as he tapped his temple. "I was talking to you, and you didn't answer. You're blocking me." He looked a little angry and a whole lot disappointed. An overwhelming flood of emotion hit Bob as he focused on his lover; embarrassment, sadness, anger, and disappointment. Then one message loud and clear.

*He doesn't want to be connected anymore.*

Bob stepped into Sam's space and gripped him hard, forcing a bruising kiss on him. Once Sam relaxed in his arms, Bob deepened the kiss.

"Don't ever think that," Bob said, and then he kissed Sam again.

*"I love you,"* he thought clearly.

"Bob—"

"I love you. Know that I will always love you." Sam needed to remember that because the future could bring many things to question that devotion. If Sam didn't believe Bob now, he wouldn't when push came to shove.

Sam reached up a hand and twisted his fingers in Bob's hair, his dark eyes filled with emotion. "And I love you," he whispered.

Bob pulled him close in a hug then stepped back. He gestured to Hal and Idris. "We need to keep going."

Sam nodded. "Yeah, let's go." The strange procession made its way to Blackwater Bridge, the last main bridge before the river disappeared out of the city. This was their last stop. If Trawl wasn't here, then it was likely they'd never find him in time to stop what was happening to Hal. Which was becoming more urgent, with Hal's breath sounding heavier with each step. Bob didn't like to think of the man's internal organs turning to stone. He'd have to encourage Sam to call in a marker or something to finish the conversion quickly to save Hal the pain, and Idris as well.

Sam held up a hand and stopped. The rest of their entourage came to a halt behind them.

"I want everyone to wait here," he ordered. He looked pointedly at Bob. "You as well," he added.

"I'm not—"

"I've seen flashes of Trawl in the last three bridges, yet we all scramble up with weapons and a fae king. He's not going to be hanging around, is he? I'll do this myself," he said.

"Sam—"

"No, Bob." He didn't elaborate, simply left and scrambled down the bank to the waterline. Bob took a couple steps closer until he could see under the bridge, and true to what Sam expected, Trawl was sitting on the bank right under it.

Sam's thoughts came back to him. Sam wasn't stressed or afraid, he was confident and knew exactly what he needed to do. "*Eww, he smells just as bad as I remember,*" he sent back to Bob. Then he looked over his shoulder right at Bob and smiled. Abruptly, everything was right in Bob's world, just with that smile, and he relaxed.

He watched as Sam approached the troll and tensed as the words failed to carry back to him. Not only that, but he couldn't get a sense of how Sam was feeling.

"I don't like this," he said to no one in particular.

"What's happening?" Idris asked.

Bob shook his head. "I have no idea."

When Sam finally turned to come back to them, he didn't look happy. "He doesn't have it anymore," he said as soon as he was close enough to be heard.

"No," Idris whispered in despair. Bob saw the king crouch beside Hal, who met Bob's gaze, determination tightened his jaw and reflected in his stern expression. The lack of the crown could be his death warrant unless they did something.

"What now?" Bob asked.

Sam's mirthless laugh didn't reassure him. "Trawl said he exchanged the crown for a love spell from a succubus in town."

"Succubi don't do spells."

"No," Sam began patiently. "She exchanged something with a witch. I lost track after the first exchange or so. Anyway. I know where this succubus is. About half a mile from here." He looked down at Hal, who was attempting to stand. "Bob and I will visit her, alone. Idris, take Hal to the harbor with your guards. Be ready at the ocean for when Bob and I get the crown. If we are going to get the trade with the sirens done in time, we have to hurry."

Idris wasn't convinced. "But, Sam—"

"No arguments. Get him ready. We're going now. We'll meet you at the bar by the harbor. Watch for sirens, you can't trust them. Smudge!" Sam called. The cat had disappeared and reappeared without warning during their search. Bob wasn't surprised when the unpredictable beast jumped out of the shadows and onto Sam's shoulder to emit a loud purr. Smudge always seemed to know when Sam needed him.

"I wish we were outside the succubus's place."

Bob quickly wrapped his hand around Sam's arm seconds before they vanished.

WHILE IDRIS HELPED Hal to stand, he missed Bob and Sam leaving. He knew it was only ten minutes or so to the harbor where the river met the sea, but it seemed like such a long way. How long would it take for Bob and Sam to find the succubus? Would it work? Was it possible to find the crown?

"They'll find it," Hal comforted him.

How could Hal be reassuring *him*? He was the one who was whole and well; he should be making Hal feel better.

"I know they will." Idris injected calm and peace into his voice, as if for that moment he actually believed all was going to be well.

They hobbled a little farther.

"I wish it didn't matter," Hal said. His voice now had a strange tone, like ice in a glass, hard and brittle.

"What?"

One of the guards came up next to them and supported Hal from the other side. Idris was extremely grateful for the help. As Hal transformed, he got heavier.

"I wish there were a million chances to turn the curse on its head, I wish this didn't matter so much." Hal cursed and stumbled, and the weight of him nearly pulled Idris to the ground.

"Keep going, love, keep going, we're not giving up now."

They kept walking, step by torturous step, Hal getting slower with each one until finally the harbor was there. They passed boats floating serenely in the calm water, the old inn at the jetty, and finally they were at the water's edge. Or rather, behind the tall six-foot wall between them and the water. Idris was informed enough of siren antics to know not to get too close to the water here. Especially when Hal would sink like a stone. The guards formed a half circle around them and each one very deliberately turned their back so they would be facing outwards to meet danger head-on. Not that sirens took their battles to dry land—well, mostly they didn't. Idris stopped himself from thinking too hard on that. Instead he focused on Hal, finding a smooth stretch of skin on his wrist to the back of his hand and stroking in a gentle rhythm.

"This will be over soon," he said reassuringly. And he meant every word of it. "We are meant to be together."

Hal leaned into him a little and smiled. "I know. I'm glad you're here with me at the end of this. I don't want to die alone."

"Don't say that," Idris pleaded. "You won't die. I won't let you die."

They kissed but the texture of Hal's lips was wrong. Instead of being pliant they were hard and unyielding. Hal tried to pull back, but Idris refused to let him go. He deepened the kiss and realized he had tears running down his face. He pulled back, and Hal reached up to wipe away the tears.

"I wish we'd found each other sooner," Idris said.

Hal nodded. "I wish I'd never run."

"I love you."

Hal rested his heavy head on Idris's shoulder. "And I love you, King of the Fae."

They sat there quietly, and Idris listened to Hal's breathing, inhaling and exhaling at the same speed as his lover. He decided then and there that if Hal died, he wouldn't remain the king. He had a place in the mountains close to dragon land. He'd go there and live out the rest of his days.

"Stop thinking sad things."

Idris was startled; he hadn't realized he'd stopped focusing on the here and now and instead lost himself in the terrifying world of what-ifs. Hal looked up with a soft smile. "Bob and Sam will make this work. You'll see."

Idris smiled even though inside his heart was breaking. They were cutting it fine if indeed they had any chance of finding the crown. Instead of saying all of this, he simply said,

"Of course they will." And he realized he meant it. That he had to think they would succeed so he and Hal could have more time together.

He was getting good at this hope thing.

SAM CLOSED his eyes and waited for the world to settle around him, wishing he'd kept his eyes closed for the entire journey. When he could focus he saw the club was shut and he quickly identified the side stairs that Trawl had told him about. He took a step toward them, but Bob stopped him.

"She'll try to suck the life out of you."

"Trawl said she didn't try it with him."

Bob sent a very graphic image of anyone sucking anything from the troll and Sam shivered.

"She won't touch me," Bob said. "I'll go first."

They climbed the stairs quickly, and Bob knocked soundly on the wood. The door shook, but no one shouted anything along the lines of "come in."

"Maybe she's not home," Sam offered. Bob tried the handle and pushed open the door. The room they walked into was a loft conversion of some sort, a wide-open room that wouldn't have looked out of place in the human world. Large leather sofas, low lighting, drapes, and a kitchen. All very normal. Bob stepped right in, and Sam followed at a cautious distance. He didn't want to get anything sucked out of him just yet.

Which is why what they discovered next was wrong. So very very wrong.

## Chapter Fourteen

THE SMELL HIT SAM FIRST. A HEAVY, SICKLY STENCH, THAT hung in the air like a smothering blanket. Sam was seconds from purging his stomach on the floor. "What the hell is that?"

*"Don't look, Sam,"* Smudge said from the floor.

"I think she tried to seduce the wrong person." Bob nodded toward the body strewn across the puce silk couch. Or it had been a body at one time. The couch had bits of the succubus spread across it. It looked like a demon's buffet of dark blood and bits of flesh had been laid out for feasting.

Sam pressed his right hand over his mouth. Smudge brushed against his leg, easing some of the nausea in Sam's stomach.

"Do you need to step outside?" Bob asked, his incisors sliding out from between his lips.

Sam swallowed a few times before replying. He'd never get this scent out of his memory. "No, I'll be fine. What about you?"

"To me she smells like food gone bad. Still, blood holds no interest to me."

"Then why are your teeth dropping?"

"Just because I cannot eat it, does not mean it won't make me hungry."

"Can you control yourself?" If Sam could stop from throwing up, Bob should be able to get a handle on his urges.

"Yes. Give me a minute."

Sam spent his time glancing around the studio apartment. Other than a doorway that probably led to the bathroom, nothing jumped out as being a magic crown. He had to glance away from what was left of the succubus and back to the case at hand. "Do you think it's still here?"

"I don't know."

Frantic, Sam scanned the room. Where would a succubus keep a crown?

"You want to check the shelves over there? I'll check the cabinets." Bob pointed to a series of bookshelves in an alcove, conveniently the farthest spot from the body.

"Sure." Sam wouldn't argue. He didn't usually like Bob taking care of him that way, but with the dead succubus making him want to hurl, he'd take the out this time without argument.

He stumbled over to the shelves. A quick glance didn't show anything. He moved a few books around, searching for a secret cabinet. If it were up to Sam he wouldn't show off a crown in his possession; he'd hide it where no one could take it away. Persuaded his line of reasoning was sound, Sam pushed and pulled books out of the way while he studied the wall behind it. What if there was a secret compartment?

"Search with your magic too," Bob called out.

"Sure, I'll do that." Sam kept his muttering low. He didn't know who Bob thought he was talking to. Sam had yet to successfully understand his magic even while using it.

"I can still read your mind."

"Sorry." He wouldn't want anyone in his mind right now. The mixture of nausea and doubt had Sam feeling unbalanced.

"Focus on finding the crown."

"Yeah, okay." Sam turned his back to the dead body. He couldn't look at all those pieces and remain sane. His mind kept trying to fit them all together despite the missing chunks.

His search of the bookshelf revealed nothing except questionable taste in literature. "I don't see anything."

Bob slammed the cabinet door. "Nothing in here either."

Sam spun around and leaned against the bookshelf. "What do we do now? If we can't find the crown, we can't get the pearl."

"Don't give up yet. If we discover who killed the succubus, we can find the crown. They must've taken it with them."

"We don't have time to solve another case."

"Well, it's the only way we'll find the crown," Bob replied.

"I wish we could talk to the succubus." He froze after the words left his mouth. Smudge purred nearby.

*Crap.*

"Sam." Bob's warning tone had Sam wincing.

"Sorry." A cold wind fingered its way up Sam's spine, like a skeleton's bony fingers had trailed a path. Sam scooted away from the wall. Too late. It was too late to take back his words as the succubus's ghost solidified beside him.

"You wanted to talk to me?" Her pale, smoky outline began to fill in, sketched in sepia shades. Luckily she looked much as she had in life and not the scattering of pieces on the couch. If she hadn't been transparent Sam wouldn't have known she was dead.

"Um, I don't suppose you can tell us who killed you."

Sam had only met one ghost before, and it still lived in the house with him.

"A fae asshole brought a demon and had him kill me."

The succubus was eerily beautiful, and the curse word seemed wrong coming from her mouth.

"Why would he do that?" Sam folded his arms against his chest.

She shrugged. "He demanded the crown. I refused. That crown was mine! When I didn't give in, he opened this bottle he had and released a demon. I didn't stand a chance."

"I'm sorry." Those words seemed weak against her trauma, but they were all he had to offer. She inclined her head at his soft words. "Do you know the name of the fae who did this?"

"Mevn." Her long hair whipped around her head as she spit out the words. "He's always trying to stiff me on payments, but he never tried to hurt me before."

"That's because he's never needed a valuable artifact before," Bob said, coming to stand beside Sam.

Sam frowned. "What does he need it for now?" He couldn't think of any instance where another fae would need the crown. Possessing the crown wouldn't mean the owner was suddenly king or queen of all fae. The crown didn't make the ruler, or the queen would've lost her title when she'd given it away.

"He said if the king didn't have it then he couldn't choose someone unsuitable." The succubus shrugged.

Facts began tumbling into place. Mevn probably thought he could become the king's consort if he had the crown. After all, if Hal turned to stone, the king wouldn't have a consort.

"Where would he go?" Bob asked.

The succubus ignored him. She didn't act as if she'd

heard anything he said. Bob nudged Sam, nodding toward the succubus.

Sam sighed. "Where would he go?"

"He keeps an apartment on the Eastside, away from the palace so no one can see what he's up to. Sometimes he hires succubi to increase his pleasure during sex, and I've heard rumors of a lot of other kinks. His partners were always willing, or I wouldn't have gone along." The succubus's wistful tone had Sam wondering if there had once been something more between her and Mevn.

"Thank you for your time." Sam didn't know how to banish a ghost. Luckily his words appeared to be enough. With a swirl of mist she vanished.

"Wow, who knew you could channel spirits." Bob kissed Sam's forehead, chasing away some of the chill that had sunk into Sam's bones.

"I don't want to make a habit of that. I don't think we've met Mevn before." Sam tried to remember all the members of the court and realized he could match very few names to the faces in that room.

"He was one of the royals sitting next to the queen when you zapped her. I've met him before," Bob said. "He's always been a suck-up. A royal yes-man."

"Huh? Sounds to me like he learned to say no. Or at least that he wants to have a say over who is on the throne somehow."

Bob shook his head. "I think he changed his focus from being the queen's mate to being the king's. He must've rushed straight here while we were talking to Trawl. There are spies in every court."

Sam sighed. "Sounds like he went from yes-man to manipulator. What's his motivation for stealing the crown? Does he think Idris will decide he's irresistible? Isn't he straight if he was going for the queen's attention before?" All these political maneuverings were beyond Sam's knowledge.

"Who knows what he's thinking. Maybe he likes power, and it doesn't matter who's his partner. Most fae are bisexual. I think King Idris is one of the few who's been exclusively with men."

"How do you know that about Idris?"

Bob shrugged. "I've heard about him from people."

"People?" Sam was suspicious.

"I've been around a long time, Sam," Bob pointed out. "So, what's next?"

Bob's blatant attempt to change the subject made Sam suspicious, but Bob's thoughts were clear of subterfuge, so Sam dismissed his concerns.

"I guess we need to ask around about this Eastside location." Sam didn't like having to hunt down this guy, but better to find him now than let him run around free and use his demon to kill others. It wouldn't be long before the demon took control. Controlling any aggressive demon never lasted. Eventually, the demon either killed its master or possessed the summoner's body.

"We'd best hurry before Hal sinks to the bottom of the ocean as a stone."

"Do you want to go back and talk to Idris about what's going on while I hunt down Mevn's location?"

Bob snorted. "I'm not leaving you alone to deal with a psychotic demon-wielding fae. Especially when we're not certain what kind it is. We'll go together. Maybe we can have Smudge send Idris a note."

"Smudge?"

*"I'll go."*

Before they could say anything else, Smudge vanished.

"He's quite handy," Bob said.

"He can be." Sam didn't know if the extra boost in magic was worth the hassle of having a powerful familiar follow him from place to place.

"Let's go." Bob waved for Sam to precede him.

Sam exited the succubus's home. "We need to report her death."

"We can do that after we get the pearl. We are on a deadline. Hal could turn to stone if we stop to answer questions."

Bob made sense, but Sam still felt bad for the succubus. She'd been doing the best she could using her nature to make some money. He wasn't that much different from her.

They hurried to the Eastside. It only took asking a few street people to be given Mevn's address. The number of people eager to turn the fae in was almost amusing. Mevn hadn't made any friends among the street people. Every one of them stated they hoped Sam and Bob took him down.

They stopped outside a set of large iron gates. "Stay behind me. A demon is less likely to hurt a vampire."

Sam rolled his eyes but didn't argue. He could be armed from head to toe and Bob would still want to protect him.

"Do you think we should ring the bell?" Sam asked.

Smudge appeared on the ground beside Sam. *"I'll open it for you."*

"Thank you, Smudge."

*"Always happy to help."* The familiar wrapped his tail around Sam's calf before unwinding it. With a crackle of electricity, the gate swung open. Blue streaks of energy chased around the metal curlicues. Sam was careful to avoid touching them.

They followed the long drive up to the house and paused outside the front door.

Sam knocked.

"What are you doing?" Bob whispered.

"It seems wrong to just march in." Sam's mother had raised him to be polite.

*"You will need to lose some of your civility to win this match,"* Smudge said.

"What are you talking about?" Sam asked. The door swung open.

"Welcome, Sam Enderson." A fae Sam recognized from the court opened the door. So this was Mevn.

Mevn's wide smile, slick as a puddle of oil, made Sam's stomach churn. The fae's eyes didn't reflect his grin; they were killer cold. His next words chilled Sam. "Did you come here to die?"

## Chapter Fifteen

BOB MOVED TO STAND BETWEEN MEVN AND SAM. HE HAD A history with the fae court, and he knew how dangerous Mevn and his kind could be. Not normal-fae-dangerous, but empire-building-dangerous. He thought the Vampire Council had dealt with all the rogue fae a long time ago, but they clearly missed one. Mevn had given the impression he was supportive of the new king, but to stand here and threaten Sam? He certainly wasn't a good guy.

"Bob," Mevn greeted in clipped tones.

"Mevn."

Sam poked Bob in the back. *"You know him?"* Bob didn't know how to answer. His secrets went way, way back and he didn't have time to explain them to Sam. This was not the time, nor the place for explanations.

*"Leave this to me,"* he sent back.

"I didn't come here to die," Sam said from behind Bob.

"Your little human is feisty," Mevn said with a curl of his lips.

Bob filed away that description. Mevn had seen what happened in the throne room, seen the power that coursed through Sam, but now appeared unconcerned about Sam's abilities. Maybe his demon was giving him a false sense of power.

"Give us the crown and we'll leave," Bob said in simple clear terms that weren't open for discussion.

Mevn smirked. "I don't think I can do that." He examined his nails then buffed them on his jacket. "I need to keep hold of that object until it's too late to save Halstein."

Sam pushed past Bob. "Why?"

Bob held out a hand to stop Sam getting too close to the fae's threshold. Mevn laughed.

"Don't tell me you haven't worked it out."

"Enlighten us," Sam snapped.

"Without the crown, Hal dies, King Idris is bereft, and I become consort. And we all know the power lies with the consort of the king."

"What makes you think you'll automatically be consort?" Sam asked the question preying on Bob's mind.

"Because I'll let my demon kill fae subjects until Idris gives in."

"We'll warn him, and he'll be able to counteract your demon," Sam said.

Mevn raised a single eyebrow. "Not if you can't leave here."

Bob didn't give away his reaction. They weren't inside Mevn's house and it was doubtful magic could extend from inside out to where they were standing. They weren't trapped.

*"What does he mean?"* Sam asked.

Then it became all too obvious what Mevn meant. Bob ducked. The rush of air over his head let him know how close he'd come to capture. He spun around to face his attacker.

*Fuck.*

A soul ripper demon stood before him. The air turned cold

as a winter graveyard with the smell of dirt and decay surrounding them. Bob struggled against memories of being buried alive in his younger years by his sadistic master.

"Bob!"

Sam's voice snapped Bob out of his trance. One way soul rippers caught their prey was by dragging up their victims' worst memories and trapping them in the past.

Magic must have hidden the demon before. Bob cursed himself for talking to Mevn when he should have been alert to the demon's presence.

Bob dodged the ripper's swipe of claws, nearly tripping over Sam as he pushed him back.

The demon snarled and leaped forward. The ripper's red eyes and razor-sharp teeth had Bob's incisors descending in defense. Instinct had him shoving Sam backward and out of the demon's reach. Without thought, he threw himself at the demon.

No one was taking Sam from him. The demon's claws sank into his shoulder and scraped bone, but he refused to scream, only using the hold to his advantage. Ducking, he threw the demon off balance, with the demon's claws still embedded in his flesh. He gritted his teeth against a scream of agony when the demon tore free. A quick upswing of his forearm blocked the next blow. The demon screamed. Vile black blood spilled from his mouth and burned like acid on Bob's skin. Bob twisted on the balls of his feet then grabbed the demon before it could strike again. The demon stumbled and before he could right himself Bob sank his teeth deep in its throat. He tore, bit and sucked down the fetid blood until the demon was a husk on the ground.

Bob collapsed. The demon's evil blood seared through his veins, liquid fire burning through him. He took slow, measured breaths; demon blood and bile was poisonous to vampires, and he knew what he'd done was give himself a death sentence. He only had an hour or two remaining to get the crown, save Hal, and then place Sam under Mikhail's protection.

A smothered gasp had Bob twisting to see Sam. Mevn had taken the moment of distraction to drag Sam into the house. The powerful fae had blocked Sam's thoughts and prevented Sam from warning Bob. He couldn't even think about leaving Sam, or what it might do to him.

Struggling to stand, Bob tried to focus his thoughts and break through the mental barrier Mevn had put between them.

*"Wish for help, love,"* he threw the words out over and over, but the connection was so weak and fuzzy he doubted he got through. After a few failed attempts, Bob stood and stumbled for the door, only to be thrown back by the magic net over the house. He tried again, and again, each time thwarted. He could hear Sam shouting and Mevn's cackling laughter.

He looked around, scanning the building for weaknesses. There must be another way in. He shook as he dragged his poisoned body up the outside of the house, finding purchase among the sickly smelling flower boxes that caged the house, and clambered to the roof. Up here the magic was thinner, still impenetrable to most, but to Bob it was nothing. Sam was inside the house, and he wasn't letting his love die.

The poison inside him was starting to work its evil, and it took almost everything he had to gather his strength and smash through the tiled roof, dropping to a crouch inside the hole. The noise he'd made had taken away the element of surprise. Running, he followed the sound of cries, sliding to a halt as he saw a ring of dragon fire surrounding a sobbing, pleading Mevn. Sam floated ten inches from the floor with his back arched and dragon fire flowing from his fingers.

The fire burned Mevn to ashes in seconds as Bob watched and Sam collapsed to the floor, the fire vanishing with a whoosh as if someone had blown it out. Bob approached his lover cautiously.

"Sam?"

Sam looked up at him. "I called for help," he said with shock in his eyes. "I didn't know what I was asking for."

"I told you to call for magic," Bob said, gathering Sam into his arms.

"I didn't hear you. I couldn't hear you." Sam's skin had an unhealthy pallor, and his voice shook.

Bob held him tight. Hal, Idris, the crown, and the poison sliding through his body were unimportant as long as Sam was okay.

"We need to find the crown," Bob reminded him gently when it was finally time to move.

"Is the demon still out there?"

"No, I dealt with him."

"I didn't mean to get dragged in here," Sam said. "I tried to stop him. I should have called for help."

"The demon is dead, Mevn is gone. Wish for the crown, Sam."

"Why didn't you have me wish for it before? It could've saved us all this pain."

Bob released Sam then stepped back. "No. Mevn would have protected his house with blocking magic. Any wishes you made to locate something would've been blocked. Now that Mevn's dead, his spells should be invalid. Wish for the crown, my love."

Sam nodded. He took a deep breath and let it out again before he spoke. "I wish I had the fae queen's crown." He held his hands palm up as he spoke. He'd barely finished his wish when the image of a crown coalesced and became whole in Sam's hand. It was a tiny thing, no jewels or shine, just a simple gold object that Sam looped his fingers through.

So much pain and death for something so ordinary.

"I'd expected something more," Sam said.

Bob opened his mouth to speak, but the room spun. He stumbled and Sam righted him with a concerned look. Bob pulled up his hidden reserves. The success of his mission depended on Sam not suspecting a thing.

"Fuck," Sam murmured. "Bob, we need to get you help."

Bob cradled Sam's face. "I heal fast. Don't worry."

"You don't look so great."

"We need to leave, Sam, now." Bob picked Sam up in his arms and tried not to hurl. "Close your eyes, babe, I'll get us back where we need to be."

Sam gripped Bob's shoulder with his free hand and tucked the crown between them. Then he very deliberately shut his eyes.

"Let's go," he said. "We have a gargoyle to save."

BOB FALTERED ONLY TWICE on the journey back to the harbor, and he didn't think Sam noticed. When they reached the point of exchange Bob set Sam onto the wooden dock before quickly pulling down the sleeves of his shirt to cover the black trails that were starting to mark his arm. The poison was eating away his blood. He didn't want Sam to suspect anything was wrong. There would be time enough for goodbyes when they had saved Hal.

Idris waited for them with the guard, crouched down beside Hal, whose head was buried in his hands. Bob didn't have to look closely to see the cracks in Hal's hand and wrist where stone had taken hold.

*"Are we too late?"* Sam asked.

Bob sighed. "*I hope not.*"

Sam held out the crown. "So now what?"

A voice from the water called to Sam. "Now," Sturgeon said with unfettered glee in his voice. "Sam brings the crown to the bottom of the sea."

Sam looked at Bob, then back at Sturgeon, who floated just beyond reach. "What do you mean?"

"I won't give the pearl to you unless you place the crown on my head in the palace."

"No," Bob said, simple and to the point. "I'll go in with you, and you toss Sam the pearl. I don't trust you to keep your word. For all I know you'll drown me and keep the crown and the pearl."

"I'll go," Idris said desperately. He stood up and shook off Hal's hold. "I can't live without Hal, and even if I die trying—"

"No," Bob said again, not bothering to keep his voice kind. No way would he let anyone else die for this quest.

Sturgeon bobbed up a little, exposing his chest and the seaweed that curled around him like long strands of hair.

"Then what do you propose as a solution to our dilemma?" he asked slyly.

"I'll go," Bob said.

"No," Sam shouted.

Sturgeon chuckled. "One lover has to die to crown me king and bring prosperity to my kingdom." Madness tinged his words. "I don't really care who it is."

Idris stepped forward. "It is my right to sacrifice myself for the man I love," he stated.

"You have a kingdom of your own," Sam said. "I should go."

Bob glanced at his right hand. Poison trailed through the

veins on the back of his hand. Soon it would reach his heart, and he'd be dead.

"I can find a breathing spell or something," Sam said with hope in his voice. "I had dragon fire, and I only wished for help. No one has to die today."

Bob turned to cradle Sam's face like he had at Mevn's house. "I love you," he said. He pushed every ounce of what he felt for Sam into those three words. Every molecule of love, desire, and want, and he hoped Sam understood. "I will always love you," he added softly.

With a quickly stolen kiss, Bob snatched the crown from Sam's hands and dived into the sea. The water closed over his head. A gleeful Sturgeon threw something up and out of the water, before pulling Bob under the water with him.

Bob didn't need to breathe, but he was dying anyway, and so he relaxed and let the ocean swallow him whole. Sam had the pearl.

His last glimpse of the upper world was Sam's face in an anguished scream and Idris holding him back.

*"I love you."*

## Chapter Sixteen

Sam watched Bob sink beneath the waves.

"Bob! No!"

He gripped the pearl in his hand and couldn't find it in his heart to care what happened to the king or his lover. What had Bob done? Had he sacrificed himself for a stupid jewel? *This can't be happening.*

"May I have the pearl?" Idris asked.

Sam opened his fingers and dropped the pearl into Idris's outstretched hand. Ignoring everyone else, he stumbled to the edge of the dock and fell to his knees.

*"Bob, please, can you hear me? Where are you?"*

His heart felt as if it weighed a million pounds as he tried to figure out how they had reached this point. After everything he'd been through over the past few months, he never would've thought he'd lose his lover. Shock froze him in place.

*"Please. Bob. Please be alive."*

"Vampires can't drown," Hal offered.

"I know, but that isn't it. I saw his face; he's not coming

back." He'd known as soon as Bob gave him that last kiss. Sam knew a goodbye kiss when he got one.

"Why?"

"I don't know. He says he loves me." Tears slid down Sam's cheeks. What had he done to get Bob to leave him? "I don't understand."

"Your and Bob's sacrifices will be remembered in the fae history books for eternity," Idris said, as if Sam gave a damn.

"Thanks." Sam didn't bother to glance at the fae king.

"I-I'm going to see if this works on Hal's curse now." Idris's shaken tone drew Sam's attention. The anxiety on the fae king's face didn't make Sam feel better.

"If it doesn't I'm going down there and insisting on a refund." Sam looked down into the water but only saw his reflection. No sirens lurked beneath the depths to stare back at him. They were all probably off watching their siren king become kinglier.

A loud shout pulled Sam's attention from the low waves. He glanced over his right shoulder to see what was going on. Hal writhed on the wooden dock. Unearthly screams burst from him as he flopped about more than a line-caught fish.

"Is he all right?" Sam got to his feet, hurrying over to see if he could help.

"I-I don't know." Idris's expression of fear and worry pulled Sam out of his self-absorption.

"Do something, Sam!"

"What?" Sam reached out and grabbed one of Hal's flailing hands. Immediately the ex-gargoyle stopped thrashing about. His breathing evened out, and Hal stopped screaming.

"What did you do?" Idris asked.

"I don't know." Sam glanced toward the water but saw no sign of Bob resurfacing. He let go of Hal's hand.

Hal screamed, arching up from the dock, his throat

bulging and veins popping to the surface with true monster movie horror.

"Grab him!" Idris shouted.

Sam wrapped his hand around Hal's arm. Once again the screaming halted.

Idris stared at Sam with wonder in his eyes. "Something about you helps. Can you do anything else?"

"I'm not a trick pony, and I have to find Bob." He couldn't leave his mate in the siren king's clutches. "He could still be alive."

Idris reached for him. "Please, just stay for Hal, if you let go of him he'll die."

"You don't know that." Sam's chest tightened.

"Bob sacrificed himself to keep you safe," Idris said. "You can't make what Bob did mean nothing by putting yourself in danger."

*Sacrificed?* That sounded so final. How could it be the end? Sam refused to think that.

"He's coming back." Sam insisted.

A tear slid down Idris's cheek. "No, he isn't, Sam. He's dying."

"Sturgeon won't harm Bob. He knows that if he does I will go down there and rip him apart." No one could hurt Bob and get away with it. Sam might not be able to control his abilities, but he could cause enough damage that the siren king would know not to screw with him in the future.

Idris bit his lip as he stroked Hal's hair. Sweat beaded Hal's forehead, and his labored breathing didn't reassure Sam to his future health. "Bob is poisoned, Sam, he knew he was dying. I sensed it right before he jumped in the water. He's saturated with demon blood."

"The soul ripper demon at Mevn's house? Bob killed it."

Idris nodded. "The only way to get rid of a soul ripper is

to drain its blood. Usually, they are hunted by vampire packs, so no one vampire ingests too much blood. Soul Ripper blood is poisonous to vampires. Over time, vampire hunters are slowly consumed by the pure evil of the demon. If Bob swallowed an entire demon's blood supply, it is only a matter of time before he dies."

"No!" Sam let go of Hal as he straightened. "There has to be something we can do."

Hal's screams of pain were ear-piercing.

"Please, Sam. We need to get Hal to the palace!" Idris pleaded.

"I'm not going anywhere!" Sam refused to give up on his lover, and as much as he wanted to help the gargoyle, Bob came first.

"I swear to you, Sam Enderson, if you help me now I will do whatever I can to help you save your mate." Idris's spoken words formed a glowing string of letters in the air. A fae's magical promise that bound him to keep his vow or suffer consequences he might not survive.

Sam crouched back down beside Hal. "You'd best hope Bob is still alive when I get there. Smudge!"

The familiar appeared beside Sam, thrashing his tail in annoyance. *"You bellowed?"*

"We need to get Hal back to the palace. Could you teleport us all there? I need to get him healed so I can go after Bob."

Smudge didn't bother to answer. From one breath to the next they were whisked from dockside to palace drawing room. A gasp went through the crowd as they spotted the newcomers.

"We can help." Idris's cousins approached. They formed a triangle around Idris, Sam, and Hal.

The triplets raised their hands and linked them together as

they chanted. Sam's entire body tingled with energy. The fae could create tremendous magic if they worked together. Sam hadn't witnessed any other fae doing magic together, but they must, at some point, to repel their enemies.

A loud bell rang through the room. Sam released his grip on Hal to clap his hands over his ears. Pain ricocheted through his skull along with the rhythm of the bell. Long after the sound ended, Sam still felt the reverberations bouncing through his skull.

"What was that?" At least Hal wasn't screaming anymore.

"The ringing spell of King Valfey, the fae who created the anti-spell to break through enchantments. This will finally fix Hal."

Sam's jaw dropped. Then it sunk in what the fae triplets had said. "Could this have cured Hal on its own?"

"Maybe," one of the fae said. They didn't seem bothered that Bob had sacrificed himself.

Sam found it hard to form words. "Why the hell didn't you do that before we went to retrieve the pearl?"

The fae to Sam's right spoke for the trio. "We had to determine Idris's attachment to his gargoyle. If he wasn't willing to do whatever necessary to save Hal, then their pairing wouldn't last."

Sam had thought he'd experienced anger before, but he'd been wrong. Every annoyance he'd felt before vanished beneath the crescendo of pure rage pulsing through him. He stood up then ducked beneath the trio's clasped hands. He wanted all of his enemies within sight.

"Bob might die because of you. He had to fight a soul ripper demon. To save me, he swallowed all of its blood. While you three were playing relationship roulette with your cousin's life, my lover was doing everything he could to help."

The trio released their hands then lined up to face Sam. "We are most sorry, Sam. We had no idea it would go this far. We thought the succubus would hand the crown over to you, and that would be the end of the matter. Idris might have had to deal with Sturgeon, but no one was supposed to die."

"Well, you were wrong!" Flames flickered on the tips Sam's fingers. He guessed once dragon fire was used he retained the ability, at least for a while.

"Sam, I will keep my promise to find him." Idris helped Hal to his feet. The ex-gargoyle's color was much better than before. He watched Sam with a guarded expression.

Sam rounded on Idris. "He might be dead because of you. I may have lost all chance."

"Idris would never have deliberately sacrificed another person to save me," Hal said, his voice raspy from screaming.

The guilty expression on Idris's face told a different story. "I think he would." Sam held up his hand to forestall the king from speaking. "I'm not saying you did; I'm saying you would've."

"You can't just jump into the ocean and get Bob, you need a plan," Idris said. "If you go there without any idea of what to do, the sirens will tear you apart."

"Well, I'm not leaving him down there." Sam didn't bother to hide his annoyance at all the fae. They were acting as if he could simply walk away and move on with his life.

A low horn sounded in the room.

"What's that?"

"The communication pool. Someone is trying to get hold of us." Idris walked over to the water.

Sam followed, almost stepping on Idris's heels in his eagerness to see the water.

Sturgeon appeared in the pool's depths. "You sent your poisoned pill my way. He is going to sicken the ocean."

"He's alive?" Sam walked closer, crowding out the king, hope in his heart. He knew vampires were technically dead, despite what Bob said, but a dead Bob who could talk and one who became fish food were yards apart.

"He's decaying before my eyes! Get him before his body sickens my fish. I can't have him in my kingdom."

Sam turned away from the pool. He stumbled a few steps away to get out of Sturgeon's sight. He pressed a hand to his heart, the pain sharp and devastating. "He can't be dead," he whispered.

Wouldn't he know if the other half of his heart had died?

Smudge wound his tail around Sam's legs. "*You must become.*" Smudge's voice was insistent.

"Become what?" Why did everyone talk in riddles?

*"The one who can save him."*

"I can't save him. Didn't you hear, Bob's gone!" Why did everyone think Sam had amazing abilities? He only had the magic he borrowed from others. On his own, Sam had little skill. Now he'd failed in the most important deed of his life. If he'd been faster, maybe he could've protected Bob from the demon.

"Don't lose faith, Sam. Let's retrieve Bob's body. See what we can do," Idris said, abandoning his spot by the pool.

"I'm not a necromancer." Defeat sat on Sam's shoulders, making him droop. He could barely function. His mind kept looping over and over that Bob was gone, and he'd never really told Bob how much he meant to him. Every criticism and snarky remark he'd made now stabbed him as lost opportunities. How foolish he'd been to not fully accept Bob's love.

"Smudge, please take me to the docks."

"Us." Hal took one arm and Idris the other. "We are as responsible for Bob's predicament as you."

"Decay isn't a predicament. It's the end." Sam didn't understand why everyone kept arguing with him about this.

"You need to stop thinking like a human," Hal said. "You aren't human—you are more."

"Now is the time to face the truth," Idris added.

Sam didn't speak as the world flipped around him and the wooden dock once more met the bottom of his shoes.

Sturgeon stood at the tip of the pier. Bob lay at Sturgeon's feet, oddly dry, as if the ocean hadn't touched him.

"Bob!" Sam tried to run over to him, but Idris and Hal held him back with a tight grip on him.

"Approach with caution, Sam," Idris whispered in his ear.

Sam nodded, and the trio walked up to the siren king, close enough to hear what Sturgeon said, but not close enough for Sam to touch Bob.

"You tried to kill me by sending this poison-riddled vampire," Sturgeon said.

Sam hadn't sent Bob; Sam had nothing to do with Bob sacrificing himself.

"I have a new respect for you, young Sam. You are cleverer than I had counted on. You are a worthy adversary."

Idris squeezed Sam's shoulder in a silent unneeded warning. Sam wasn't rising to anything Sturgeon said because he knew if Sturgeon was wary of Sam, he had better odds of survival.

Sam shrugged. "Just leave now."

Sturgeon smiled, baring rows of sharp teeth. "Since you gave me the crown, our agreement is finished. May you live through a thousand storms at sea, Sam Enderson."

Sam stood unmoving until Idris elbowed him in the side. Sturgeon wasn't moving.

"Finish the siren greeting," Idris whispered.

"And may your coral be bright, your ocean be clean, and

your children be many," Sam rushed out quickly. Anything to get to Bob, and he added a small bow. For a race intent on so much hate and pain, the sirens had many protocols.

Sturgeon bowed back. Before any more words could be exchanged he jumped off the pier and back into the water.

"Well done, Sam," Idris said. Sam made a move toward Bob, but Hal held him back.

"You can't go over yet, what if it's a trap?"

Sam wrenched his arm free. "I don't care," he snapped. Sturgeon didn't reappear as Sam raced to Bob's side. He dropped to his knees, his heart breaking all over again.

Bob lay like a corpse in a coffin, pale and perfect.

*"We need to take him to the vampire castle."* Smudge's voice snapped Sam out of his reverie.

"What?" Sam said, unfocused and terse. "What vampire castle? You mean beyond the Fire Mountains?" Sam desperately tried to recall anything he had read about the center of vampire power. Millennia old, the fortress stood a thousand miles beyond places that Sam had seen; the last bastion of an older time. No one went to the castle. No one.

"The castle? That's a good idea." Hal said. Of course, he hadn't heard Smudge but the words appeared to light a fire of purpose in Hal's eyes. "If anyone can bring back a vampire it would be his people."

"Agreed," Idris added. "Do you know if Bob has any family?"

Sam shook his head. For the first time he realized there were tons of things he didn't know about his lover, and he felt sick not knowing. Had Bob ever been to where his ancestors ruled the paranormal world for so long? Would he have ever wanted to? The castle was shrouded in mystery. As unreachable as a dragon's horde, it had a million legends attached to it. Great battles, wars over land, a peace held and ruled by the vampires.

"I don't know about his family." He stood shakily and Idris supported him. "I'm willing to take a chance. They can't hurt him more than he is already. Let's go."

## Chapter Seventeen

THEY COULDN'T TELEPORT TO THE CASTLE ITSELF. NOT EVEN Smudge had that ability, apparently.

*"The ancient vampire castle is the center of vampire magic. Wards press outwards from the center of it. I can't get us close."*

"So where should we go? What should we do?" Sam asked desperately.

*"Dragons,"* Smudge said.

"Dragons," Sam repeated. "Okay, we'll go and see dragons."

"I'm going with you," Idris said.

"Me too," Hal added.

Sam looked at the two men. He should hate them for this. If they hadn't appeared in his life, then Bob wouldn't be lying here, lifeless. But he didn't have it in his heart to hate the king for wanting to save his lover, and both men could be useful. If he remembered correctly from Bob's explanations of the para world, fae and dragonkin had long ago parted ways; a misunderstanding over a missing horde or something.

Still, Idris was king; his presence wouldn't hurt. So he

nodded, and with the pull of magic in the pit of his belly, Smudge transported them to the dragons, and to the very center of the dragon mountain itself.

They transported into the middle of some kind of feast. Surprised dragon shifters swarmed toward them, only parting when two men stepped through. One a dragon shifter bare to the waist and with beautiful tattoos over his golden skin, the other a vampire who stood very close.

"Sam!" The vampire shouted over the growls and snarls of defensive dragonkin.

"Enough," roared the dragon shifter.

Sam had never been happier than to see Bob's best friend Mikhail, and his lover, the king of dragonkin, Ryujin. "We need your help," he blurted. "We have to get to the vampire castle." There was no time for discussion in Sam's head.

"What's wrong?" Mikhail asked as he looked left and right. "Where's Bob?"

Sam stared wordlessly at Mikhail, then, like his strings had been cut, he literally fell into his arms. "Mikhail, he's dying."

"What?" Mikhail looked at Hal, at Idris, then held Sam a little away from him. "Tell me."

"There was a battle, and he was infected with a soul ripper's blood," Idris explained when Sam couldn't find the words. "There's nothing we can do for him, so we're taking him to his people."

"We're taking him to the vampire castle, but we can't get there on our own," Sam snapped, energized by the unwavering statement. Why was everyone giving up on Bob? Why was it only he who refused to let Bob really die? "They'll heal him."

"He's dead?" Mikhail asked. "He can't be dead."

Sam's cat wound in and out of the table legs nearest them,

the food and place settings above vanishing. He weaved swathes of gold magic, until Bob's body coalesced onto the tabletop, a white shroud covering all but his face. He was as still and icy pale as he had been at the dock. Lines of black poison marred Bob's features before disappearing under the sheet. Mikhail let out a sound of horror, stumbling back and away from Sam, and going straight to Bob's side.

Mikhail touched Bob's cheek.

*Not dead, he's not dead, just unconscious.* Sam repeated that mantra in his head over and over.

"What can we do?" Mikhail snapped. He looked over his shoulder and Jin was there immediately. "What can the dragons do?"

"Nothing," Jin said softly. "His soul is gone from here."

Relief flooded Sam at the words. "His soul? But we can retrieve that, Smudge you can bring back his soul."

Smudge leaped up on the table and sat between Bob and Sam. The tip of his tail twitched.

*"This is beyond even me,"* Smudge said. *"His soul has vanished."*

"Vanished where?" Sam snapped. "How can a soul vanish. Is he a ghost?" Sam looked up with hope in his heart. Teddy was a ghost, and he could talk and move and if they could have Bob back like that, at least Sam would be able to see him and speak to him again.

*"We need to get to the vampire castle,"* Smudge said. He turned his head and very deliberately stared at Jin.

Were they talking? Dragonkin could talk to familiars.

"What?" Sam asked. "What are you saying to each other."

Jin nodded at Smudge, then back at Sam. "I can take Sam, Bob, and Mikhail, I'll need volunteers to take the others and a few guards to accompany us." He said this softly, and Sam only recognized one of those who stepped forward. Nillon bowed to Jin, then to Sam. Four others joined them. Sam didn't know their names, but he appreciated their loyalty to the dragon king.

"We leave now," Jin said.

In little time, they took to the skies. Sam clung to Bob for dear life, his stomach swooping, his head hurting. The movement of the dragon's wings as they flew across high mountaintops left Sam feeling like he was in a boat on heaving seas. When they crossed the forest, he couldn't look down for fear of being sick. This journey high in the sky, was torture to someone who didn't like heights, but for Bob he would do anything.

They flew low over houses, with smoke curling from chimneys, through valleys with rivers carving into rock, and close to emerald meadows speckled with scarlet and yellow flowers. Sam wasn't sure they were in the vampire kingdom yet but what he saw was beautiful.

So this was where Bob was from?

The dragons slowed as a castle came into view. It was nothing like Sam expected, not some monstrosity in black stone with gates and bars; no, this was a white castle, standing on the peak of a snow-capped mountain, and the dragons didn't hesitate to land in the wide courtyard inside.

"I didn't think we'd be able to land right inside," Sam said to Jin as he slid off the dragon's back, with Mikhail close after bringing Bob with him. Jin shifted from his dragon form to human, clothes covering him in kingly finery.

"Ettore, the leader of vampires, is my friend."

"He is?" Sam asked. He glanced at Jin with new respect.

"As of last week when we took down a witch in the badlands together," Jin added.

A commotion had Sam's heart stopping in his chest. Swiftly and silently a group of vampires moved closer. At their head was a tall, slim man with black hair, and the smooth, steady gait of someone in charge. The others formed a guard behind him Mikhail set Bob on the ground beside them before sinking to his knees and bowing his head.

"My king," Mikhail said.

This was King of the vampires?

"Ettore." Jin inclined his head.

"Ryujin," Ettore said with that same subtle nod of deference.

Sam stayed silent, not wanting to draw attention from the kingly greeting. For once diplomacy was important. They were outnumbered in the vampire HQ; that had to be a test of their bravery.

"Mikhail," Ettore said with a smile in his voice. "Good to see you again." Mikhail rose, and the two vamps embraced. Then Ettore looked at Sam. Right through Sam, like he could see inside him, and he paled. "What is he doing here?" he said.

Mikhail placed a hand flat on Ettore's chest. "We had to," he said. "It's Bob. We had to bring Sam and Bob here."

Ettore's expression changed so quickly. He'd looked calm and pleased, and now he looked nothing short of shocked. "What? This was not part of the agreement."

"Bob is dying," Sam said a little desperately. He stepped forward into Ettore's space and damn it if Ettore didn't step back, right onto the foot of one of the group behind him. Sam stopped. Ettore stopped. "Help him," Sam said. "Please."

Ettore finally looked past him to the shrouded form lying on the ground at Nillon's feet. In seconds, he was at Bob's side, on his knees, pulling back the shroud and let out a sound of pure grief.

"No," he whispered. "My brother. Roberto."

Sam joined Ettore and crouched by the vampire. "Demon's poison," Sam explained.

"No," Ettore repeated. "He can't be dead." Ettore's eyes were bright with tears, and he reached out to trace the black lines on Bob's skin. "His soul has gone," he said. "What happened?"

Sam looked at the abject grief on Ettore's face. "Bob was your brother?"

Ettore nodded mutely. "My older brother, always the sensible one, the hero. When he heard there was a—" Ettore stopped and looked directly at Sam. His grief-stricken expression slid from his face and temper took its place. Ettore's incisors extended and in seconds Sam was on his back with Ettore's teeth at his throat. "I will kill you."

Sam shut his eyes. He didn't fight. If Bob was dead, what was the point? But it seemed like his body had other ideas. He convulsed as power coursed through him and in seconds Ettore was laying flat on his back ten feet from Sam.

Sam scrambled to stand, staying as close as he could to Bob's form.

"I don't care what you do to me," he shouted, "but save him, help him."

Ettore stood, his hands in fists at his sides, and he bowed his head, visibly trying to get back control. Only after the longest few minutes of Sam's life did Ettore raise his gaze. The temper had gone, in its place was icy calm.

"If we're lucky, then his soul is still in waiting for Aset Ka."

"Aset Ka?"

"The vampire god," Mikhail said, then made a sign of something on his chest. Sam winced. Did Bob have a god of sorts? This Aset Ka? Was this something else Sam didn't know about the man he loved?

"And this Aset Ka, they, he, she…" Sam was tripping over his words. "They could have Bob's soul, and we could get it back."

"There is only one way to retrieve a soul," Ettore pointed out. He looked at Sam pointedly.

"Whatever it is, I'll do it," Sam said.

"Not you. Whoever goes to Aset Ka has to beg for the life of their loved one," Ettore said.

"I can do that."

"They would need to love beyond all else."

"I do."

"You can't—"

Sam interrupted the flow of being told what he could or couldn't do. "How do I do that?"

Ettore shook his head. "You can't go," he snapped.

"He's my mate," Sam said.

"And he's my brother!"

Sam stepped forward, but Mikhail got between the two of them. Very deliberately he turned his back on Ettore. "Sam, you can't go to Aset Ka, only a vampire can go and make a deal."

"What kind of deal?"

"A soul bargain," Ettore said.

"Leaving you nothing more than a ghost," Mikhail said, although he didn't turn to face Ettore as he said that.

"There is nothing I wouldn't do for my brother," Ettore said.

Mikhail stepped away until the three of them were in a triangle and he placed a hand each on Ettore's and Sam's shoulders.

"You would have to make your peace, Ettore, and Sam, you would have to decide if this is what Bob would want from his brother." Then he walked away.

"What does he mean, a ghost?"

"Aset Ka keeps your physical body, and your soul is separate."

"So you die."

Ettore shook his head. "You can't understand."

"I want to."

"I need to save my brother; I *want* to save him."

"He wouldn't want you to die in his place," Sam said as they stood and stared at each other. Inside, Sam's heart was dying. He couldn't ask another man to sacrifice himself for Bob, but he wanted to. How desperately he wanted Bob back in his arms.

*How will I live without him?*

Ettore held out a hand. "He would do it for me."

Sam took the hand, and they held each other for a few seconds.

"I know he would."

"He has sacrificed so much for me," Ettore said. "Now it is my turn."

"Bob is the kind of man, vampire, who would die for a chance to keep someone alive," Sam said sadly. Then he added fondly, "He was always stupid like that."

"You love my brother."

"With all of my heart," Sam said.

Ettore closed his eyes. "You need to become what you were meant to be, Samuel Enderson," he said. "For Bob, for vampires, for all of paranormal kind." He dropped his hold, and with a muttered sentence he vanished.

Mikhail made a noise of pain and stumbled to Sam's side.

"Where did he go?" Sam asked.

"To Aset Ka." Mikhail cross-legged next to Bob. After a minute, Sam joined him.

"I didn't want him to do it," Sam kept saying, over and over.

He didn't know how long he'd sat there when there was a moan from Bob, and the shroud moved a little. Sam and Mikhail pulled back the white cloth and watched as the black lines vanished bit by bit.

"He did it," Mikhail said, sadness in his voice. "Ettore saved his brother."

Sam held tight to Bob's hand, leaned over and pressed a kiss to icy lips, and waited. Finally Bob opened his eyes, blinking at the light.

"What happened?" he mumbled.

Mikhail gripped Bob's other hand but didn't say anything.

"I love you," Sam whispered.

A soft smile curved Bob's lips. "I love you, too. Did I sleep?" His words were still low, and he sounded confused. Then an awful clarity hit him, and he attempted to sit up with Sam and Mikhail's help. With darting glances, he looked around him.

"Home? Where's Ettore?" He looked right at Sam. "What did he do?"

Sam's heart broke all over again at the grief in Bob's eyes.

"He made a deal with Aset Ka. He saved you, Bob."

And that was when big, strong, brave Bob, cried.

## Epilogue

"YOUR HEART IS HURTING," JIN SAID TO HAL.

Hal looked up from his plate of food and directly into the dragon king's concerned expression. Too many stories of dragons eating fae had Hal squirming back in his chair, his hand clasping Idris's tightly. Idris didn't seem to care that a dragon shifter was staring down at them, but then, Idris was a king himself. After the vampire king had vanished, they quickly returned to the dragon palace for Bob to recover. They hadn't gone farther in case they needed to return to the vampires.

They'd moved back indoors, and Sam and Bob had vanished with Mikhail and Smudge into an anteroom. Bob was distraught, Sam pale, and the cat seemed twitchy and crabby. That left him and Idris in the middle of a whole lot of dragons.

"What do you mean?" Hal said.

Jin frowned and tilted his head. "Loneliness," he said, then crouched in front of Hal, making him look down. Jin held out a hand and pressed it palm flat against Hal's chest. "Your heart feels like stone."

"It does?" Hal had lost all his intelligence, it seemed. His heart was pounding in his chest, so what did Jin mean that it was made of stone? The pearl and the bell had fixed him; he wasn't turning back into a gargoyle now. He was safe, with Idris.

"I think you need to come with me," Jin said. His tone didn't allow for argument. He stood and held out a hand, but Hal balked. "Both of you."

Idris paid attention when Hal stood. He'd been talking to one of the dragon shifters who had come with them this morning, but he wasn't letting go of Hal's hand it seemed.

"What's wrong?" Idris asked.

"I need to show you something," Jin said.

Idris and Hal followed Jin down a long corridor, and Hal hoped to hell this wasn't the place dragons took unsuspecting fae to eat them. Instead, Jin opened a door and gestured inside. Hal and Idris went in, and Hal gasped. High ceilings that were nothing but the roof of a cave were studded with pinpoints of diamond light. The walls shimmered with rubies, emeralds, and sapphires, and gold lay in piles. At the center of all of this was a pool, a small fall of water that widened into a space big enough for ten men.

"The healing pool," Jin said proudly. He waved his hand expansively. "Until it is time for you to leave I suggest you use the pool to mend fully. It is a space meant only for mates."

Hal looked over the edge into the deep pool and frowned. "Is it going to burn us alive or something?" he muttered.

Jin also peered over, and he looked confused. "It's water," he said.

"Yeah, right," Hal added. "Water with dragon acid in it."

Jin tutted, and then in a smooth move he yanked at Hal

and pushed him into the water, and another shove had Idris following.

"My apologies, King of the Fae, but your lover is an ass."

Then with a toothy smile he left and shut the door after him.

Hal paddled to the side where Idris clung to the rock.

"Not acid, then," Idris smirked.

Hal smiled at his lover, then sobered. "It's my fault Ettore is gone."

Idris sighed. "I knew you would say that. It wasn't your fault you were cursed, or that Sam and Bob are two of the bravest people we will ever know. Or that Ettore wanted to save his brother. This was all fate."

"You think they will be okay? Sam and Bob?"

Idris let go of the side and pressed his toes to the bottom of the pool before gathering Hal close.

"If their love is half as deep as ours, then they will get through this. Maybe find a way to get Ettore back from Aset Ka."

Hal hugged Idris. The dragon king was right, the pool was making his heart feel less heavy. He moved away and floated in the warm water, stripped off his sopping clothes then floated some more. Bit by bit the pain in his chest eased and when Idris floated next to him, he knew he was finally healing.

"I love you," he whispered.

Idris released his hand and gathered him into a heated kiss. "I love you, too."

---

ASET KA STOOPED to touch his newly acquired soul. The vampire kneeled before him, but he wasn't cowed by the fact he was doomed. In fact, he looked up at Aset Ka and smiled a soft, steady smile.

"Why?" Aset Ka wanted to know.

And the vampire smiled despite the fact his life was over, even though he was forever part of this hell.

"For love," he said, simply. "Always for love."

**THE END**

# THE CASE OF THE

*Guilty Ghost*

## END STREET VOLUME 3

# Prologue

"You are my greatest prize yet," Aset Ka's deep voice rolled across Ettore.

Ettore almost impaled his tongue on his fangs to keep from speaking his mind. Angering the vampire god when he was stuck with him for eternity wouldn't be a good idea. He remained kneeling before Aset Ka, not eager to receive any punishments for his actions.

His stomach growled. Hunger haunted Ettore. Aset Ka wanted those in his presence to suffer—to know they only ceased feeling pain by his grace. If one pleased Aset Ka, he granted a reprieve from agony. That was more than enough reason for most of the inhabitants to bow down to the mighty vampire god.

Unfortunately, Ettore had difficulty being a good little peon. Wariness of the god's power didn't lend to worshipful adoration, and Ettore had been a king for far too long to find satisfaction at anyone's feet. He might fear Aset Ka and be mindful of the god's ability to torture his minions, but deep in his soul, Ettore longed to escape.

He hungered. For food. For light. For salvation. Time had ceased to have any meaning as soon as he entered the realm.

"I have decided to free you," Aset Ka said.

Ettore turned his attention back to the imperious god. He shouldn't have let his mind wander in the first place. The god's words were like icy water to the heat flaring inside him.

"Why?" He didn't try to hold back his suspicious tone. The most feared god in the afterlife didn't have a reputation for his warm and loving ways. To grant one of his minions escape was unheard of. How could they suffer properly if they were free to go?

Aset Ka exposed his long fangs in a grim smile. He towered above where Ettore was kneeling on the ground. A combination of the most dangerous creatures formed the god's body. Aset Ka had the strength and fire of a dragon, the soul of a demon and the ancient blood of a vampire flooding through his veins. "Your noble, self-sacrificing aura is dampening my hell."

Ettore remained silent waiting to hear his fate. There would be a price for his return.

"I'm releasing your spirit to travel back home." Aset Ka crossed his scaled arms over his broad chest, and his long tail flicked and wrapped around him. "For new duties."

A good minion would ask no questions and do what he was told, but Aset Ka was a cruel, capricious god, and Ettore sensed a trap in the Aset Ka's unexpected benevolence; he didn't send people to freedom.

"What new duties?" Ettore winced after the words escaped. Whatever Aset Ka was thinking, Ettore didn't imagine it was rainbows and unicorns. It also didn't sound like he was being sent to the end of things to have his skin ripped from his bones and his soul sucked into the abyss.

Aset Ka said nothing, so Ettore tried something simpler.

"Why?" That was the shortest way of summing up the hundreds of questions in his head.

Aset Ka narrowed his eyes, and Ettore waited for some nonsense about lesser beings not needing to know what a god wanted from them. Instead, he tapped his long nails against the arms of his throne.

"Something is wrong in the balance of things," he said. "There is a man, and his magic is wrong, and so strong that it ripples into this realm. You have seven days to find out who, or what, is threatening my afterlife, and report back to me."

"Seven days."

"Seven."

"Do you have anything else for me to go on?" Ettore knew he sounded confused. Seven days wasn't a large amount of time to find whatever mystical something was bothering a god.

"When you find it, you will know. Seven days, Ettore second son of Kurius."

Ettore hesitated before bolstering his courage, "And my reward?"

For a second Aset Ka looked like he wasn't going to answer, then he bellowed smoke and flames, and his eyes turned scarlet.

"I won't flay you alive then revive you to do it all over again," he spat. Aset Ka's acid breath burned Ettore's skin. He fell to the floor in agony, the pain only easing after he couldn't scream anymore and the chamber had silenced. Ettore curled up into a ball, the acid on his skin had vanished, but the residual pain kept him on the ground.

"Any more questions?" Aset Ka asked in a soft voice. For a second Ettore welcomed the noise in the silence of the stone chamber.

Before he could unwisely say anything else, Aset Ka

began to speak in a strange language. Words spilled from his lips without form or shape, but in a long string of syllables Ettore couldn't decipher.

A strange buzzing went through him like a low crackling electric wire. Then he was free. Floating above his collapsed body, Ettore drifted away.

"Remember you have seven days, then you will be back."

Ettore didn't respond. Instead, he focused on the pulling sensation. Someone, somewhere was thinking of him. No doubt his brother Bob was cursing him out for taking the deal and dying. Smiling, Ettore floated away.

## Chapter One

SAM TOOK THE STAIRS TWO AT A TIME, ALL ONE HUNDRED and sixty of them, to the top of the tower, leaving him gasping for oxygen. He'd seen Bob heading that way, or dreamed it, or half woke and imagined it. He didn't know what exactly, only that somehow, he knew he would find Bob at the top of the black tower. He ducked the low lintel, slid to an ungainly halt on the stone floor, unbalanced and grabbed at the wall to hold himself upright.

"Bob?" he called into the dark corners of the tower, but there was no reply. His vampire lover didn't step from the shadows with a smile or words of love. The place was empty, and the only presence Sam sensed was spiders. Knowing his luck, they were man-eating spiders.

"Sam!"

Sam winced at the shout up the stairs, and then heard huffing and cursing as the owner of the deep voice appeared in the doorway. Jin, who had never quite gone home, citing that he was responsible for Sam, was way past pissed. At least Jin, being a dragon shifter, could light up the room.

Then Sam recalled *he* could light up the room just by thinking about it.

"I want there to be light," he murmured, and then held up his hand to block his eyes as a pure white light exploded in the center of the room, filling every corner before receding back to a steady glowing orb.

He blinked, the light burning his retina. He closed his eyes tight, willing the spotted vision to go.

"What are you doing up here?" Jin asked. He sounded wary, like everyone else tiptoeing around Sam these past two weeks.

"Bob," Sam said. When he opened his eyes again, he could see the entire room. An elaborate altar took up the far side of the circular chamber, built into the wall and covered in years of dusty cobwebs, likely from the imagined killer spiders. He stepped toward it, a low humming drawing his attention. Jin moved to block his way.

"Leave it, Sam," Jin said. His hard tone left no room for discussion.

The noise of more footsteps stomping up the stairs, then Lambert, Sam's vampire liaison, appeared at the top. Lambert, a tall stretched-skinny vampire with eerily cloudy eyes, had a propensity to follow Sam everywhere, spouting fear at everything and anything.

"Sire, you can't be in here," Lambert said, waving his hands ineffectively.

Sam spun back around to face the altar. "Stop calling me sire," he muttered under his breath. He was getting pretty sick of how people treated him in the damn castle. Half the vampires lauded him as a ruler of supernaturals, the other half wanted him either locked up or gone. The first group assigned Lambert to him. They felt Sam needed an escort in the vampire kingdom because he was, in their words, special. Lambert was the kind of paranormal stuck firmly in the past. The historian kept talking about the old days like they were better times.

Sam wasn't sure why Lambert had been so accepting of him given he was A, human, and B, with Bob.

Jin held up a hand, glowing with the remnants of dragon fire magic and placed it flat on Sam's chest. It didn't burn, only fizzled, and popped sending a small shock through his body.

"Sam, talk to me," Jin demanded.

The humming from the altar intensified, and a voice in Sam's head was saying the same things over and over, *Sam, I am here, and I need your help.*

"I can hear Bob in my head, he called me up here," Sam repeated.

"No, you can't have heard him," Lambert corrected. "The mate link is blocked in times of mourning. You are hearing something else, dark magic maybe. You need to come back down to your chamber where you are safe."

A mixture of exasperation and fear crossed Lambert's face when Sam stepped back toward the altar.

"I want to see him." He'd been too long without Bob. Their separation was causing cracks in his sanity.

"It's not much longer until he's done," Jin reassured.

"Please come away, Sam," Lambert pleaded. That was new. Lambert never called him Sam.

"Just take my hand," Jin said, holding out his hand.

Sam stepped backward, more toward the altar, and he heard Lambert let out a small curse.

"Take my hand, Sam," Jin said. "This is stupid and dangerous."

Sam turned on Jin, sparks flying from his fingers. Jin

stepped back from him, narrowly avoiding the biting magic. "Stay away from me."

He shook his fingers, electricity passing up his arm. Usually when that happened, Bob was there to hold his hands, settle him and take away the pinpricks of pain.

"Come away, Sam," Jin said.

"Listen to the dragon," Lambert added, his voice thick with fear.

"You and Jin do what I say," Sam snapped, not knowing where the superiority in his voice was coming from.

Sam fought his loss of control. *So much for me being a higher supernatural.* Every day without Bob felt like torture, and Sam was lost without his vampire lover next to him. The headaches, the sparks of energy from his fingers, and the pain in his chest grew more intense with each hour that passed. He knew Bob was in mourning. Hell, Sam respected the traditions, but right then, all he wanted was his lover by his side.

*Hurry up,* the voice in his head said. *I need your help.*

He shook off the words and concentrated on Lambert. "Take me to the Sanctum, let me see Bob, convince me he isn't calling for my help, and I will come with you." He wasn't being unreasonable, they were.

"This is an ancient rite." Lambert seemed stunned that Sam was asking this. "No humans."

"Something is wrong." *With me? With him? Something is terribly wrong, but no one is listening.*

"What is wrong? Is it your head?" Jin asked, his voice low, and his expression concerned.

*Yes. No. Hell, I don't know. I know Bob loves me, and I love him. I just need to kiss him.*

Instead, he said, "I have to help Bob with his grieving. We can't be apart like this."

Sam didn't know what made him say it that way; he wasn't needy, it wasn't a normal need for lovers to be together. His instincts had been screaming at him that he and Bob shouldn't be apart.

*Ever!*

Lambert gasped as he did every time Sam suggested he should be part of any ancient vampire rite. "A non-pureblood cannot help with the rituals of grieving."

Sam knew Lambert was winding himself up to that whole vampire purity speech and he sighed. Jin must have sensed his irritability because he rounded on Lambert and roared, fire sparking around him. Lambert stumbled back in shock.

"Wait for us outside," Jin ordered.

Lambert looked torn between staying to keep an eye on Sam, his job, or evading the dragon fire that Jin was breathing all around the room.

Lambert's eyes narrowed. His calculating gaze flashed from Jin to Sam and back again a few times before he sketched a small bow and left the chamber. "I will go down exactly the seven steps of Aset Ka," he announced over his shoulder. He was kind of stuck on numbers and more than a little obsessive about the freaking vampire god.

The same god who had made a bargain with Bob's brother Ettore before returning Bob to Sam, and taking Ettore to some kind of hell, or heaven, or whatever.

"Bob needs me," Sam said, firmly. "I was asleep and heard him calling me. He must be out of mourning."

"Sam, you have to stop, he isn't up here."

"He must be, he called me." Maybe if Sam said it enough times one of them would listen.

Jin shook his head. "You heard that through your mate link? In your mind. You can't have because the link is muted when Bob is mourning."

Sam shook his head, confused. "No, it was like an image of the stairs, and this room, and there was an altar, only it wasn't this old. It had gold all over it, a chalice in the center, and Bob was examining it, and he called me over, and there was magic…." Sam pressed his hands against his temples, attempting to ease the tension building from that incessant humming. "He needs me."

"Sam, it was just a dream. You're tired. Let's go get some sleep, and we'll re-examine this in the morning." Jin took his arm, encouraged him back to the doorway, but Sam wrenched away and shoved Jin to the side, and with a flick of his hand there was a thick wall of ice between them. Sam stood on the side of the altar, and Jin beat on the ice trying to get through.

Bob needed him, and nothing or no one was stopping him. He'd felt Bob's grief, through their bond, for four long days and then without warning; the bond was severed. He'd been told that had to happen as part of the rituals of mourning.

Sam was lost. Not even his daughter Mal arriving had helped. At that moment, it didn't matter that she was the light of his life, he wasn't whole without Bob. There was no *family* without Bob.

"Watch Mal," Sam spoke clearly through the ice, which wasn't giving way, and Jin snarled at him. "Please."

"Don't do anything stupid, Sam! We'll go down and find Bob."

But Sam wasn't doing anything stupid. He was doing what he should have been doing all along, finding Bob and making sure he was okay. Something had happened, someone had come into the castle, stolen Bob from his mourning and only Sam could help. He turned his back on Jin to face the altar. Something there was calling him. *Help me, help me.*

Bob's voice? Or was it softer the closer that Sam got to the altar? A whisper of a voice?

He stepped closer, the hum louder, and then another step, and as he neared the low resonating noise stopped, and for a moment he was motionless.

He reached a hand toward the altar, expecting a barrier, or magic, or some booby-trap that would whisk him to killer spider land or some other awful, horrible place.

A crash behind him had him looking back. Jin was nearly through the barrier, melting the ice as fast as he could with his dragon fire; in seconds he would be through. Sam flicked his hand to create another level of ice, but nothing happened.

"Just when I need magic, it isn't there," he murmured.

Something inside him began to hurt, an insistent tug at the base of his neck that ran down his spine then back again. The sensation was weird, moving his feet, guiding him, and he had no control over his own body. He was a marionette, and someone else was pulling the strings.

Fear began to spread in the pit of his stomach, Jin screamed his name and the heat of dragon fire warmed his back, but none of it mattered.

Because his hand touched the altar.

And everything went to hell.

## Chapter Two

THE VORTEX WASN'T PRETTY. INSTEAD OF A BEAUTIFUL kaleidoscope of colors, it was hellfire, rain, and the taste of ash in his mouth. Sam screamed as he slid out of the room, something grabbed him and yanked him away from the castle. He tried to grip Jin's hand, to snatch at his only bit of security, but he failed.

The vortex collapsed behind him as the castle disappeared to a pinpoint, a tiny speck among mountainous terrain. He couldn't stand against the turbulence tossing and turning him. Hurled through space and time, Sam saw demons, dragons, trolls, humans, werewolves howling in pack formation, and beyond them, nothing but wasteland. Though he closed his eyes, the images burned them as the light had before.

And then, when he thought he would never breathe again, he landed in a boneless heap on a hard, cold floor, surrounded by papers, dust and envelopes covered with scrawled writing. Tall filing cabinets flanked the room like silent, dented metal soldiers guarding their secrets.

He lay on his back, aching and stared at the familiar watermarks on the ceiling. Sam knew where he was.

Home.

Somehow, he had returned to the End Street Detective Agency.

He pushed up to his knees, shaking as nausea hit, and then a few stomach-churning minutes later to a wobbly standing position while leaning on the nearest cabinet for support. Or at least he tried to lean on the cabinet. His hand vanished through the metal furniture, soon followed by the rest of him as he tumbled right through, crashing back down to the floor.

The floor didn't move, though.

This was new.

He sniffed, the smell of brimstone a reminder that Jin had tried to grab him. Had Jin followed Sam through? There was no sign of his friend. Sam thumped the back of his head on the floor a few times in a futile attempt to awaken from this strange dream.

*Can you smell things in dreams?* Hell, if Sam knew.

He stood up, smacked his temple on the bottom of the table, and ended up crawling out from underneath it. How come he'd fallen through it, but managed to hit himself on the now solid table when he stood up? What rules governed this weird universe of partial solidity?

He pressed a hand to the cabinet. Nope. Solid as a rock.

"Bob!" he shouted. "Where are you?"

"Sam, you made it, you're here, it worked, You're home!" Someone shouted gleefully. He recognized the voice immediately. Teddy, the agency's resident ghost.

The words spun as fast around him as the vortex had, and he felt his balance wavering. He steadied himself by bending his knees a little, no sense in leaning on cabinets that were phasing in and out of being real.

Teddy stopped in front of him, his mouth moving, but the

words weren't making sense. Was Teddy even speaking English?

"What the hell?" Sam asked no one in particular. Teddy was a ghost with attitude and a fine line in flitting from here to there, but he never held serious conversations. Sam wouldn't be getting any useful explanations from his specter-in-residence.

"Yes, hell," Teddy said, floating around Sam agitated. "You're quite right."

Sam reached out to stop Teddy and make him stand still, but of course, that was like grabbing air and Teddy floated away and toward the wall. Just as he began to disappear, halfway through, he stopped. Instead of his usual half-here/half-there appearance, like he didn't belong in the real world, he was suddenly robust and real.

"Ouch," Teddy said, although it was muffled given half his mouth, his chest and all of one arm were embedded in the wall.

Sam stared. What was going on?

"Have you seen Bob?" Sam asked. Maybe his lover had come before him?

Teddy looked guilty. "Bob is still at the Vampire Castle," he mumbled. Although it sounded like Bampire Asshole.

"No, he's here, I heard him," Sam insisted. "He called through our mate link."

"No, you heard me."

"What the hell, Teddy?" What game was the ghost playing to pull him from the castle? Bob still needed him.

Silence, and then in a very small voice Teddy said, "A little help here?"

Sam resisted the spiteful urge to ignore the ghost. Instead, he walked up to the wall, and to the half-embedded ghost, and something about Teddy had him touching a solid body of skin and bones instead of air and nothing.

"What the hell?" he said for the second time.

"Long story," Teddy muttered. "Get me out of here."

"You're…I mean…Teddy?"

"Get. Me. Out. Of. Here!" Teddy shouted as best he could with only half a mouth available.

Sam didn't know what the hell to do. He began stating what he wanted and waiting to see if each wish was granted. Sometimes that worked.

"I want Teddy out of the wall." Didn't work.

"Release the ghost from the bricks." Didn't work either.

Frustrated Sam slapped his hand on the wall, and it went straight through. In a panic, he pulled it back. He stared at the offending hand, and then the wall like he could find all the answers by staring.

"Do that again," Teddy ordered, well, more grumbled. "Yank me out."

Sam hesitated, and he knew he was going into shock. After all, it wasn't every day that a person became a ghost, or whatever it was that he'd become.

"Am I dead?" he wondered out loud as he reached in, grabbed Teddy then yanked hard. That wasn't physically possible, right? After all, Teddy, *the ghost,* was corporeal and stuck in a wall. Somehow, though, he came free, and the two of them tumbled back—Sam to the floor and Teddy right through the floorboards, vanishing below.

"TEDDY!" Sam shouted at the top of his voice. He heard banging from below, and then steps on the stairs, accompanied by cursing.

"Not again," Teddy snapped. "Having to use the stairs all the time. Floating is better." He was more mumbling to himself than talking to Sam, but Sam had questions.

"Sit," Sam ordered, waving at the floor in front of him.

Cautiously Teddy lowered himself on the floor not daring to talk until they saw he didn't fall through.

Sam counted on his fingers. "One, why am I here? Two, how did I get here? Three, why am I half ghost and half human, and come to think of it why are you? And four. What. The. Hell?"

Teddy didn't look him in the eye. His brown gaze remained fixed firmly at a point over Sam's shoulder. Up close like that, not quite so transparent, Sam could observe Teddy's colors; his long chestnut hair, the hint of auburn in his beard, and the soft pink of his lips which were pressed into a hard line.

Teddy was as real as Sam.

He wasn't a ghost.

"It's a long story," Teddy said.

"I have time," Sam snapped.

Teddy finally met his gaze, and worried at his top lip with his teeth. "Can I have a shower first? I haven't had one in a hundred years."

"No." Sam needed answers, and he needed them fast.

Teddy sighed and slumped a little, his ass vanishing through the floor. He raised himself above so they were eye to eye.

"I have never told anyone this story."

"First, is Bob still at the castle?"

"Yes."

"But you called me here by pretending to be Bob in trouble."

"Yes."

"And you don't see the problem with doing that?" Sam pressed.

Teddy didn't take the time to think about his answer. "No."

Temper snapped inside Sam. "Remind me, Teddy," he began smoothly. "Can you re-kill a ghost? Because I'm this close to finding out." He held his right index finger and thumb about a half an inch apart.

Teddy scooted back and away from Sam, his shoulders hitting the wall and not vanishing through.

Sam waited. His story had better be good.

## Chapter Three

ETTORE DRIFTED THROUGH THE AIR. THE TRANSITION BACK from the afterlife spun his senses and sent stabbing pains through his head. Time had lost meaning in Aset Ka's realm, and he'd gained little on the way back. How much time had passed since his death? It could have been hours or centuries.

At first, Ettore's surroundings were vague and cloudy like a foggy landscape. Eventually, things began to clear and the castle he called home came into sharp, brilliant relief. What had brought him there? Who had called him? Was it the first step in Aset Ka's obscure quest, or something more personal?

"I doubt it will be that easy," he muttered. If Aset Ka's reason for sending him here could be found in the Vampire Castle, he would have never accepted Ettore's soul. He would have demanded help and taken souls as he needed to.

Ettore wished he could resolve his own issues while trying to figure out Aset Ka's problem. Sadly, Ettore's difficulties went deeper than a quick patch of emotional glue. His soul would never heal from the separation from his beloved. If Aset Ka ever released him permanently, maybe then he could go find his mate. As a spirit, his heart shouldn't still hurt at the thought of his lost lover. With his soul already claimed by the vampire god, he would never see his soul mate again.

Thoughts swirling, he floated past familiar faces noting that they looked no older than when he'd left them, and that the castle still had an aura of mourning about it. He heard his name whispered in the halls, and knew it hadn't been long since he had given his soul to Aset Ka. He watched them for a while, noting which of them were more upset than the others. A good way to learn which of his people missed him. His friends appeared crushed, and his known enemies wore smug smiles causing him to pause and contemplate mischief.

No one could see him; it didn't seem that anyone could even sense him. Maybe small revenges could be applied later, when he could focus on letting himself be seen.

He pushed away the ideas running playfully through his head and decided to concentrate on his brother instead. He closed his eyes, focused hard and imagined Bob.

A gentle tug urged him forward. Time meant nothing as he drifted from room to room. He had no way of measuring how many hours, or days, it had been since he'd died. His brother's voice pulled at him. Following the sound, he floated to a small room where he found Bob kneeling on the hard stone floor in front of a small shrine of Aset Ka. Prayers spilled from Bob's lips, and the sorrow on his face tore at Ettore. His brother had always been the one who tried to do the right thing. He'd even given up the throne to answer the call to find his soul mate.

After he'd found Sam, Bob had pulled away from the other vampires, but from his letters, Ettore knew his brother had found happiness with his mate. Why was Bob alone? Where was Sam?

Bob's soft, heartfelt, prayer pulled Ettore's attention back to him. "May Aset Ka guide your steps, Brother, and keep you out of the torturous halls of the damned."

A quick slice of a knife across Bob's palm split the skin to allow blood to drip down his hand. "I sacrifice my blood as my brother sacrificed his life to ease his way into the underworld. May Aset Ka accept my offering."

Tears dripped down Bob's cheeks, and a soft sob followed his words.

If Aset Ka hadn't already released him, the god would've been forced to grant Ettore a boon due to Bob's bloodletting. Each time a family member offered blood to their dead relative, they bought goodwill from the vampire god. In the dark ages, vampires had drained humans for their offerings until Aset Ka informed them only blood willingly given from a true relative by blood or marriage counted. They could flood the altar with gallons of human blood and not garner an ounce of goodwill.

Ettore smiled at his brother's devotion as he floated down to kneel beside Bob. His older brother had always been the caretaker of the family. He ghosted a hand across Bob's hair. Bob shivered but didn't look up from where he'd bent his head to whisper over a chalice of bloody water.

Bob's broken expression surprised Ettore. Yes, they were brothers, but they'd grown apart over the past few centuries; Bob, in his quest for his soul mate, had thrust Ettore into being King even though he'd never wanted the throne. He hadn't imagined his older brother would be that upset over his death.

Maybe Sam had given Bob back his heart?

Too bad no one could do the same for Ettore. Some hearts were fractured into so many pieces, it was impossible for them to be stuck back together with super glue sentiment.

He'd lived with a broken heart for so long that the pain was part of him.

Bob whispered a charm for Ettore to rest in peace.

That same peace eased through Ettore, for the first time since his death. Kneeling beside Bob and feeling how much his brother truly cared made his sacrifice worthwhile. Better to have Bob there and alive than have him join him in the afterworld. The world wouldn't stay in one piece if Sam lost his soul mate.

Sighing, Bob slowly stood. He pulled a handkerchief from his pocket then wrapped it around his hand. He turned his head, and Ettore smiled at him, dropping the smile when Bob, gasped, jerked away, then tumbled off his feet and onto the floor.

"Ettore!"

Ah, so Bob could see him. Interesting.

"Surprise." Ettore gave a half-hearted wave. The shock on Bob's face made returning worthwhile. It had been a long time since he'd gotten the upper hand on his brother.

Bob spluttered, "What the... how... how did you get here?"

"Aset Ka released me."

"Why did he let you go? Why did you sacrifice yourself for me?" Bob pressed his hands to the floor to push himself up, "Ettore, why?"

Ettore paused, those two questions were so far apart, but the answer to one was simple. "You know why I made the deal," he said.

Bob shook his head. "There could have been another way."

Ettore smiled at his older brother. "There was no other way, and you know it." The secrets the brothers shared, the ones passed to them from their father to his three sons, meant that Bob had to be the one to live. Ettore, Bob, and their wayward youngest sibling Radim, had always known their destinies.

"I hate this," Bob said.

Ettore changed the subject. "I have been given seven days to finish my task; I want to use the time to settle things, not point fingers over what we could've done better."

Bob got to his feet. "What task and why seven days? I thought once a soul was in a bargain with Aset Ka that was it. I've never heard of him rejecting a soul. Was it something I did wrong?" He looked pale, even for a vampire, and his eyes were wide. Not with fear, nothing scared Ettore's big brother, but with absolute shock. "Is Sam in danger?"

It always came back to Bob's soul mate, the inevitable end to everything, Sam who would be the one to unify all supernaturals.

"No, this isn't about Sam."

"Then what's it about?"

"I don't know. Aset Ka said there was something I needed to do. Maybe it is the succession. I am dead, you abdicated, that only leaves our brother Radim, and he cannot be allowed the throne. He will take us back to the dark ages and bury our people there."

"I won't let Radim back on the throne," Bob said fiercely.

"How will you stop him, Bob? He's next in line. You have to take the throne and rule in my stead."

"What?" Bob's mouth dropped open before he snapped his jaw closed.

"You have to take—"

"I heard you." Bob shook his head. "But I can't. What about Sam?"

Ettore frowned at Bob. "What about him?"

"I can't abandon my life with him to be here. You know I was on a different path, that I needed to find Sam."

"Yes, yes, you love him, but I don't mean you have to rule forever, just until you can train someone to take your place. It's the least you can do after my sacrifice." Ettore winced at his own words but didn't take them back. Although he hadn't sacrificed himself so his brother would owe him a boon, it didn't take away from the fact that the vampires still needed a ruler. There was no way in hell that Radim, their sadistic younger brother, should be given a chance to take the throne.

Bob scowled. "That's not fair. You know I had a different fate."

"I know you need to be there for your mate, but our people need a leader. Sam can still be with you; he can stay here while you straighten things out."

"You know half the vampires out there hate him, and the other half are terrified of him." Bob's jaw tightened as if contemplating all the things that could happen to Sam in a castle filled with vampires. "I don't want anyone to hurt him."

"Yet you sit here lost in the mourning rituals and leave him alone to the whims of the court."

"Not alone. Jin, the Dragon King, is here."

"You shouldn't be stuck in here," Ettore pointed out.

"I need to complete the rituals to make sure your afterlife is settled."

"Bob," Ettore sighed. "That is a moot point now. I'm here."

Bob reached out to touch Ettore and check that he was real. When his hand went straight through him, it was all Ettore could do not to ask Bob if he thought he imagined him. Instead, he wanted to refocus back on Sam, because maybe *that* was why he'd been sent there.

"Sam has so much magic in him that it was felt in Aset Ka's kingdom, he'll be okay," Ettore said to change the subject.

Bob shook his head. "He's impetuous, brave, and tends to get into trouble if left to his own devices."

"Really?" Bob's mate had a fascinating aura, but Ettore didn't know anything about Sam except for rumors, and most of them were pretty unbelievable.

"Yes. The prophecies were right; he really does have a bit of most supernaturals in his blood."

"How does he taste?" Ettore couldn't imagine having that much power beneath his fangs and not draining him dry.

Bob sighed. "Like the best and worst of everything. Remember when we had those siren twins?"

"Yeah," Ettore thought that only his mate had tasted better.

"Think of them, but ten times better."

"What's the downside?"

"I can't drink from anyone else anymore."

"Because they aren't your mate?" Ettore hadn't experienced that symptom when drinking from his, but maybe Sam was different.

"No." Bob gave a sad laugh. "Because everyone else tastes sour, like rotting fruit, and makes me sick."

"Oh." Ettore nodded. No one tasted as good as his lost mate, but he could still drink from others without too much trouble, he'd had to, his soul mate had been dead for over a century. Sam and Bob's connection must go even deeper than Ettore's old bond. "You must be blood bonded."

"You think?" Bob rubbed his chin. "I always thought that was just a romantic story mother used to tell us."

Ettore couldn't stop the surge of jealousy. Even dead he

couldn't completely suppress his envy of Bob, not one of his greatest personality traits. "I think you have a true double bond, big brother. The kind that the books talk about; blood and soul."

They sat in silence to soak in the ramifications of Bob's relationship with Sam. If Sam had truly bonded with Bob in all ways, they were linked past death. "Aset Ka won't like that he can't claim your soul when you die."

Being the god of vampires, Aset Ka couldn't claim anyone not a vampire. If Bob were truly bound to Sam, he would follow Sam into the human underworld upon death and completely bypass the vampire god. Ettore smiled, then began to laugh until the sound reverberated against the chamber walls.

Bob eyed him with a strange expression. "Your echoing laughter is really creepy brother."

"Thank you," Ettore said, once he stopped chuckling. If he were still corporeal, he'd have had to wipe tears from his eyes.

"You're welcome." Bob shook his head and sighed. "I miss you Ettore. I know it's been a long time since I last visited, but you were never far from my thoughts."

"You could've visited." He let his built-up resentment color his words. For years, he'd tried to understand Bob's withdrawal, but sometimes he hated the distance between them. Ever since it had been foreseen that Bob would find the one supernatural to be the figurehead for the paranormal world, he had been distant. Ettore had never wanted to be king—that had been Bob's birthright. Bob leaving put the pressure of ruling on Ettore's shoulders. It was difficult not to resent his older brother when Bob's actions changed Ettore's life forever.

Bob folded his hands together and gave them his total

attention. "You know, communication and visitation works both ways."

Ettore didn't look at his brother; instead, he examined the altar, letting his gaze rest on the flickering candles.

"I've always had more pride than sense," he admitted.

Bob nodded, then he spoke from loyalty. "Can't be king and admit to being wrong," he said. "There's no time for reflection when you're running from problem to problem. You forget I was the heir apparent for the longest time."

"I didn't forget. You'd think such long-lived beings as we are, some of our fellow vampires would think for themselves, but they brought me all their problems."

Sitting there beside his brother, Ettore he could admit his regrets. He had nothing to lose at that point. All the reasons he gave himself for putting on an impassive face vanished after death.

"If you were corporeal, I'd give you a hug," Bob said with a wry smile.

"Thanks," Ettore returned the grin. "We've never been the hugging sort of family, but I appreciate the thought."

"Maybe that's where we went wrong. More hugs and less hate might've changed everything. Maybe Radim wouldn't have become such an asshole." Bob's regret hung in the air like acrid smoke.

"Somehow I doubt anything would change our little brother. Radim was born a vicious, nasty jerk." Radim had damaged the kingdom with his dedication to keeping born vampires in charge despite some of the made vampires being just as strong. He'd vanished a long time ago, and Ettore never wanted to see him again, not after he'd killed the only man Ettore had ever loved.

"Do you think he's still alive?" Bob asked.

"He's not in Aset Ka's domain." It had been one of the

first things Ettore had asked the vampire god. He had struggled with disappointment when he learned his brother was still alive. Radim deserved an untimely death more than anyone Ettore could think of.

"He is the next in line for succession to the throne since I abdicated," Bob pointed out.

"I'm surprised he didn't come running as soon as I died. How much time has passed?"

"Ten days."

"And my body?"

"In the family crypt, next to father."

Ettore wasn't ready to see his corpse just yet. "Radim might turn up when the news of my death spread out from the castle. He's always wanted the crown."

"Depending on how good his contacts are, he might not know yet that you are gone," Bob mused. He ran his fingers up and down the seam of his jeans. His eyes were distant as if he were considering the different possibilities. "But when he does find out I don't know what will happen"

"Exactly. This is why I need to leave someone strong in charge. It would be best to have someone born from our bloodline so Radim can't get his blood purity fanatics behind him to overthrow anyone we put on the throne. You said you weren't going to stick around." Ettore tried to keep the bitterness out of his voice.

Bob must've heard it anyway. "I'm sorry, Ettore. Even if I wanted to stay, Sam has too many enemies for it to be safe here. The fewer people around him, the better off we are. Besides we have a daughter we need to watch out for. She's in the castle now, and she'll be an adult before we know it. We can't risk anyone using her against us."

Ettore's mouth dropped open. "You have a daughter? You adopted?" A spear of hurt followed his surprise. He'd thought they were close enough his brother would've shared information about a new addition to his family. He didn't expect Bob to gossip about his mate's favorite sexual positions, but he thought he'd tell Ettore about adopting a daughter.

Bob ducked his head, his expression embarrassed. If he were human, he would've blushed. "I should've told you. She's a born vampire. Cutest little thing. She adores Sam. He tries to be the firm one, but she easily twists him around her little finger."

"And I suppose you're the tough one?" Ettore asked not bothering to keep the ridicule out of his voice. Bob had always been the best big brother, allowing Ettore and Radim too much leeway.

"Maybe not so much," Bob admitted with a shrug.

Ettore laughed. "Tell me about her. Is she a handful?"

"She can be, but she's a good kid. I fear for her future boyfriends, or girlfriends, though."

"Plan to show them your fangs?" Ettore asked. He couldn't imagine Bob letting any average suitor near his daughter.

"Sam might set them on fire," Bob mused. His gleeful expression had Ettore smiling.

He couldn't remember the last time he'd just sat and talked to his brother. Too many bad memories about Radim, and then Bob's quest for his mate, had pulled them apart over the years. Neither of them spoke as they watched the candle flames flicker.

"Who should we make king? Hardrien?" Bob asked after a few minutes of silence. "His leadership of the army is exemplary."

"He's not royal." Trying to appoint someone outside the family could cause a revolution, although technically anyone could be king. If the people were unhappy, it could cause a crack in leadership big enough to let Radim in. "We need a logical line of succession. We need you."

Bob bowed his head. "I'm sorry, but please don't ask me to take up your mantle, brother, I can't leave my mate. This isn't just because it's my destiny to be with him; he is everything to me."

"I understand." For once he really did. Over the years, he'd rarely understood his siblings, but he could bond with Bob over this one thing. They knew the prophecies, and if Sam was the missing piece to everything, then he needed Bob as his protector. Ettore tried to put a hand on Bob's shoulder, but it went through causing his brother to shiver. He understood far more than Bob probably expected. "We have to be careful who we choose to be king. The entire vampire community has to find him acceptable."

"How about Tarren? He's a first cousin. Technically he's in line for the throne if something happened to all three princes."

Ettore couldn't argue about that. "True."

Tarren had grown into one of the more influential members of the kingdom, the leader of the council, wise and settled, and more importantly, he wasn't one of those who believed born vampires were superior to everything. He also wasn't given to violent outbursts or random kills. He might lack imagination, but with the proper advisors, he'd make a steady leader. "He might work."

"I can't stay," Bob repeated. "We need to find someone."

"I know." Deep down Ettore did understand about sacrificing everything for love. Hadn't he done the same? "If you decide to give up a kingdom for one guy, make sure he's worth it."

Bob smiled, his eyes lit with a joy Ettore had never seen

on his brother's face before. "Trust me; Sam is worth everything. Stubborn, gorgeous, soft-hearted and filled with so much magic he can barely contain it. He's perfect."

"I'm glad you finally found him." Bob had searched long and hard before he found Sam. The seers couldn't give him too many details about where Bob would find his soul mate, or it might change fate. Bob finding Sam among the populace of the entire planet only proved they were meant to be together.

"Me too. And I'll do anything to keep him." Bob's voice dipped into a low growl.

Ettore raised his hands defensively even though Bob couldn't harm him. Instinct had him wanting to calm his brother. "How about we concentrate on how we're going to persuade cousin Tarren to take the throne. Then you can go and cuddle with your mate for the rest of your lives."

Bob winced. "I owe Sam some attention. I've been conducting your rites and pushed him away to mourn, but we have another eleven days of ceremony, and I can't let him be a distraction."

"If I could kick you, I would," Ettore warned. "I'm here; you don't need to mourn me now."

"I suppose not." Bob's soft laugh told Ettore they would settle everything between them. "I'll go find my mate and apologize. It would be nice if you could meet Sam properly before you return to Aset Ka."

"I'd like that." Ettore didn't particularly want to go back, but his afterlife would be happier if he knew his brother was content with his mate. At least one of them should have a good life. "After this, we'll go visit your Sam. Where is he now?"

"Somewhere around here. I had to block the link between us for mourning."

"Haven't we discussed there is no more mourning to be done? Contact him." Uneasiness added an edge to Ettore's tone. There was something about Sam that lit up all his instincts and told him that Bob's mate was this important center of everything. When Aset Ka had spoken of a man with magic that sent ripples into his realm he had to have meant Sam. There was too much evidence for it not to be true.

Bob frowned. He closed his eyes then opened them less than a minute later. A panicked expression crossed his face. "I can't feel Sam. He's not here." He jumped to his feet. "Sam is gone."

## Chapter Four

SAM WAS COLD. ACTUALLY, WAY PAST COLD, HIS SKIN HAD A blue tinge that wasn't looking all that healthy. Teddy didn't look cold, if anything he looked flushed and like his world had ended; a mix of miserable and shocked.

"Tell me everything," Sam said, and began to shiver. He looked down at himself, aware he was only in thin pajama bottoms and a short-sleeved T-shirt.

"Wait, I'll be right back," Teddy said, walking toward the door carefully. He pushed a hand out, and it passed through the wood. He pulled it back quickly, then huffed in disgust. Screwing up his eyes he reached for the handle, managing to grasp it, then yanking the door open.

"Teddy?"

In a few moments, Teddy was back, blankets in his hands, one that looked like it had been chewed by a wererat, then spat back out. Sam ignored that one but gratefully pulled all the others around him.

Teddy sat opposite him, cross-legged and thoughtful. "So, something happened," he began, in his usual vague Teddy-speak.

"You'll have to be more specific."

"I fell in love when I was a young man."

Sam considered Teddy; he didn't look that old as a ghost. He had long hair that reached his shoulders, glossy and curled; it hid the glint of gold in his earlobes. He also had quite the beard going on, and his chestnut hair didn't show a single sign of gray. Not that ghosts aged, Sam guessed. The ghost Teddy was now must reflect the age he was when he died. That's how ghosts worked, right? Sam hadn't quite reached the ghost chapter in the Handbook of Private Detecting.

"And?" Sam prompted.

"Everyone hated us being together. His parents wanted him to find a wife."

"It was a man then."

"No," Teddy frowned. "A vampire."

Sam hadn't quite meant that, but at least it moved the story along.

"Which vampire?" He abruptly had an awful thought that it was Bob. But that couldn't be right. Could it? Teddy or Bob would've said something.

"Ettore," Teddy said, miserable, and sunk into the wooden floor a little.

"Bob's brother? That Ettore?" Sam felt the knot in his chest loosen but only a little. There were too many coincidences in his life. Inheriting a detective agency that just happened to have the ghost of Ettore's mate inside became one too many.

"I loved him so much, but he was the second heir to a vampire ruling family. When Bob decided to undertake a quest, to begin searching." He looked at Sam. "For things," he finished a little lamely, "that moved Ettore up to the next heir to the throne. Where before his family only disapproved of our relationship, they vocally denounced my human status once he became the next potential king."

"So, you were a human, before… things happened."

"You mean before I became this," Teddy said, sadly, and pointed at himself.

"Yeah, that."

"Human, yes. I worked in the castle and grew close to Ettore as I got older, but no one liked us seeing each other."

"Not even Bob?" Sam didn't want to hear that Bob was an ass that disapproved of vampire/human relations. His lover had never indicated as much, but people's perceptions sometimes changed as they got older.

"Bob? No, he left before everything went to hell, I don't think he even knew about his brother and me. I never told him, even after he came here; he wouldn't have understood."

"He wouldn't have cared, even if he knew," Sam defended.

"I am, I was, a human."

"And so am I. And Bob loves me," Sam snapped.

Teddy looked at him sadly, like he wanted to comment on the human part. Sam had all his arguments ready. Instead, Teddy carried on with the story. "There was a third brother, Radim, younger by several years, and he was determined to keep the purity of the royal blood line. He was part of a small group of vampires who called themselves The True Vampires." He lifted his wet, shiny gaze to Sam. "No one knew they were even operating anymore."

"And they believe what? That non-vampires were worth nothing?"

"Not just that, but a born vampire is superior to every living being, that a vampire who is made by a bite is an aberration."

That wasn't a story Sam wanted to hear; he knew it couldn't end well.

"Radim befriended me, said he understood that love was love and that me and Ettore were forever. He pretended to be on our side, but it was all an act. He convinced us we needed to leave everything behind if we wanted to stay together. He helped us plan our escape, but when I got to the cellar tunnel where we were meeting to leave…." Teddy cut off as if the words were too painful to speak.

"Teddy?"

This wasn't the sarcastic ghost Sam was used to; it was a man who had the weight of grief dragging him down.

"Radim had a cursed knife, one cut and it would kill any living thing it touched. He pointed it at my heart and told me that the relationship Ettore and I had was wrong and that I wasn't going to ruin his family name."

Teddy pressed a hand to his chest, and grief flooded his expression. "Ettore arrived and heard what Radim said. They fought. Radim had Ettore pressed against the wall with the knife at his throat. I pushed myself between them; then Radim stabbed me and ran while I lay dying."

"What did Ettore do?"

"The snap of our soul connection knocked Ettore out. He was unconscious."

"Teddy, I'm so sorry." Nothing he said could make up for the sorrow of losing a soul mate. If he could touch him, Sam would've given him a hug.

They were silent for a short time. Sam didn't know what to say, imagining him and Bob in that situation made him sick to his stomach. Teddy looked different, not from switching between ghost and corporeal, since there wasn't the scratchy irritating expression he normally wore, but true grief etched his face.

He sighed. "I suspect whatever demon curse lived in the blade prevented me from passing on. My body was dead, but my soul couldn't leave this plane of reality."

"You were stuck here?"

"Yes, and I couldn't stand the thought of spending the rest of my undead existence watching Ettore move on with his life. My spirit left just as he was waking, as guards found him."

"Oh, Teddy…."

Teddy paused again, his eyes wet with tears. "I hoped he'd move on after I died. I didn't want him clinging to a lost soul. So, I moved to the old city and ended up here watching over the detective agency. I found the cases interesting, and the supernaturals could see me which gave me someone to talk to. I'm invisible to humans." He gave Sam a pointed look, which Sam ignored.

Sam sighed noisily. How many times did he have to put up with people trying to guess what his paranormal inheritance might be? "So, you're not a ghost, you're what, a wandering soul?"

Teddy shrugged, and his elbow knocked against the cabinet beside him. Idly he rubbed his arm. "I don't know what I am anymore."

"So, what happened? Why are you now half solid, and half not, and what the hell is happening to me? I'm not a spirit; I shouldn't be phasing through things," Sam complained.

"I don't know. Maybe it's the vortex swirling us up together."

"What vortex."

"The thing that brought you here."

"Why did you pull me back home?" Despite his interest in Teddy's situation, Sam still wanted to know what was so urgent that he needed to be yanked from the Vampire Castle.

"I'm not sure I did, but I need your help," Teddy said.

"I was busy dealing with Bob. He's in mourning."

Teddy frowned. "Why?"

"Because Bob was dying and his brother traded his soul to revive him."

Teddy blinked at him. "Bob's brother? Radim? Please tell me it wasn't Ettore." Suddenly Teddy looked like he was going to shake Sam to get the words out of him.

"Ettore," Sam said, reluctantly, knowing the news would hurt Teddy. "He made a bargain with Aset Ka to save Bob."

Teddy let out a sharp gasp.

"Ettore made a soul deal?" Teddy's words were tight with grief.

"Yes, in exchange for Bob's life."

"With Aset Ka? A proper deal?"

"Yes," Sam frowned. Teddy looked absolutely horrified. "Once Ettore agreed to go with Aset Ka, Bob sat up like he'd just been sleeping instead of dead. It was incredibly brave of Ettore. He was clearly a good man; I can see why you loved him." He winced at the sound of himself using a past tense.

Teddy stood up and paced, sometimes floating just above the floor, other times walking on the wood itself without appearing to notice the difference. He went from shock to anger, to crying, to looking thoughtful. Then he sighed heavily and sat back down. "Oh Ettore, my love," he finally said, and wiped away tears with the back of his hand. "You stupid vampire." Teddy was agitated. "This must be why I feel so strange."

"What do you mean?"

"Ettore and I… it must have been Ettore's death that has affected me, and made me want you here."

"So, because Ettore died you decided to drag me away from my mate and my daughter and any, and all vital diplomacy, just to chat? Why? What could I do to help?"

Teddy shrugged, and Sam knew he wasn't getting any more out of the ghost. What was the connection between Teddy and Ettore? And what did that have to do with him being half ghost?

"Why are we phasing in and out?" Sam asked.

Teddy shook his head. "I told you, I think it's the vortex, they tend to scramble the people connected, and I used myself as an anchor to bring you here. It shouldn't last long." The last part he said with great hope, like it would reassure Sam.

It didn't. Not at all.

"How long?"

"I don't know." He waved his hand again, which was really beginning to frustrate Sam. Then Teddy's eyes widened, and he bit his lip, and hell, was that blood there? Teddy went cross-eyed trying to look at his lip, and in the end, he pressed a finger there and stared in horror at the scarlet drop on the tip of his finger. "Balance, harmony, fucked," he said, like he was stringing random thoughts together.

"Teddy?" Sam watched the corporeal ghost with more than a little apprehension. Teddy had gone from ranting to throwing out words that made little sense.

"There's a balance okay. You must have read about it in your reference book on paranormals."

Sam felt guilty. "Is it past chapter five, the one about the dwarves? I think that's where I got to when we had that siren-in-our-bathroom issue."

Teddy looked at him aghast. "You need to read it all, Sam. If you had, you'd know that balance is everything, and this is wrong," he thumped himself on the chest, "I am wrong, you are wrong." He looked anxious, scared, and a whole host of other weird expressions which Sam couldn't decipher. Teddy's breathing tightened, and he closed his eyes to concentrate, but it didn't help.

Teddy hyperventilated, then fell through the floor.

As he disappeared a voice said from Sam's left, clear as day, "Samuel Enderson. Savior. Lover of my brother and holder of his heart. We need to talk."

Startled, Sam turned, looking right into Ettore's dark eyes, the vampire king was a little hazy around the edges. Sam scooted back and away, because, hell, Ettore was dead, right?

Sam wanted to feel shocked, or be surprised. But, he knew, given the way his life went, two dead guys in his company was just the start of a regular day.

"Call me Sam," he managed to force out.

"Bob is looking for you," Ettore said, as he crouched down next to him. "He's worried. You left without a word."

"I didn't exactly get a chance to chat before I was teleported here. Is Bob with you?" Sam asked, trying not to get his hopes up.

"No, he's at the castle, searching for you." Ettore's irritated tone set Sam's back up.

"Well, I'm not at the castle, am I?" he snapped back.

"I can see that. Speaking of which, you can see me, can't you?"

Sam sighed heavily. "Don't tell me; I'm the only one that can see you."

"Humans rarely can see ghosts and usually only those they are related to. I guess I heard correctly that you aren't human."

Sam eyed the dead vampire. "Did you come all this way just to bother me?"

Ettore scowled. "Yes, to settle my brother's state of mind.

He's oddly fond of his mate. I followed the signature of your magic. I didn't want to tell Bob in case I couldn't locate you, but he's becoming frantic."

Sam groaned. "I would've contacted him if I could, but he isn't connecting with our bond while in mourning, and I wasn't expecting to come here." He didn't need a guilt trip over abandoning Bob on top of his own issues. It wasn't like he chose to leave.

Sam knocked the back of his head against the wall, only the wall wasn't there, and he fell, panicking as he passed straight through. He scrambled to get back up before he was stuck.

The door slammed open, and a pissed off Teddy stalked in, his white flowing shirt billowing around him. Next to him Ettore gasped and let out a strangled whisper. *Teddy.*

Sam waited for Teddy's reaction, but there was nothing. In fact, Teddy was looking right at Sam like he was the only person in the room.

"I really hate this," Teddy growled and kicked the filing cabinet. His booted foot contacted with the metal, and he let out an oomph of pain.

"Aset Ka, save me," Ettore said in a soft whisper. "He looks so… real."

"He is real," Sam explained. "Right now, at least. Other times he falls through the floor."

"Sorry?" Teddy said.

"I was just talking to…." Sam waved at the space next to him, not sure about what to say. Teddy didn't show any signs of seeing Ettore, and his next words confirmed Sam's belief.

"Who are you talking to?" Teddy asked, coming to a stop in front of him.

Sam glanced at Ettore, should he tell Teddy that Ettore

was there? The vampire inclined his head, but his terrified expression didn't reassure Sam.

"Ettore," Sam said.

Teddy huffed. "For a minute, I thought you said Ettore. That's not funny, Sam."

"I'm not trying to be funny. Ettore is here in the room."

Teddy scowled. "There's no need to be so hateful. I did what I did to bring you here because this is all so weird. I thought with your magic you might be able to do something or be willing to try. I guess I was wrong."

*Not as weird as having two dead men in the same room and them not being able to see each other.*

"I'm not being hateful," Sam defended. "Ettore is sitting right beside me."

Teddy looked at Sam's left, then his right. "No, he isn't."

"He can't see me," Ettore said, his tone wistful.

"Why can't he?" Sam asked Ettore, and Teddy cursed.

"Why are you lying?" Teddy asked, a hurt expression on his face. "I told you my past in confidence, and you throw it back at me. I thought better of you, Sam."

Ettore waved a hand in front of Sam's face. "Our soul connection is lost. He doesn't acknowledge me as part of him anymore. Tell him you're not lying," Ettore demanded.

"Teddy, I'm not lying or mocking you," Sam said. Before he finished the sentence, he knew Teddy wouldn't believe him.

"Yes, you are," Teddy snarled.

Ettore snapped his fingers. "Tell him about the pond."

"What pond?" Sam asked Ettore. His head was really starting to hurt. Why couldn't he have a simple day of sitting around drinking coffee and reading a trashy novel?

"Tell him I still remember he said that I had the best ass out of all the vampires in the castle."

Sam stared at Ettore in horror. "I'm not saying that."

Teddy stalked closer. "What? Not saying what?"

Ettore moved a little closer as well, and suddenly Sam felt more than just a little surrounded.

"You have to; it's the only way he'll know," Ettore said, sounding tired.

"Okay, okay!" Sam held up a hand as Teddy opened his mouth to speak. "Ettore says, that at the pond you told him that you thought he had the best ass out of all the vampires in the castle."

Teddy's mouth fell open, and then he collapsed to his knees, luckily he was solid, and the floor caught his graceless slump.

His eyes were bright, emotion sparking in them, and all he said was one single word, filled with equal measures of fear and hope.

"Ettore?"

# Chapter Five

ETTORE STARED AT TEDDY. SEEING HIM AGAIN, BROUGHT back all of the old feelings he had for his soul mate. Saying he missed Teddy, barely scratched the surface of the soul-deep longing and desperation, he felt at their separation.

"What happened to him? Why is he a ghost?" Ettore asked Sam. He struggled to think of ways he could make Teddy see him. He wasn't a witch with an arsenal of spells at his disposal. Vampires didn't have any abilities more than their higher-level senses, and they didn't gain any after death.

"We think the demon blade your brother used to stab Teddy left him in this half form. This sometimes solid, sometimes not phase is new," Sam answered Ettore, although his eyes remained on Teddy.

"I can't believe he's here," Teddy whispered from his spot on the floor. "I wonder why I can't see him. Maybe it's because I'm solid right now. If I go back to being a ghost, maybe I'll be able to see him. He's really there?"

Sam sighed at the despondent hope in Teddy's voice. "Why would I lie?"

Teddy squinted, his gaze tracing around the room as if he were trying to see Ettore. "I don't know."

"Look, we need to figure out what's happening and why our bodies are destabilized. I'm not going to spend the rest of my life fading in and out. Falling through walls and floors isn't how I plan on living or not living." Sam scowled.

"I told you I think it's the vortex. It should stabilize soon." Teddy didn't sound overly confident, and Sam wasn't buying his far-fetched ideas.

Ettore smiled as he floated over to Teddy. His beloved. Unable to resist he brushed a finger across one sculpted cheek. He'd forgotten his lover's beauty. They had never gotten around to having a painting made of Teddy. They had planned to have one made before their bonding ceremony, but never had the chance.

Teddy shivered, his eyes going wide. "Ettore?" he asked in a hushed whisper.

"He's standing right beside you," Sam said.

"I felt him." Teddy's eyes went wide with surprise. He looked around, then sighed when he didn't appear to find Ettore

"I can't feel you," Ettore whispered, pain spiking through his translucent chest. If he couldn't have a solid body, he shouldn't have physical responses. It wasn't fair to have an aching heart if he couldn't truly have a physical heart.

Sam's pitying expression didn't help Ettore's resentment over the situation. How could he put his old life behind him if he couldn't even talk to his old love? What had happened to Teddy? If Aset Ka captured Teddy's soul, then he could use it to force Ettore to obey Aset Ka's whims.

Ettore would do anything for Teddy.

*Anything.*

He couldn't let Teddy be harmed even more. Aset Ka

controlled Ettore well enough without the added security of possessing his loved ones.

"Radim should suffer for what he's condemned you to, Teddy," Ettore whispered, then he spoke to the room, not quite certain where to speak. "Do you know what happened to Radim?"

Sam looked at him, and then repeated the question to Teddy. "Ettore wants to know if you know what happened to Radim?" Teddy must have said something because Sam nodded, then turned back to Ettore. "He doesn't," Sam replied. "Do you know anything at all?"

Ettore shook his head. "Radim disappeared, and he isn't in Aset Ka's realm, so he isn't dead. Bob and I believe he'll return to the castle once he finds out I died. With Bob gone, and me dead, the throne could be his."

"Is that a bad thing?" Sam asked. "Beside the fact he killed your mate and ran? Could he be a better vampire now?"

"I will never forgive him," Ettore snapped.

"I know you won't," Sam sounded so patient. "But a hundred years is a long time."

"He was an extremist, believing that born vampires are superior, and that made vampires are lesser. With his political views, I don't think the majority of the vampires will support him. His ideals are outside of everything he'd been taught. Bob and I never believed in blood purity. Sure, some of our cousins believe born vampires are superior, but they never killed humans as far as I know. Radim was a danger to the vampire kingdom, and I can't allow myself to believe he could have changed. If he starts slaughtering humans, he will draw too much attention, and his human prey will become predators and kill us all."

Sam's brow furrowed as he considered Ettore's words.

"Maybe it was your relationship with Teddy that caused Radim to snap."

"No. He had those twisted ideals long before I met Teddy. It was one of the reasons I hesitated to introduce Teddy to the family." Ettore missed Teddy with every bit of his being. "I don't know what we should do next. Aset Ka thinks there is a problem with the balance in the world. I have no idea how to fix it."

Sam nibbled on his bottom lip for a minute before asking in a cautious voice. "Teddy mentioned that also. How is Bob doing? I haven't been able to see him in so long."

"Better. I asked him to take over the kingdom," Ettore confessed. He didn't want secrets between him and his brother's mate, and he considered maybe Bob would never admit to Sam what Ettore had asked of him.

"Wh-what did he say?" Sam asked.

"He refused the crown, so we are still trying to decide which of our cousins can take over since I obviously can't rule. I only have a few days before I have to return to Aset Ka."

Sam walked over to sit in a chair. He froze after sitting before wriggling as if uncertain it would take his weight. He ran his fingers through his hair then asked, "If Bob has to help, how long do you think it will be before he can come home?"

"I don't know." Ettore shrugged. "He knows all of the royal responsibilities, and it could take years before the new king will be ready to rule. It would be best if you returned to the castle and talked to him. Between the two of you, I'm sure you can work something out."

Ettore hated the thought he might be responsible of ruining Bob and Sam's relationship. He was certain they could work something out if they didn't turn stubborn and just talked.

"There might not be a place for me in his life anymore," Sam said, brokenly. "He might have turned down the crown, but I know he'll want to be there to advise anyone you guys choose for a king. Before anything else, he is a vampire."

Ettore floated over to Sam and attempted to put his hand on his shoulder. "Bob is your soul mate, and he is giving up ruling our people to be with you. You're the other half of him," he added. "I know how it feels to lose a soul mate and Bob won't let anything take your spot in his heart, especially not to achieve power he never wanted."

"That doesn't make the separation hurt any less." Sam wiped his eyes with his palms.

"I know. Can you tell Teddy I still love him?" Ettore pleaded with Sam.

Sam wriggled uncomfortably. "I wish you could see each other to talk."

He yelped as light filled the room, a curious purple color, like the acid breath of Aset Ka, and then as Ettore blinked he realized he could see Teddy.

"Ettore!" Teddy exclaimed. He moved toward Ettore and stopped a foot away from him. "I can see you."

"You can?" Ettore asked, cautiously. The joy in Teddy's eyes warmed Ettore's heart. So many years had passed he'd worried Teddy might not feel the same way. There had never been a study of bonds between humans and vampires since it rarely happened.

Teddy's beautiful eyes filled with tears. "Oh Ettore," he said, his shoulders slumping.

Ettore reached out a hand, but there was still no way to touch. He gave Sam a pleading look over his shoulder.

Sam was staring at them, still blinking after the blinding flash. "I wish Ettore and Teddy could touch," he said.

Nothing happened. Ettore's hand still slipped through Teddy's fingers. He squashed down his instinctive cry of despair. He could see Teddy and talk to him; he should be thankful for even that ability.

"I need to... uhm... call Bob... bye."

Before Ettore could say anything else, Sam stood and left the room leaving him alone with Teddy. Ettore turned to face his dead lover who looked surprisingly solid. "I missed you." The words were insufficient for the aching hole in his chest, but they were all he could push out over the lump in his throat.

Teddy examined his fingers as if they were the most fascinating things he'd ever seen. "I don't know what to say now; I missed you." He looked up at Ettore, his eyes shining. "I couldn't stay as a soul at the castle to watch you happy with someone else. You understand that, don't you?"

Ettore nodded. Of course he understood, didn't mean he had to like it. He'd always imagined Teddy safe in whatever version of the afterlife a human had. He never once thought Teddy might have his soul ripped from his body and be cursed to wander the earth in ghost form. "There was never happiness after you died," Ettore admitted. "And I never touched another like I touched you, no one. Not for a hundred years."

Teddy sniffed back tears but didn't move closer. His expression was one of despair and unhappiness.

"What about you?" Ettore asked. "Do you... have you...?"

"There was no one," Teddy said.

"Oh my love," Ettore murmured, his head full of things he wanted to say.

"A soul like mine becomes sadder and more unfocused as the years go on. And I was lost without you."

"What about Sam?" Ettore asked, unable to shift the suspicions that curled inside him.

"What about him?"

"Why did you call Sam back home?" Ettore couldn't think of a single reason to drag Sam to Teddy. "Do you have feelings for him?"

Teddy looked aghast and then frowned. "Of course not. I'm not sure why I wanted him here. It's like I felt a compulsion to have him back."

"Do you think it was your own?" There were plenty of things that could cast mind tricks, but few that could compel ghosts.

"I don't know." Teddy's confused expression didn't give Ettore any sense of reassurance. "Now that he's here I'm no longer confident over why I brought him back," Teddy confessed. "I didn't mean to; I don't think. But I was thinking about you, and Bob, and Sam, and suddenly I was in the middle of creating a summoning vortex and calling for Sam."

"Hmm. You had no control?"

"I thought I did."

"Then, either someone wanted Sam out of the castle, or they wanted him here, and they used you as a tool."

"Yeah." Teddy tapped a finger to his chin. "I can't imagine who else would care if Sam was here or not, but strange things often happen around Sam. He's also phasing in and out like I am."

"Ah, that explains the chair," Ettore said.

"The chair?"

"He didn't look like he was certain it would hold him."

"He's going from transparent to solid. I don't know that it is truly a ghost state, but it has made him fall through solid objects a few times." Teddy adjusted a ruffle on his shirt. "Do you think Aset Ka will let me join you in the afterlife?" Teddy asked, a longing expression on his handsome face. "I know I'm not a vampire, but maybe he'll make an exception."

Ettore hated to destroy the flash of hope in Teddy's eyes, but he refused to make him false promises. "I doubt it. I think it would need the magic of a god to overturn anything Aset Ka has done."

"Why did he send you away?"

"I don't know, but I think I probably went off plan because I just wanted the chance to say goodbye properly to Bob, to everyone."

"Will he be upset that you've deviated from your task?" The doubtful expression on Teddy's face made Ettore really think for a minute.

"He wasn't that specific about what he wanted me to do, but I doubt anything would make him happy." Ettore silently cursed. As a king, he should've noticed another's manipulation, even if it was a god. "I have no idea. He wants me to figure out what's going on here. He thinks the balance is wrong in this word, and it's threatening his Underworld. Since you think the same thing, we should work together to fix whatever is happening. Maybe he'll give you a boon if you help me fix it. Maybe then we could both move on and meet again in our next life."

Ettore didn't bother to mention he still had no idea where things had gone wrong.

Teddy's solid body faded to a transparent ghostly outline. Silvery tears dripped from his eyes.

"You are still so handsome," Ettore said. "I missed you so much. When you stood between me and the knife…." he stopped talking, smiled and floated closer, reaching out.

Teddy's hand reached back and in their ghost states their fingers passed through each other, then something snapped into place and their fingers entwined. The burning was intense, a fire racing up his arm, and Ettore gasped. Teddy winced. Was he feeling the same pain? Abruptly, the pain vanished, and in a crash of noise and blinding light they both solidified and dropped to the floor in a tangled heap.

Memories slammed into Ettore's head.

In clarity, he recalled the final day, Radim with his cursed knife, the scuffle, the knife at Ettore's throat, and Teddy forcing himself between them, boldly stating that Radim would have to go through him to kill Ettore.

The look of pure hate was in Radim's eyes as he plunged the knife into Teddy's chest.

Ettore pressed a hand to his mate's chest and buried his face against Teddy's neck, inhaling the somewhat dusty smell of his lover's skin, but touching the warmth there. Their soul mate bond flickered between them, and he could feel the phantom pain of the knife. He could feel the tendrils of poison under his skin and see the pull of Teddy's soul from his body.

Was it that simple? That Teddy had to be in a ghostly state for them to connect? Had Sam really cast magic that would make that possible?

Teddy moved them a little, so they could lie side by side amongst the files and folders that had tumbled to the floor. Still entwined, Teddy pressed a kiss to Ettore's lips before pulling back.

"I never stopped loving you," Ettore murmured.

"Nor I you," Teddy said and kissed him again. The tenderness on Teddy's face warmed Ettore's cold soul. He leaned forward, unable to resist the close proximity of his beloved. At the first feather-soft brush of their lips, Ettore sighed. Quickly following a firmer kiss was the first tentative touch of tongues. Then the kisses became faster, harder, and more intense. At some point, they needed to get up off the floor. But for just a moment, all he wanted to do was touch Teddy and remember their love.

## Chapter Six

Ettore pulled away. "I think we need to figure out how to remain solid before this goes any further. As amazing as it is to touch you, I can't exactly take off your clothes while you're a ghost." Pent-up yearning pressed at the edges of Ettore's temper. He'd waited for so long to see his beloved again, and although they could touch lips and hands, much else was out of the question.

"Sam!" Teddy shouted.

"Why are you calling Sam?" Ettore had appreciated his brother-in-law's discretion when he left.

"Because he got us this far, and maybe he can channel some extra energy and make us more solid. It didn't work the first time, but that doesn't mean Sam can't fix this." Teddy scowled. "I refuse to be this close to you and not be able to touch you."

Ettore laughed. A century of stress rolled off his shoulders. He'd forgotten the joy he received from just being close to his beloved. No one else saw the world like his Teddy, and he'd buried how much he'd appreciated Teddy's no-nonsense approach. His beloved never held back when he wanted something.

"You called?" Sam peeked inside the doorway, his expression wary as he looked from one to the other as if trying to determine what they wanted before committing fully to entering.

Smart man.

"Fix us!" Teddy demanded, crossing his arms.

Sam frowned. "I can't fix you. You're dead. I can't bring back the dead even with my wonky abilities."

Teddy huffed. "Technically we're between the present and the afterlife, but let's not be picky."

"Teddy, that's enough," Ettore reprimanded. He'd forgotten Teddy's bossy and opinionated ways; luckily they were balanced by being his soul mate and incredibly sexy.

Teddy didn't stop; of course he didn't, he never listened to Ettore. "Why don't you do that wish thingy again and demand us to be solid."

"It doesn't always work," Sam defended.

"I swear, for a man with so much power at his fingertips you don't do a hell of a lot with it." Teddy sounded half annoyed, half destroyed.

Sam rolled his eyes and shook his hand, the bracelet charms knocking. "The power I've been given is tricky. I'm not always certain of how things will work out. I did try to make you solid a few minutes ago if you remember."

Ettore smiled at the exchange. A new affection rose in him for his brother's mate. Sam seemed like he was a good guy. After his own experiences, Ettore hadn't been thrilled when he learned of Bob's human mate, but maybe he'd been too quick to condemn Sam as completely human. If Sam was *the one,* then he was more than *just human.* Being a spirit gave Ettore a different kind of sight. Finally, he could see the auras of the living, and Sam's was a kaleidoscope of colors. He'd never seen such brilliance. Ettore couldn't begin to separate the different layers of Sam's magical essence. Whatever Sam might be, the human portion was probably the smallest bit.

"Try again," Teddy demanded, and then added a soft *please*.

"I can give it another go, but I can't promise anything. When I said I wanted you to be able to touch, I was envisioning you as solid, but that isn't what happened." Sam scratched the back of his neck as if he were embarrassed at his lack of results.

"Hey, don't take it too hard. How about you give it one more shot." With the amount of magical power seething around Sam like a snapping storm, Ettore couldn't imagine there was much Sam couldn't do with the right incentive. Aset Ka would want Sam's soul, vampire or not. The vampire god was a collector of the powerful, and Sam definitely had power in spades. With Sam being Bob's soul mate it would bring him to Aset Ka's notice.

Was that ultimately why Ettore had been sent back? To collect Sam for Aset Ka?

"I guess it can't hurt to try again," Sam said after several minutes of silence. "I can't hurt you, right?" The trepidation on Sam's face made Ettore smile.

"It's not like you can kill us again," he offered.

Sam laughed. "That's true. All right. Give me a second to center myself."

Ettore watched with mounting anticipation as Sam closed his eyes and began to take slow, measured breaths. The air sizzled with pent-up magic like a sleeping beast daring to be awakened.

A new anxiety built in Ettore's chest. Maybe it hadn't

been such an amazing idea after all. He cast a quick look over at Teddy and his resolve hardened. He needed to be more than a ghost if he wanted to give Teddy a proper goodbye in the limited time he had left. He barely had a minute to wonder if Aset Ka would feel Sam's interaction with him before Sam began to speak.

"I wish for these two bonded beings to be on the solid plane of existence," Sam said, formally, like he had considered the wording carefully. Magic poured down Sam's arms, swirling in long streams like shimmering snakes before surging from his hands in bolts of white lightning that zapped into Ettore and Teddy. They jerked at the impact. Ettore couldn't help it; he screamed. Teddy's shout soon followed.

Ettore had never experienced anything that powerful before. Overwhelmed, Ettore forced himself to stop fighting and welcome the magic into his body. Immediately the pain stopped, and Ettore relaxed more. He could do this. He would endure any pain to be back with his beloved.

Time lost meaning between the crackling white fire and fighting to accept the weird energy. He gasped when it cut off, and dropped to the floor. Blinking his watery eyes, Ettore tried to understand the sensations hitting him from all sides. The hard floor beneath his hip from where he fell, and the cool air of the room surrounding him sent information to his brain he had difficulty processing. It took him a few minutes and a groan from the person beside him.

"It worked." Ettore smiled.

Teddy sat up, watching him with wide eyes. "We're solid."

"Does that mean you're alive now?" Sam asked standing over them.

Ettore shook his head. "No. I don't think so. That would make things too easy."

Sam swayed where he stood. "Trust me, that wasn't easy."

Teddy jumped to his feet. "Hey, sit down before you pass out."

"I wanted to connect to Bob, but I can't, I need to get a hold of Jin, I have to get back to the castle."

Ettore forced his gaze from Teddy to notice Sam really didn't look that great. His skin had taken on an unhealthy pallor, and his eyes had a glassy sheen. He climbed to his feet to check on his brother's mate. "Are you going to be okay? How do you feel?"

Sam took so long to answer, Ettore almost asked him again. "I have a headache." Sam blinked rapidly as if trying to clear his head.

"You need to lie down before you fall down," Teddy said. He wrapped an arm around Sam's waist. "I'll help you."

Ettore resisted the urge to say Sam could get there on his own. There was no need for jealousy. Sam had helped them, and it didn't look like Sam would walk more than a few feet before passing out. The last thing he needed was for Bob to come hunting for his blood because Sam fell down stairs after helping them out.

Instead, he made no arguments only following the pair to Sam's room so he could get a good layout of the building.

"I need Bob," Sam half-whispered.

"Sleep first," Ettore said. "I'll talk to Bob."

"You promise?" Sam swayed, and his eyes rolled back in his head before he blinked at Teddy unfocused. Teddy tightened his grip and cast a worried look at Ettore. "I'm so tired," Sam murmured.

"We'll wake you when we have Bob."

Light filled the corridor, and a cat appeared mid-pounce, sliding to a halt right in front of Sam.

"He knows?" Sam asked, looking down at the cat. Were they talking to each other? The cat must be a familiar, imbued with magic and connected to Sam. "I don't want to sleep," Sam said, and then ruined the effect by yawning.

"What is the cat saying?" Ettore whispered to Teddy.

"I have no idea," Teddy replied. He turned his attention to Sam. "What do we need to do? Is Smudge bringing Bob here?"

Sam closed his eyes and leaned on the doorjamb for support. "No. He felt the magic I used and says I need to rest. Bob knows I'm safe."

That seemed to be enough for Sam to relax a little, and he fell onto his mattress face first. The cat, Smudge, curled into Sam's side, then stared right at Ettore and Teddy.

"There's a guest room next door," Sam muttered. "Smudge will look out for me."

Teddy shut the door, and for a moment he wouldn't look Ettore in his eyes.

"Teddy?"

"What happens now?" Teddy asked. He looked up, and there was an endless sadness in his eyes.

Ettore held out his hand. "We will make the most of our time." He gestured to the half open door and guest bedroom beyond. "Sleep maybe?" After years without Teddy, he wanted to renew their acquaintance as soon as possible. He doubted Aset Ka would let Ettore stay because he wanted to have sex with his boyfriend. If the god had ever had sex it had been so long ago, Aset Ka must've forgotten the meaning of pleasure.

He didn't bother to ask Teddy if sleep would be enough, or if he wanted more. Just to have Teddy in his arms was the best thing he could imagine.

He let himself into the guest room, Teddy close behind,

and smiled appreciatively at the cool blue walls and green bedding. It was a room meant to soothe weary guests. His mind wandered to the type of people who might come and stay with Sam and Bob but quickly lost interest when Teddy hugged him from behind.

"What do you think?" Ettore wriggled free and lay down on the bed bouncing up and down lightly. "I think it's big enough for us both to hug and sleep."

Teddy smiled. "And other things," he said. "There's really only one way to find out."

Before Ettore could say anything else. Teddy pulled off his shirt and let it flutter to the ground.

Ettore stared with his mouth open at the masculine beauty before him. So many years had passed since he'd seen Teddy naked he had forgotten all the delicious details. Teddy's sleekly muscled body and smooth, flawless soft-looking skin almost had him drooling as he regarded his mate. It wasn't until his gaze reached Teddy's chest that reality struck him. A long, ugly knife wound marred the skin over his heart.

Entranced Ettore slid off the bed to get a better look. He slid a finger along the line. "Is that where?"

"Yes, that's where Radim stabbed me." Teddy's casual tone took Ettore by surprise.

"You don't seem upset about it."

Teddy shrugged. "At this point, it's been so many years I barely remember it happening. I tend to remember the loneliness and missing you instead."

Ettore didn't know how to respond to Teddy's statement. He couldn't say he had missed Teddy; it was too quiet a word for the gut-wrenching heartache that had weighed him down for the past century. "Same here. I never thought I'd see you again."

Teddy snuggled up closer. "We're together now."

They stood there absorbing the feel of flesh to flesh. Ettore soaked up Teddy's body heat, amazed the ghost had any even in solid form. He pressed a kiss to the side of Teddy's neck and snuggled in close. He'd longed to hold Teddy again almost more than sex. As a vampire king, Ettore didn't have anyone to lean on, not since Teddy died.

In unspoken agreement, they stripped down and climbed on the bed. Ettore admired Teddy's long frame while Teddy licked his way down Ettore's body. Long, languid laps of his tongue brought Teddy to Ettore's erection. "I never forgot how you tasted." Teddy inhaled. "How you smelled. The amazing noises you made when I sucked you. I've been craving you for almost a hundred years, and I'm not letting you out of the bed until I'm done." Teddy's eyes darkened with need, and Ettore didn't doubt any of his words.

"Sounds like a good idea to me." Ettore stroked Teddy's head, encouraging his attentions. "I'd keep you here for the next century if I had the chance."

Seven days sounded more like a wishful dream than a proper period of time. He'd rather stay with Teddy for an eternity, but he doubted Aset Ka would wait that long. How many times would they be able to make love before Ettore had to return? A soft tug had Teddy climbing back up his body until their mouths met.

A groan ripped from his throat. He lifted his chin for another kiss. Savoring the taste, flavor, and warmth of his mate's mouth, Ettore wallowed in the contact. While they kissed, he slid his hands across the silky texture of Teddy's back, touching as much as he could to relearn the shape of his lover's body through his fingertips.

"I love you," Teddy's whispered words brushed across his skin.

"I love you too, never forget that." Time, space, and level of being wouldn't change Ettore's mind.

He flipped Teddy over onto his back. "Lube?"

Teddy frowned then rolled over and opened the drawer to the small table beside him. "Nothing."

"Give me a minute." Ettore pulled on his pants without bothering with underwear. He walked down the hall to the only other closed door and banged on it.

"Wha?" Sam's voice was blurry.

"Sam? May I ask you something?"

Sam opened the door, leaning heavily on the wood, with tousled hair, a frown, and an angry hissing cat wrapped around his shoulder. "Is it Bob?"

"No."

"Then what?"

"We need lube."

Sam's eyes widened, then he sighed on a yawn. "Just a second." He vanished and came back with a small tube. "Here you go! Use it liberally. It's been a long time for Teddy."

"Thank you." Ettore turned around, ignoring Sam's advice.

Teddy hadn't moved from where he left him, Ettore noted when he entered the room. He closed the door behind him and let his gaze trail across the firm muscles and smooth skin forming Teddy's body. He swallowed the moisture pooling in his mouth since it wouldn't be sexy to let drool slide down his chin.

"I stayed put," Teddy teased as he spread his legs and let his right hand slide down his inner thigh.

"So I see." Ettore hoped Teddy didn't notice the roughness of his voice. He cleared his throat before crawling on the bed and wedging his knees on either side of Teddy's hips. "I've got you."

"And I struggled so hard to escape." Teddy's dry tone made Ettore smile.

"You did, but I, in my wisdom, captured you." Ettore set the lube on the pillow beside Teddy's head and took off his pants.

"You are a clever fellow." Teddy grinned up at him.

Ettore leaned down and kissed Teddy. Pressing his lips against his lover's, Ettore slid his tongue alongside Teddy's entangling them together. A soft moan left him. Years of memories of dreaming about his beloved had been dull shadows compared to the reality of Teddy's touch. When Teddy ran his hands up Ettore's back, he melted into the embrace. Need spiked through him, and he grabbed the lube. He lifted his mouth long enough to ask his question. "I want to be inside you?"

Teddy shook his head. "Please."

During their time together, they had traded back and forth, both enjoying the give and take of each position. However, Ettore needed to be inside Teddy. A burning desire to reclaim the man who should have been his for eternity, instead of the little time they had shared.

"I love you." He made sure to show everything he felt in his eyes. Teddy should have no doubt about his feelings. "I will always love you."

Teddy blinked rapidly as if fighting off tears. "I know. I love you too."

Ettore opened the tube and coated his fingers with the clear lubricant. More kisses to relax his lover were followed by Ettore pushing one finger into Teddy. He slowly eased Teddy open before adding another. Ettore didn't rush prepping Teddy for his cock. If Teddy had been a ghost for that long, he doubted sex had been an option. Even Ettore had been unable to do much sexually. Teddy's tight, warm hole had Ettore gritting his teeth while trying to hold back coming before he'd entered his partner.

Finally, he was ready. With Teddy pushing back on his fingers and making obscene noises, Ettore wouldn't last much longer. He spread the lube on his cock then hooked his arms beneath Teddy's knees and lifted him up for easy access. His hips pushed forward almost as if his cock was a divining rod and knew where to find pleasure. With careful movements, he pressed against Teddy. A groan tore from him as Ettore pushed inside.

Teddy gasped, but with enthusiasm, he pushed down with equal passion.

"Oh, yes right there," Teddy groaned.

"Anything for you." Ettore spent the next ten minutes making sure he hit the right spot over and over until Teddy cried out and spurted his release, finally giving Ettore permission to come along with him.

Grunts and moans faded once the last drop had been squeezed from his body. A sated Ettore pulled out of his lover. "You are everything I remembered and more."

Teddy's mouth spread into a goofy smile. "I'm glad you're here."

"Me too," Ettore agreed as he wrapped himself around Teddy. He wisely didn't mention again how short their time together would be. Instead of dwelling on future heartbreak, Ettore planned on milking each minute for every bit of joy, to last him through his future dark years.

Hours later they were woken up by someone banging on their bedroom door. Groaning, Ettore stood up, and slid on his pants. He yanked open the door scowling at the intrusion.

Sam stood there with his hair mussed and eyes bright. "Smudge says it's time to take us back to the castle."

"Good." Ettore considered whether it was Teddy's connection to him that pulled him to this location. Was Teddy part of his mission for Aset Ka? He needed to go back to the castle and see if anything obvious could be found there. He couldn't help thinking that the task he'd been given was utterly and completely connected to Sam and Bob.

Maybe Teddy could help him find clues to the lack of balance, whatever the hell that meant, and then Ettore could fix it all.

But then he'd have to say goodbye to Teddy.

And his heart would be destroyed all over again.

## Chapter Seven

BOB WATCHED FOR SAM AND THE OTHERS' ARRIVAL BACK from the agency. It had been a full night. Although Smudge had reassured him with a new and entirely creepy way of drawing words in the air, that Sam was safe, Bob still worried.

Before Sam could say a word, Bob pulled Sam into his arms as soon as they materialized in the courtyard. For the longest time, he simply held on. He could see his brother, standing a little way off with another man whose back was to him. He didn't want to think about what was up with that situation. Ettore was more solid than he had last seen him, but he would worry about that later.

He had too much to catch up on.

"I love you, I love you," Sam was repeating over and over in his head. He wasn't the only one; Smudge was winding between Bob's feet, purring loudly. Seemed it wasn't just him and Sam that missed being together.

They kissed, and Bob carded his hands through Sam's hair, wanting him closer, wanting them in a quiet space where he could be naked and against his lover, and to right all the parts of himself that felt wrong.

And Sam was gripping him tight in return.

"I was so scared when you went missing," Bob said close to Sam's ear, and all he felt was an answering shudder and blackness that clouded Sam's thoughts.

"I missed you so much."

The only thing that separated them was Mal, launching herself from the castle wall and leaping up between them.

"Daddy! Pop!"

The three of them stood in a tight hold, and Bob slowly felt like he regained control. The mourning rituals relied on isolation and prayer, and he was never going to do that again.

Unless it was Sam or Mal who left him, and then he wouldn't be mourning the same way, he'd be trying to pick up the pieces of his broken heart or following them quickly into the afterlife.

"I have brought him back, Brother," Ettore said. He was holding hands with another man, not in a ghostly way, but a solid clasp of skin and bone.

Bob frowned. The other man looked familiar dressed in old-fashioned clothes, layers of cotton and a waistcoat; with long hair to his shoulders and a beard.

"Hello, Bob," the man said, and Bob abruptly knew exactly who it was.

"Teddy? What happened? How?" Bob looked at Sam.

"Don't ask," Sam said, shaking his head slightly.

Then Bob focused back on the fact that Ettore and Teddy, who seemed solid and not at all the annoying ghost he normally was, were holding hands.

"Ettore?" he asked.

"Bob, I know you know Teddy, but actually this is Theodore Constantine McMurray, my soul mate."

"Teddy is your soul mate, the one who was killed a hundred years ago?" Bob said.

"The same."

"The man you were with? That Radim killed?"

Ettore nodded. Bob was lost for words; he'd been at the agency with the ghost of his brother's soul mate all that time and had never known. Something about that was incredibly wretched.

"Why didn't you tell me who you were, Teddy?" Bob asked.

Teddy just looked sad and wouldn't meet Bob's eyes. Sam squeezed his hand in reassurance. He guessed everything would be explained later.

Finally Bob pulled his brother into a hug, and then Teddy, which was the weirdest thing he'd done in a long list of weird things. Finally everyone, by silent agreement, separated, although Sam held Bob's hand and stood so close that they might as well have been one person.

"I think we have things to talk about," Bob finally said, everyone looked at each other, and then at him.

Sam nodded. "You won't believe what's happened."

Jin landed next to them, his wings wide, and then vanished as he transformed from dragon to man.

"Sam," he said, gripping Sam's free hand. "Don't ever leave like that again. When you disappeared into the vortex…." he stopped talking like he was waiting for Sam to explain.

Bob didn't give Sam time to think up a reply; he doubted that Jin telling Sam what to do would work. Instead, he tugged Sam sideways, and the group trudged into the castle. Sam was quiet, even his thoughts were still, and Bob attempted to calm his own worries knowing Sam would see them all. Smudge leaped onto Sam's shoulder, curling around his neck, and Mal chattered behind them with Ettore. She called him Uncle, and that made Bob smile a little, easing some of his tension.

Lambert was waiting just inside, his serious face even more tightly focused than usual. Bob hadn't missed the vampire the last week or so; he had an annoying way of getting right under Bob's skin.

"The council has called a meeting for the morning," Lambert announced, slightly breathless, stooped, his hand pressed to his chest. "They are calling for a decision on the succession." He looked past Bob to Ettore behind him, then bent further at the waist. "King-in-passing," he added, with respect.

Teddy appeared to be blocking any and all vampires that wanted to show their respect for Ettore. Bob guessed his younger brother couldn't very well act like a king; he wasn't king anymore. He also looked tired, and not up to facing all the questions.

The name King-in-passing would stick to Ettore until the day Ettore was finally back with Aset Ka, and that was a whole other subject for Bob to think about.

He'd already lost his brother once, what would it be like to lose him again, when they'd finally reconnected.

And what about Teddy? Would he become a ghost again? He didn't have a place in Aset Ka's vampire afterlife.

Lambert bowed to Teddy as well, "Welcome King-in-passing-mate," he said, formally.

"Call me Teddy," Teddy said, and extended a hand, dropping it when Lambert frowned at him. He doubted Lambert would be calling Teddy by anything other than the official, approved, name for however long he and Ettore were there.

"I have a room prepared for you, King-in-passing,"

Lambert said. As if there was nothing unusual in welcoming a dead vampire and his human mate. Then he strode down the long hall. Bob and Sam followed, and Bob knew the others would too.

"I'm going to go play," Mal announced as they reached a large oak door, surrounded by intricate carvings.

*The Library—as good a place as any to discover what the hell is going on.* Sam squeezed his hand in answer and knocked shoulders with him.

"I would rather you stayed with us," Bob said, understandably shaken by everything.

"I will accompany the princess," Lambert announced loftily.

"I'll go," Sam said. *We need to talk, but Mal being alone with Lambert scares me.*

*Why?* Bob asked.

Sam shook his head. *I don't know. Lambert is fixated on the old ways, and I don't trust him.*

*Then we will both go with her,* Bob decided.

"I've got this," Jin said, and muscled his way past everyone. "I'll watch over young Mal here." He must have picked up on the silent communication, and Bob was thankful that a powerful dragon would guard Mal with his life.

"I want to play," Mal said doubtfully, looking up at Jin, who crouched down in front of her.

"I like playing," Jin murmured.

She considered him carefully. "Can we go flying?"

Bob winced, as did Sam, but both stayed quiet. Jin would die before letting harm come to Mal.

"We can," Jin said. "We shall visit my mate, Mikhail, if that is okay with your dads."

"Yay, Uncle Mikhail," Mal said, looking up at her dads with wide eyes.

Bob could hear the longing in Jin's voice. He likely missed his lover as much as Bob had missed Sam. But it was Mal's entreaty that grabbed his heart the most. How could he refuse their daughter anything?

*I'm okay with it,* Sam said. *Better Jin who we trust with our lives, than Lambert.*

Lambert looked at Sam sharply, like he'd heard the unspoken words, but Bob realized that A, this wasn't possible and B, he was likely looking past Sam at Teddy and Ettore.

*Then I am too,* Bob replied.

"Of course," Sam said out loud.

"Have fun," Bob added.

Unspoken was, *look after her.*

They watched Jin transform in the courtyard, lying down so Mal could climb on his broad back. Bob refused to feel scared. When Jin swooped into the air, Mal yelled her enthusiasm and glee. Bob wanted to call Jin back. He exchanged a look with Sam, who appeared just as worried. But, Jin was long gone, and Bob and Sam trusted him.

Mal would be fine. Safe. Protected.

Lambert indicated they should go inside the library, the whisper of cloaking magic like a warm breeze on Bob's neck. Once inside Lambert closed the door behind them.

"King-in-passing we need to talk succession," he said to Ettore, who paled and sat on the nearest chair, right next to a teetering pile of lurid fantasy novels. Ettore tugged Teddy onto his lap and held him.

"I need time," he said, his voice ragged.

"We need to consider that Radim is next in line," Lambert said.

"No," Teddy gasped and clutched at his chest. What Radim had done was lost in the history books, consigned as nothing more than sibling rivalry. Or at least that was how the

True Vampire movement were playing the fact that the youngest of three brothers had murdered the King's soul mate.

"No, not Radim," Ettore said and glanced at Bob for his agreement. Bob nodded. "Radim would be a tyrant. He thinks of himself first and not his people."

Lambert pursed his lips and gestured to Bob. "Roberto is here, and he had first succession, we could reinstate him in line."

"I have other duties to perform," Bob said, in a tone that brooked no arguments. He wouldn't let anyone set the crown on his head. His responsibilities to Sam took enough effort, and it was what he'd been born for. One day there would be no vampire king, just a unified community with The Chosen One at the center of it. He was becoming more and more convinced that Sam was that person, and Bob would be part of making that happen. That was his destiny. His and Sam's fate.

Lambert nodded, his eyes darting from Ettore to Sam and back. "If that is what you want, I will research the archives for precedence on skipping one of the royal family in order for another."

Sam leaned on Bob, exhaustion passed through their connection, and abruptly Bob didn't want to talk about matters of state or be part of making world-changing decisions. Let Lambert do his research, he and Ettore would decide after a full night's sleep.

"I need to sleep, *we* need to sleep. All of us." Bob waved a hand to indicate the entire group.

Sam nodded. "Please."

*I need you*, Sam thought.

They agreed to reconvene in the morning and headed to their chambers. Bob, as befitting a member of the royal family had a suite of rooms in the tallest tower, the walls curved, and a huge oak bed stood in the center, draped with covers that glinted with gold in the soft waning light of the evening.

Sam closed the door behind them and pressed a hand to the door. "I don't want anyone to disturb us until morning," he murmured, and a soft light traced each grain in the wood. "Unless, Mal needs us, or there is danger." The light sparked and then vanished.

"You're getting very good at that," Bob said, with pride.

Sam shrugged, "Magic always comes with drawbacks, like every time I wish for something there is a downside or a consequence but…."

"But?"

"I need to touch you."

Bob smiled as Sam began removing his clothes, one layer at a time, dropping them to the floor, until his slim, toned body was on display, his cock hard.

Bob copied him, and watched as Sam clambered onto the bed and lay spread-eagled on the covers. When he too was naked, he stalked up the bed, caging Sam and kissing him. As normal, his fangs descended as soon as he tasted Sam, but he didn't want to drink and fuck, he wanted it all to be slow, and Sam writhing under him was perfection.

They kissed and tasted, and when Sam tilted his head, exposing his throat, Bob scraped his fangs over Sam's soft skin, enjoying Sam whimper.

"I'm so sorry," Bob began, even as they ground against each other. "I never meant to shut you out when I mourned."

"You had to," Sam reassured, and moaned up into a kiss. Bob thought he saw a flash of a sharp and extended white canine in Sam's mouth but dismissed it as they kissed again. He stretched Sam, seated inside, dragging Sam up to straddle him, and gripping his hair. He needed to taste Sam, and when his fangs sank into Sam's soft throat, he recalled every single perfect moment he'd had with his lover, and listened to Sam's soft moans as he drank. He stopped, licked off the scarlet drops, watching as the wounds healed, and then Sam buried his face in Bob's neck, and began to move.

*I love you, I love you...*Sam said, again and again, his thoughts a growl of want and need. Bob felt a sudden pain, teeth sinking into his skin, Sam drinking from him, gasping and messy. Bob's orgasm slammed into him before he even questioned what was happening, and the answering flood of Sam's release had him shouting Bob's name.

Bob scrambled away, Sam falling to one side, his eyes scarlet and wide, with bright red blood on his lips, fangs descended, and Bob watched his lover, terrified over what had just happened.

When Sam tried to move, he began to convulse, arching off the bed, before falling utterly silent, eyes closed, body still, and as cold as ice.

Bob went to the door, attempted to pull it open, but the magic was stopping him, and Sam was unconscious.

Sam was sleeping, or was he dying?

Was Sam asleep?

Or was he now a vampire?

What had Bob done? What had happened? Had Sam wished for this?

Horror and shame were a sickness inside him as he finally crawled onto the bed, pulled Sam into his arms and held him close. "Sam," he said against his paling skin. "Sam, please wake up."

Sam opened his eyes. They weren't crimson anymore, but his normal color, and his skin was warming to its usual pinkish hue.

Bob would have thought he'd imagined the whole thing except there were traces of blood on Sam's mouth.

"Wow," Sam murmured, "That was the best orgasm I've had since the last time we had sex," he teased.

"Sam, you…."

"What?" Sam looked up at him, confused. "Are you okay?"

Bob kissed him, tasting the blood there, and kissing it away.

They'd talk about it tomorrow.

## Chapter Eight

ETTORE DIDN'T KNOW WHAT HAD WOKEN HIM. HE UNTANGLED himself from Teddy when he felt a change in the castle. Something evil had entered. He quietly slid out from between the covers, careful not to awaken Teddy. Although they were both already dead, some things could still hurt ghosts, solid or not. They could end up in a hell far worse than just being separated.

Slipping on his clothes Ettore fastened up his zippers and buttons with careful precision not allowing any noise to escape his movement. A few minutes later he let out a sigh of relief as he closed the door behind him. Teddy remained sleeping, unaware of any danger. Ettore nodded at the guards outside his door.

"Keep an eye on him, don't let anyone inside."

"We will," the guard on the left said. The one on his right nodded her agreement.

"Thank you."

Ettore closed his eyes and centered his focus before letting his senses flare out. There! By the front entrance, a dark presence stood like a stain on the castle's soul. Curious and slightly afraid, Ettore made his way down the long staircase to the front doors.

He held back a gasp at the sight that greeted him.

"Ettore, my brother, I had mistakenly heard you were dead!" The tone indicated overwhelming disappointment at the turn of events.

"Radim."

Radim inclined his head. "The same."

"Are you here to check on my health?" Ettore didn't miss a step as he continued down to greet his brother.

"Among other things."

A quick raking of his dark eyes up and down Ettore's body had a feral smile crossing Radim's handsome face. "Ahh, so you *are* still dead. How delightful, and how is our older brother, Roberto?"

"Bob is here with his mate," Ettore emphasized the dig. What was Radim doing there? And why was there so much malevolent evil coursing around him?

Radim smirked. "I miss so much when I am working and traveling."

"You've been gone a long time, and you need to leave before I tear you limb from limb." From the dark energy soaking his brother, Ettore was willing to bet Radim hadn't been up to anything good.

"You still bear a grudge brother?" He sounded incredulous that it was true.

"You killed my soul mate," Ettore snapped.

"I have atoned for that."

"You can never atone for murder and attempted fratricide."

"I've been at a monastery." Radim ran a hand down his dark gray traveling coat. The fine weave screamed wealth. "Contemplating my future and repenting my past."

"Not a modest one I see." Ettore searched his mind for any monastery he could think of that might celebrate monetary wealth.

"Hmm, modesty is overrated. As long as I serve my god, I will be rewarded in the afterlife." Radim's smug smile set alarm bells through Ettore.

"And what god would that be?"

Radim stepped forward into the light, and Ettore got his first look at the runes marking Radim's face. They pulsed and oozed, moving across like an ill tide. Ettore felt sick. There was nothing of his little brother left in the vampire that stood before him.

"Kation, the god of the dark and deadly." Radim's deep voice rumbled with malicious pleasure.

Ettore froze. Kation was a sworn enemy of Aset Ka's and the chief god of dark wizards. "You've turned on your people, Radim." Ettore didn't bother trying to hide his distaste of his brother's choice in deities.

"My people?" Radim indicated the castle with a wave of his hand. "They abandoned me." He paused and then pointed to the people behind him. "Let me introduce you to my new *people*."

A small posse of men and women moved forward into the light. Evil pulsed from them like a living heartbeat. Ettore took a cautious step backward. They emitted a sense of wrongness Ettore couldn't bear.

"Who are you? *What* are they?"

Radim laughed. "They are other members of the monastery I studied at. We spend our days worshipping Kation and learning his dark magic."

"Vampires can't do magic," Ettore said. His mouth dried at the cold expression in Radim's eyes. His stomach clenched as he waited for his brother to speak.

"Maybe not, but we are strong powerful beings and we *can* control those who have magic. I've learned many skills in the monastery. I learned that if I drink enough dark sorcerer blood, I can make these lesser wizards do my bidding."

A quick glance at the people behind Radim revealed they all had glassy gazes as if under vampire compulsion.

"What are you doing here, Radim? You think you can just saunter in here and claim the crown? I will kill you first."

Radim shook his head. "Poor brother, you can't hurt me, and I don't have to claim anything. You will *give* it to me."

"Why would I do that?"

"Because if you do, then I will make a deal with Kation to let your dear Teddy go with you into the afterlife. That's more than your pathetic Aset Ka will agree to."

Temptation bright and terrible flashed before him. Images of him and Teddy together forever glowed and wavered in his head. The thoughts came tumbling after the images. *What do I really owe the living?* The living had done few things to make life easy for him and his lover. The dream of having Teddy by his side for eternity glowed in front of his inner eye. He took a step closer to Radim, extending his hand, ready to make a deal.

"Forget it." Teddy's voice shattered Ettore's beautiful daydream. Something snapped from him, the images and words in his head vanished, and he realized what he'd just been about to do.

He spun around to face his mate. "Teddy, it's not safe. Run."

Damn, he had told the guards to keep anyone from going in, he hadn't said anything about Teddy coming out.

"I'm not going anywhere. I woke up and found you missing." Teddy narrowed his eyes at Radim. He stepped forward, but Ettore blocked him from going closer. "I heard an unfortunate voice and thought I'd investigate."

He was tense, and Ettore knew that if he let him go, he would fly at Radim. They'd never liked each other before Radim killed him, and since then the hate was like a living thing.

"You remember Radim, don't you?" Ettore asked although he knew the answer already. He didn't know what to do about his lover's hateful glare. It wasn't as if Radim hadn't earned it.

"Yes, I remember stab-him-with-a-demon's-knife Radim. I wish I could say it's a pleasure to see you again, but I don't like lying." Teddy bared his teeth at Radim in a horrible facsimile of a smile.

"Nice to see you again Teddy. How is being dead?" Radim sneered.

Teddy glanced at Ettore, hate in his eyes and a snarl on his lips. *I want to kill him.* The words snapped between them, for only Ettore to hear. Should that even be possible?

*Don't go near him. Please.* Ettore returned. Teddy nodded briefly and looked back at Radim.

"Being dead? Just peachy. Why don't you come and judge for yourself?" Teddy offered.

"No thanks. I'm happy here about to claim my kingdom and take my rightful place as king." Radim waved his hand to indicate the castle around him.

"I wouldn't count your serfs before they storm the castle," Teddy muttered.

Radim laughed. "You are just adorable." He turned his attention back to Ettore. "So, do we have a deal?"

"What deal?" Teddy snapped. Ettore chanced a look at his lover, and then focused back on Radim.

He tried not to show how painful it was to turn his brother down. "No. No deal."

"Shame we'll just have to do it the old-fashioned way," Radim said in silken tones before turning to face the wizards. "Kill everyone."

Teddy turned around and screamed. "Sam!"

The wizards behind Radim looked a little confused; there certainly wasn't a concerted effort to attack Teddy and Ettore. A black ball of lightning flew from one of the wizard's hands straight into Teddy. Teddy looked down before turning a puzzled look at his attacker. "Was that supposed to do something?"

Radim smacked the wizard on the back of the head. "He's dead imbecile; he's not going to be taken down with a soul-severing spell. He's all soul."

Ettore took the opportunity of their distraction to run up and punch the wizard closest to him. The idiot thought he'd sneak up on Ettore. He let out a sigh of relief when his fist made contact with his enemy's chin. A grunt had poured out of the wizard before he tumbled to the ground.

"Glass jaw." Ettore gave the fallen wizard a disgusted look before turning to the next wizard only to be blasted by a burst of energy and slammed into the wall behind him.

*Ouch.*

Ettore shook his head. He was getting to his feet when Sam and Bob appeared at the top of the stairs. Bob's eyes widened when he spotted his brother.

Radim held out his arms as if he was going to rush up and hug Bob. "Oh good, the whole family is here."

Bob snarled at Radim. "What are you doing?"

"I'm here to take on the responsibility of the kingdom. I know you need a king and face it, Bob, you've never wanted to rule."

Bob smacked away the wizard who stepped too close to Sam. The wizard crumpled to the floor and made no motion to get up again. Ettore smiled. His brother didn't let anyone near his beloved. Super powerful Sam might as well be a delicate china man with all the care Bob took in protecting him.

"The kingdom isn't yours to take. We are handing it off to another."

"Who!" Radim demanded.

"It doesn't matter as long as it isn't you," Bob taunted.

"I'll kill you all!" Radim roared.

Ettore tensed as the group of wizards moved forward, and he could see Bob doing the same thing.

"Stay away from Bob," Sam shouted.

Ettore had been so focused on Bob that Sam hadn't been on his radar. But a pulse of power washed over him. Sam's magic flared in the air around them like sparks of light.

"Who are you?" Radim asked.

"My mate," Bob's proud announcement made Ettore smile.

Bob stood shoulder to shoulder to Sam. Ettore watched Sam's eyes turn nearly white from the glow of power. Damn, the man was scary.

"Get him, kill the others," Radim said to the people behind him.

The wizards only made it two steps forward before Sam raised a hand. They were blasted back with a ball of white fire that slammed them to the stone floor. Sam then created a shield of magic around the remaining wizards who stared right at him, blinking. Only Radim remained outside the cloak.

Ettore stepped forward, careful to keep out of the line of fire. "Take your wizards and get out."

Radim's face flushed red and blotchy as he spit out his words. "Don't think you've won, brother. I already have what I wanted."

With those words, Radim turned around and marched back through the front door. Sam released his magic net, and the wizards stumbled out after Radim.

"What do you think he meant by that?" Teddy asked.

"I don't know." A sinking feeling twisted Ettore up inside. "I don't like it, though."

"We should have killed him and his wizards," Bob said.

"He gave up too easily," Teddy agreed.

Ettore nodded. It wasn't like Radim to leave without burning everything down behind him. "He's up to something."

"What?" Sam asked. "His wizards weren't very powerful, and I couldn't kill them, they were enthralled."

Ettore ran the encounter over again in his mind. "They were a diversion."

"What for?" Teddy asked.

Before Ettore could come up with any answers, Jin stumbled down the stairs holding his arm. Blood dripped down between his fingers. "They took Mal," he said before collapsing on the floor. "Mikhail is hurt."

## Chapter Nine

SAM GRIPPED BOB'S ARM HARD; HE COULDN'T PROCESS everything that was happening. Jin was covered in blood. Mikhail was hurt.

And Mal was missing.

"I couldn't stop them," Jin coughed, blood on his lips. "Their magic was too strong."

Horrified, Sam released his hold on Bob, and ran for the open doorway, throwing a wish for light but seeing nothing more than an empty courtyard and no sign of Mal, the wizards or Radim.

"Radim took Mal," Sam moaned and stiffened as Bob slid to a stop next to him. The light began to dim, and Sam shook his head. "Bob…."

"Ettore is seeing to Mikhail," he said. The words meant nothing at first, and then it hit Sam, Jin was hurt, Mikhail was… was what?

"Is he… is Mikhail dead?"

Bob shook his head. "No, he's alive. He'll need you, Sam."

Sam looked at the sky. "Mal," he said, weakly. "We need to go after Mal."

She'd be lost, alone and in the grip of a madman. All Sam wanted to do was hold her and not let her go. A crash of lightning illuminated the darkening courtyard, a blaze of fire so hot it burned Sam's skin, and he threw up protection to keep everyone behind him safe. It was instinctive, and he still felt like he had no control over all the power he allegedly possessed. The fire raged on the ground, snarling, and snapping and turning from scarlet to orange to blue until it vanished.

"What just happened?" Teddy asked warily.

"I want there to be light," Sam murmured, and the courtyard was illuminated. There in the grass and soil was a message.

"The kingdom and Sam for Mal. You have one day."

Ettore cursed, Teddy shook his head, Bob scrubbed at his eyes and bellowed at the sky, and Sam? Sam fell to his knees right by the message and prayed to every god there was that Mal was okay.

Vowing he would find her, and stop Radim.

LAMBERT ARRIVED as they gathered around the message. He sniffed the air and frowned. "Dark Wizard magic," he murmured. "Not a good sign, not a good sign at all. A horrible, tragic sign, actually."

Sam wanted to hit him and his peculiar mannerisms. "He has our daughter; he has Mal."

Lambert nodded. "Look at me." He paused until all four were looking at him. "In summary, the child princess has been kidnapped, Radim has control of dark wizard magic, we have until darkness tomorrow to come up with a way to stop this and rescue the princess. Meanwhile, the half vampire/human Mikhail is in a coma, and your pet dragon is hurt."

Sam stood and took a step toward him, wanting to hurt the vampire for his matter-of-fact assessment of what had happened. Did he have no emotions at all?

"Next you'll be telling us that Mal's kidnapping is some multiple of seven," Sam snapped.

"Leave him," Bob said, holding Sam's hand. "He isn't worth getting upset about."

Lambert cleared his throat. "Mal was taken at seven twenty-eight," he pointed out. Sam didn't argue. He was sick of it all, and Gods, and evil, and did no one understand that Mal was gone.

Jin joined them, blood dotting his skin; he hadn't even shifted to heal, his expression looked broken. "Sam? Mikhail…."

Sam turned sharply on his heel and stormed back into the castle, climbing the wide stairs to the bedrooms. Jin caught up with him.

"I'm so sorry Sam, she was playing and—"

Sam rounded on the powerful dragon shifter, shoving him back into the wall, the visceral need to hurt someone burning inside him. Jin didn't fight even with his back pressed to the stone and guilt mixed with fear in his expression.

"Let him go," Bob said from his side, but he didn't touch Sam to stop him.

Jin's eyes widened, Sam was lifting him from the floor, and the prick of Sam's canines were cutting into his lips.

"Sam, please," Bob said; he reached for Sam, but an invisible force threw Bob away. He hit the ground with an alarming smack of bones on stone. Sam didn't flinch at what he'd done. He wanted to hurt, smash and kill, and Jin was right there, letting him do whatever he wanted.

Sam tightened his hold across Jin's throat. Jin struggled at first, his nails turned to claws, scraping at Sam's hands, until finally, his eyes closed as if he was giving in, with a murmured sorry. He didn't shift, and abruptly the fury that roiled inside Sam vanished. He let go of Jin, stumbling back in horror at what he'd just felt. The blackness inside him that was stealing everything positive receded so fast that Sam whimpered.

"Sam…." Jin said, his head tilted, exposing his neck.

Sam couldn't even look at Bob, despite knowing his lover was still on his knees, his head bent like he was waiting for the anger and hate to be turned on him.

"No," Sam said. "I can't do this."

He left Jin there, with Bob scrambling to stand, and went into Mikhail's room, crossing to the prone vampire, some instinct telling him to put his hands on Mikhail's chest. The darkness had gone, and from deep in his heart, he pulled out every ounce of magic he could find. Nothing happened at first, and then Mikhail let out a sharp breath. Sam wasn't shocked as Smudge jumped up on the bed and curled by Mikhail's side. The cat looked up at Sam.

*I have this, Sam.*

However, Sam had to face what had just happened. Jin stood inside the door, his expression downcast, his arms crossed over his chest.

"Jin…."

Jin looked up, and there was some new expression that Sam had never seen in the dragon shifter's eyes. Fear. Sam had put that there. A human had put fear in the Dragon King's eyes.

"Jin, I'm sorry," he said.

Jin inclined his head. "As long as Mikhail is okay, I don't care."

"I didn't mean to hurt you," Sam said, "I was just… Mal…." He crossed to Jin, seeing the fierce bruises on Jin's skin. Sam had put them there, and Jin looked, not scared, but respectful, and couldn't quite look Sam in the eyes.

"Sire," Jin said, and half bowed.

"Stop that," Sam snapped, the taste of blood in his mouth. Cautiously he pressed a finger to his own lips; he'd definitely extended his canines, like Bob did.

Memories of tasting Bob's blood flooded him. When had that happened?

Jin sidestepped him, his eyes still averted, and crossed to Mikhail, and then there was nothing between Sam and Bob.

*I hurt you,* Sam thought, and horror flooded him at what he'd done. He knew he'd hurt Bob, as badly, if not more than Jin. But at least Bob wasn't treating him differently. *Yes.* There was caution, but no fear.

*Are you okay?* Bob's question was soft.

Sam nodded sharply and extended a hand. It was a test of how much he'd messed up. He felt shaky, needy, and all he wanted was for Bob to touch him. To ground him.

They stepped toward each other in the otherwise empty corridor, and Sam fell into Bob's arms.

"What happened?" he asked.

Bob held him tight, burying his face in Sam's hair. "I don't know," he said, "I don't know."

***

LAMBERT WAS the one who guided Sam to the council meeting. The huge ceilings in the central room of the castle were dark with protection spells. Sam had put them there. He didn't know how; all he'd thought was that he didn't want anyone outside of the council and his friends to hear a single word of what was said in there. Then with a soft puff of something from Sam, an exhalation, there was magic protecting everyone.

The council was made of seven.

Of course, it was.

Seven ancient families, including, Sam guessed, a member somehow related to Bob, Ettore and the evil that was Radim. They sat on a raised curved dais, half in the shadows cast by the magic. Not one of them bent to talk to the vampire next to them, not one of them took their eyes off Sam, which was starting to make him uneasy.

"And now we sit," Lambert finally said, after they murmured words of an official nature that Sam only half listened to. In front of the dais was a platform with runes carved all around the base.

"The symbols of the families," Bob said in a hushed tone. Clearly not hushed enough when Lambert side-eyed him in disapproval.

A commotion at the door had Sam turning. Jin stepped in, supporting Mikhail, Ettore, and Teddy close behind. No one spoke. No one said that a dragon, or a half vampire, or humans, shouldn't be in the council chamber.

Sam wanted someone to say something, even if only to argue. Anything so he could release some of the tension inside him.

"Radim's not having the kingdom," Ettore announced.

"He's not having Sam either," Bob muttered.

Sam ignored Bob and rounded on Ettore.

"He has your niece; the kingdom might be the price. And he can have me if we get Mal back in exchange. I can handle myself." He almost wished for the opportunity to see what he could do against a horde of dark wizards, needing something to vent his frustration on.

Bob placed a hand on Sam's shoulder. "He can't have you, and he can't have the kingdom," he said, evenly.

*He has Mal,* Sam thought desperately. Why didn't Bob see that?

*And we will find her,* Bob answered with a reassuring squeeze of his hand.

Sam slumped under Bob's gaze and the comfort of their shared thoughts. They'd been in worse situations; they would find Mal and rescue her. Sam would use whatever magic he had inside him, and everything would be okay. *We're always okay, aren't we?*

Bob didn't answer with thought, but he nodded, and his expression shouted that he didn't doubt they would win in the end.

So why was Sam feeling so scared?

The council began muttering among themselves, and Lambert, as master of ceremonies, allowed it. Everyone else stood in silence.

"That is agreed," Lambert announced, banging the staff he carried on the floor three times. "The kingdom is not to be ruled by a purist. That concludes the meeting."

"What?" Sam snapped as Bob bowed, and Ettore did as well. "No. I thought this was a meeting to discuss strategy. This isn't just about the kingdom, what about Mal?" Why hadn't they talked about the important issues? What was going on?

The council members began to stand, one at a time, and Sam wrenched free of Bob's hold. He walked forward, standing on the raised platform in front of them, and crossed his arms over his chest. "Stop right there," he commanded.

"Sam, get down," Bob hissed, stepping toward him, a horrified expression on his face.

"No!" Sam shouted, his voice echoing in the high-ceilinged chamber. "We need to make a deal with Radim, for our daughter. We need to be considering what to do here."

Six of the council sat down, the last member, a vampire with hair to his waist, his eyes a dark red, left his seat and joined Sam on the platform. There was a curiosity in his expression, and then he poked Sam in the chest with a sharp nail.

"There is no part of your destiny that includes a child," he announced.

Sam spluttered, and looked to Bob for help, but Bob's expression was one of confusion; like he had no idea what the hell to do next.

"Our child has a name," Sam snapped.

"Your destiny is to protect the old ways, be the balance between light and dark, and to keep us safe," Red-Eyes announced, his tone condescending, arrogant even. "Best you remember this."

Bob inhaled sharply, and Sam knew why. Because Sam was not going to take that tone with good grace. "Sam, careful," Bob warned.

Sam was way past being careful. Bob was acting like Mal wasn't the most important thing to both of them. Temper spiked in him, and those damned canines cut into his lips again. Red-eyes looked startled, and also, there was fear in their scarlet depths.

"Holy mother of Aset Ka," Red-Eyes cursed, a little breathless. "The change is already there. We are too late to stop you."

Sam saw the knife as it arced up in the vampire's hand, watching the trajectory as the blade headed for his throat, everything slowed to a stop, the blade inches from his neck, and Sam stepped back, stumbling from the dais and to the stone floor. Everyone was frozen. Even Bob, who was in mid-stride, his hand outstretched to the dais, his mouth open in a shout of alarm, shock on his face. Jin was mid-shift, scales overcoming skin, his teeth sharp, and Ettore was only a step behind Bob.

All frozen.

Apart from one other person in the chamber.

"He's right, everything is moving too fast for us to control," Lambert announced, and moved closer to Sam, extending a hand to help him to his feet. "I knew he was one of those who wanted you dead before you came into your full power."

"What? Who?" Sam stumbled over his words as he accepted Lambert's assistance. "Why aren't you frozen? What did I do? What just happened?" Finally he got the words out.

"You cannot freeze me. What you did is far more vital to understand at this time. Seems that the sevens are in alignment."

Sam snapped. "Don't give me that shit, don't talk in riddles. What sevens, and why the hell is everyone frozen?"

Lambert frowned at him, and then down at the ever-present file in his hands. "That is nothing to do with anyone else and everything to do with you, Samuel Enderson."

"What are you talking about?"

Lambert blinked at him like he'd lost his train of thought after being interrupted. "You froze them," he pointed out, and looked across at Bob. "You can release them."

"I didn't."

"You did, Sam, you saw the knife, and you stopped time."

Sam felt defeat flood him. "I can stop time?" he asked. "Of course I can," he sighed, "why did I think I couldn't?"

Lambert looked at his notes. "Among other things," he said.

Sam felt way out of control. "I don't want to stop time. Time is dangerous; everyone knows that."

"You'd rather your throat was cut by a traitor?"

Lambert had him there. Freezing people was infinitely more preferable than dying. "Who is he?" Sam pointed at Red-Eyes, and the expression of hate, the lips curled back in a snarl, the knife a wicked blade in the air where Sam had been standing.

Lambert considered the question. "Clan Vendore. I always suspected that they were loyal to the True Vampire movement. One of three on the council that are. Information led me to believe that the council isn't as balanced as you would expect, given that their average age is three hundred and fifty."

"Don't tell me, their ages are all multiples of seven," Sam said.

Lambert huffed. "Now that would be stupid. They do have to age each year. It would be impossible to keep them in multiples of seven no matter how tidily mathematical that is."

In a quick movement, Sam snatched at Lambert's notes, holding them up to the light. The pages were empty and abruptly turned to ash in his hand. He winced at the heat and rubbed his sore fingers. Lambert said nothing; he didn't move, watched Sam cautiously.

"You're no clerk, who are you really?" Sam asked. Because his instincts told him that Lambert wasn't just a man holding the past close to him and bustling around, annoying people.

Lambert snapped his fingers, and a thump caught Sam's

attention. Bob and Ettore sprawled in a heap on the floor. Quickly Sam went to his mate's side, helping him stand, startled when Bob hit out, before realizing that the situation he'd been reacting to had somehow miraculously stopped being an issue.

"What happened?" Bob asked, his gaze darting from Sam to Lambert and back.

Sam gestured to the rest of the chamber, and Bob checked around at the frozen expressions. Then he looked at Lambert standing still and let out a shocked gasp when Lambert moved.

"I love doing that," Lambert chuckled.

Sam couldn't help but see that something had changed in Lambert, he didn't seem as stretched thin, or as pale and edgy. He looked different.

"Sam?" Bob asked, and then he pressed his fingers to Sam's throat like he needed to check Sam was okay.

"I'm fine," Sam said, and stole a quick kiss of reassurance before Bob could say anything else. For a second they held each other, then both turned and faced Lambert who was watching them with a placid expression on his face. Sam was still cautious and made sure he was facing the council, in case he accidentally unfroze them.

"Who am I?" Lambert said, "That was your question."

*What is going on?* Bob asked.

Sam shrugged. *I don't know anything, except that just now I froze everyone.*

"And that is only part of your powers," Lambert said. Like he'd *heard* what Sam and Bob had been talking about telepathically. Sam sent a worried look at Bob. No one could hear them normally.

A movement out of the corner of Sam's eye caught his attention, Smudge padded around the frozen figures ending up next to Sam. Lambert glanced down at the cat and huffed a laugh.

"Still here?" he asked. Smudge lifted a paw and licked it, extending her claws deliberately. "Put them away little one," Lambert said, with another laugh. "I'm not going to hurt him."

Hurt who? Hurt Sam? Or Bob? Sam moved protectively in front of Bob who cursed and shoved him back behind him. They tussled to protect each other for a while, and then stopped and stood side by side instead.

"I'm the vampire here," Bob grumbled.

"I freeze people," Sam responded.

Then they fell quiet.

Lambert stood on the edge of the dais, shoving Red-Eyes until the vampire tumbled back onto the ground, and then brushed his hands in distaste.

"My name is Samuel Lambert, and Sam, I'm your great, great, great, great…" he paused and counted on his fingers, "great, great, grandfather. You have my name."

Sam said nothing.

"That's a lot of greats," Bob said, like he didn't want the silence. "That explains the ummm…." he tapped his teeth, and then touched Sam on the shoulder. "Fang thing. Vampire blood."

Lambert nodded. "Among other things. Dragon, fae, demon, even a touch of troll which was an unfortunate liaison two centuries back, and of course, human." He stopped and looked at Sam considering. "A small part human," he added.

"How small?" Sam was lost for words.

Lambert ignored him. "You were shielded until the magic inside you has become too much. Now it can't be kept inside."

"What. The. Hell?" Sam snapped.

"You're the perfect storm of paranormals, Samuel. You were always going to be The Chosen One. The seventh descendant, after seven centuries of breeding."

"What. The. Hell?" Sam repeated.

"I could explain," Lambert began. "I could go into details that would make your head spin, but for today I will just say one thing. You were destined to be the most powerful of all paranormals, a demigod, and you will ultimately save us all by balancing light and dark, evil and good."

"This isn't happening," Sam said. "My parents would have told me who I was—"

"Your step-father never believed the stories," Lambert shook his head. "He always thought they were something made up, and although I could prove that I was a vampire, he refused to believe we were related. That's how you grew up not knowing about your legacy."

"My step-father?"

"You had to be hidden with a human family."

Something broke inside Sam. He'd never been close to his mom and dad, hell he hadn't seen them in years, but he always thought they were at least his real mom and dad. Why would he think anything different? "Where are my real parents?"

Lambert pursed his lips and shook his head. "A tragic unforeseen accident," he murmured. "Your human mother died, and you father gave up on life. He passed on a few months after her from a broken heart."

Sam wanted to grieve, to understand what had happened to him and his family, and why his real dad had given up so quickly when he had a son. But he had to get Mal back. That was his priority; grieving was for another day.

"What about any other Endersons? Real ones. Could it be their legacy instead of mine?"

Lambert's lips thinned. "All dead. You and I are the last," he said.

Sam shook his head. "I don't... I don't care about some legacy. I just want to be able to get Mal back."

"Yes," Bob said, his voice a little shaky. "We want our daughter back."

"Finding Mal? That part will be easy." Lambert smiled up at Sam. "It's saving the entire paranormal world, the good parts anyway, from evil. Now, *that* Samuel Enderson, is going to be the hard part."

## Chapter Ten

SAM STARED AT THE FROZEN PEOPLE BECAUSE HE COULDN'T look at Lambert who seemed to want something from Sam. "What do I do to unfreeze them? The council and my friends."

Lambert sighed. "Are you sure you want to do that? They are so much better behaved when they can't talk, or move or anything."

Bob nodded. "They are, aren't they?"

Ettore walked over to kick the knife-wielding vampire. "There are always bad ones in every crowd. Since Bob is currently king, we should have this one thrown in the dungeon for plotting to assassinate the king's mate. That will keep at least one of the bastards out of commission."

"I'm not King," Bob defended. "I don't want it."

Lambert shook his head. "You have no choice; Bob, your destiny is twisting every hour that Radim is back in our lives and the council pronounced you king."

"I do have a choice—"

"No, you don't," Lambert interrupted him. "There are

powers only available to the ruler of the vampire kingdom, and it can't be Ettore, so it has to be you."

Bob went quiet and glanced at Sam with fear and resignation in his eyes. "We should put him away." Bob added his own kick. "I never liked Frantz anyway. He always cared more about blood purity than leadership."

"Wait, are you accepting this?" Sam asked, "That you have to be king?"

Bob cradled his face. "Until we find a better vampire for the job, until we get Mal back, until I know you're safe."

*I love you,* Bob added silently. *Trust me.*

Sam didn't have time to think because Lambert let out a noisy sigh. "Sam, you'll have to release the rest of the council," he said.

"Why?" Sam admired the frozen figures. "I kind of like them this way. They can't hurt us like this."

Bob snorted and tried to cover up his amusement with a forced cough.

Sam smiled tentatively at his lover. He could try and handle Bob being king if their priority was Mal and each other.

"You need to release them so they can arrange a search for Mal," Lambert said. His reasonable tone irritated Sam, who wanted the heartless council to pay for their harsh words over Mal being kidnapped.

"But you said there were three traitorous families."

Lambert held out a hand, and a burst of energy shot toward the fallen vamp he and Bob had kicked, and then another to two of the other vampires still in their seats. All three vanished to nothing more than dust.

"Not anymore, now the heads of those families are dead."

"Good. The rest better fall into line over our priorities. They have some crazy idea of what I'm supposed to do, and I refuse to let them get away with dismissing Mal's kidnapping as an inconvenience in their kingdom." Sam ended up shouting the last few words.

Bob wrapped his arms around Sam from behind, crossing them over Sam's chest. He rocked Sam gently from side to side as he ended his rant. "Easy, Sam. I know you are worried, but offending possible allies isn't the way to get help."

"That's the thing, isn't it? Even the ones that are left are only possible allies. Real allies would be interested in saving a poor innocent vampire girl, even if they didn't agree with the way we want things to be run," Sam protested.

Lambert patted Sam's arm in what Sam considered a condescending manner. "It isn't that they don't believe you, Sam, it's that they think the good of the kingdom is more important than one person. You can't assign humanity to a group of vampires. They aren't going to suddenly understand why you think they are going to change their ways just for you."

Sam nodded as if he understood, and he almost did. An entire culture wasn't going to change just because they were backward and wrong. They still thought they were the ones in the right.

He stepped away from Bob in slow motion, so his vampire lover didn't feel rejected. They had enough issues with everything going on. "I'll release them, but if they try to stop me, I'm freezing them again. With Mal's life on the line, I don't have time for bureaucratic bullshit." He could tell these vampires would happily spend centuries arguing over a comma in a treaty.

Sam turned to the door and started walking. Inside he trembled as he thought over a plan to get Mal back.

Unfortunately, strategy had never been his thing. He cast a hopeless glance over his shoulder.

"I'm coming." Bob made a disdainful noise. "As if there was any question."

A relieved smile crossed Sam's face. He couldn't help it. As many times as Bob reassured him that he would stick around, a little sliver of uncertainty remained behind just big enough to wedge a gap in his insecurities.

Bob grabbed Sam's hand and tangled their fingers together. "Always Sam, I'm always here for you."

Sam sighed. "Always suddenly got a whole lot bigger."

A startled laugh burst out of Bob. "It did, didn't it?" Satisfaction oozed from the vampire as he tightened his grip on Sam's hand. "You're stuck with me now, Sweetheart."

"That's a horrible Bogie impersonation," Sam scoffed.

Bob grinned. "No, it wasn't. That's how he sounded when he wasn't acting."

"You knew him?" Although he knew vampires lived a long time, he never expected them to do anything interesting in that time. Naïve of him, maybe, but his worldview was constantly expanding.

"I knew a lot of people." Bob tugged Sam toward the exit. "Don't forget to release the council."

"Oh yeah, the vampirecicles." Sam hadn't forgotten, but he gave a pout for show. Waving his hand, Sam concentrated on heating up the frozen men. Several yelps later the vampires jerked into action, patting themselves down as if they were on fire.

"What did you do?" Bob's smile showed he didn't particularly care; he was just curious.

"I imagined them not frozen." Sam tried for an innocent expression, but Bob's smirk didn't reassure him of his success.

"Well, they aren't frozen now." Bob nodded. "Good job."

"Where are you going?" One of the council members shouted.

"To get our daughter." Sam didn't bother to turn back around. They needed to plan, and he was beyond done with these imbeciles.

"Your Highness, surely you don't approve of your mate's actions," one of them pleaded to Bob.

Sam turned around to face the council. Surprisingly none of them commented on the missing three or the piles of gray dust in their place. Their baffled expressions almost sent Sam into a rage.

"I stand by my mate," Bob said, enunciating each word with a careful patience that belied his anger.

"Thank you." Sam kissed Bob's cheek.

"He's bewitched you," one of the council members shouted.

"I'm done with you all." Sam let his power fill the chamber. "Don't stand in my way and I won't have to hurt you."

Bob cleared his throat. "What my mate means is that it would be in your best interests to keep an eye on the kingdom and out of his business. I trust my mate to do what is best while we pursue our daughter."

"If you go, who is going to watch over our people?" A red-headed woman asked.

"Isn't that what you are for?" Bob's voice filled with steel and his eyes glowed with power. "You are the council. You are supposed to have more value than to just sit around and wallow in your superiority. If problems arise, I expect you to take care of them. If you cause problems, I will take care of you."

Again, Bob dragged Sam away. This time no one tried to

stop them. Their small posse made it to the hall before Sam asked the question he knew they were all secretly thinking. "What now?"

"We need to scout the area. The scent of dark wizards should lead us to them," Bob said.

Smudge popped into existence at Sam's right.

Lambert stumbled. "You have a powerful familiar, king mate."

"I do." Sam turned his attention to the black cat. "Smudge, can you find Mal?"

"A location spell?" Bob asked.

The cat tilted his head for a moment as if thinking. *No, they put something up to block location magic.*

"Damn, I thought that sounded too easy." Sam sighed, raking his fingers through his hair.

Bob patted it back down with a fond smile. "Babe, we'll find her. Radim isn't going to hurt his only bargaining chip."

"Maybe." Ettore walked around to face them, seemingly not affected by his quick freeze. "But what if he's not in charge?"

"What do you mean?" Sam asked.

"Aset Ka isn't afraid of a jumped-up vampire who is too impressed with himself. He kept going on about balance. I fear that Radim has turned his will over to someone stronger. Those weren't ordinary dark wizards at his side. Those were worshipers of Kation."

"Of who?" Sam asked.

"Kation the god of the dark and deadly," Lambert replied. "He is the darkness to Aset Ka's light."

"Aset Ka is light?" Ettore grumbled, "I'm not seeing that."

Lambert shrugged. "It could be worse, but whatever Aset

Ka's intentions, there always has to be a steadiness of light versus dark."

"Great." Sam groaned. "I could handle vampires, zombies, dragons and merpeople, but gods are beyond my ability."

Lambert stared right at him, and for a moment he looked like he was going to say something profound, then he closed his eyes briefly.

"Possibly," he finally said.

All Sam could think was that wasn't what Lambert was going to say. "How strong is this Kation compared to Aset Ka?"

"They are enemies, and neither has won over the other since existence began," Lambert said.

"Could someone bring me good news just once?" Sam begged. Despair dug its greedy sharp claws into Sam's soul, dragging him into depression.

"I'm pretty sure this is the imbalance Aset Ka was talking about," Ettore said. "If we save Mal and take care of Radim, maybe he'll have mercy and let Teddy into his lands."

"Then we could have eternity together." Teddy smiled, then jumped at Ettore forcing the vampire to wrap his arms around him to prevent Teddy from falling.

"Yes, my love, we'd be together forever," Ettore whispered.

Sam heard him clearly with his enhanced hearing. All his senses had an extra clarity to them these days. His hearing, vision, and sense of smell were much sharper than before.

"Don't lose hope," Bob said, planting a kiss on top of Sam's head.

"It's hard." For the past few months, one battle after another had beaten down Sam's optimism. He tried to stay positive for his mate, but Bob's almost-death had torn something in Sam that would take longer to heal. The loss of their daughter further weighed him down.

*Stay here,* Smudge said. *Allow me the time to assess our best course of action.*

*What your familiar said,* Lambert added.

"I don't know what to do," Sam murmured.

"Shh," Bob whispered pulling Sam close.

Sam didn't even know he was crying until sobs broke the silence of the men surrounding him. Once started, he couldn't stop. The rush of air around him, let him know Bob had removed him from the situation. Minutes later a soft mattress met his back. A flurry of motion later had his shoes off and a cool vampire pressed against him.

"Shh my love, it'll be fine. We'll get Mal back and make Radim pay," Bob's low, vicious tone soothed Sam more than anything had before.

"I-I'm sorry." Sam brushed away his tears. "I hate crying. We need to find Mal."

The breakdown of emotion left him hollow inside.

"I think it's been coming for a while. You've had to go through a lot lately. I'd be surprised if you remained calm over everything."

Sam gave a broken sigh. "I've been far from calm, or did you miss the room full of frozen vampires a minute ago."

"True, but I thought they looked good that way, maybe a new art form. Shame you had to release them."

"Yeah, it was. What are we going to do?" Sam rested his head against Bob's chest, snuggling into his lover's hold. "How will we find her? We should be out there searching."

"Smudge told us to stay," Bob reminded him. "Your familiar will be using everything to get Mal back."

He couldn't remember the last time they took a quiet

moment or two to enjoy each other. They still didn't have time. "We have to talk to the others and strategize."

"Give it a minute." Bob squeezed Sam, hugging him tightly. "I want you to listen to me."

"About what?" Sam looked up to meet his lover's gaze. Bob didn't usually take a serious note with Sam.

"I want you to know that no matter what happens, I am there for you. I don't care if the gods themselves think we should part, it isn't going to happen. Now let's find Smudge and Lambert and see what they have decided."

"Okay." Sam kissed Bob, not a brush of lips but a meeting of souls. No one could part them any longer.

They moved off the bed and headed to meet the others, finding them all in the dining hall. Sam and Bob joined them at the lower table, no sense standing on ceremony when they had a battle to plan. The grim faces of everyone around the table told Sam he wasn't the only one prepared to fight. He had wanted to head out immediately, but he knew they would last longer if they ate first.

A server rushed over to give them some food. They ate in silence for a bit, eventually talking about nothing important while Sam tried to think of all the ways they could locate Mal. "If Kation is working with Radim to block Mal, do you think Aset Ka can help us find her?"

"Sam, you can't ask for favors from a god," Lambert said. "They want something in return, and it is rarely pleasant. A god such as Aset Ka will ask for something truly unbearable."

"There is nothing more unbearable than losing a child," Sam said, conviction in his voice.

Silence blanketed the air around him telling Sam he hadn't kept that musing silent.

"Do you think Mal is okay?" Sam asked, poking at his

eggs. He could barely concentrate on the conversation with worry weighing him down.

Bob squeezed his knee under the table. "We will save her. Now eat something."

"I'd like to fly over the territory and see if I can find anyone," Jin said.

"Not alone," Sam protested.

Jin shook his head. "I'll have a few of my dragonkin take a portal here if the vampire king gives permission."

Bob snorted. "Don't start getting all polite now Jin; I wouldn't know what to do with you."

Mikhail glared. "You'd best not do anything with him."

"Your boyfriend is safe from me," Bob said, ignoring Jin's smoky chuckle.

"I am right here." Sam waved a hand. He knew they were trying to bring a light-hearted edge to the serious meeting. None of them were taking Mal's abduction easily. Jin and Mikhail, in particular, had a haunted look in their eyes.

"My eyes have never strayed," Bob said, wrapping an arm around Sam.

"That's because I would stab them out," Sam said, resisting the urge to shrug Bob off. His nerves were on edge, and he couldn't handle the thought that there was nothing he could do. "I don't want to sit around and hope someone finds her. I want to go and look for Mal too."

"What makes you think you'll be doing nothing?" Lambert asked. "Your familiar and I, have a plan. You are going to the tower, and we are going to put your magic to good use."

"How?" Sam tried not to let despair strip him of hope, but he was sinking fast. Memories of his daughter's big innocent eyes shining up at him tugged at his heart. No, he couldn't let her down.

"All that meditation you've been doing is going to come into use. If we can focus your magic, you should be able to sense the pockets of emptiness that will symbolize the dark wizards blocking us. If you find that, then you find their hideout."

"But if you locate them, won't they just kill Mal in order to get back at you?"

Bob glared at Mikhail as if he was about to rip off his face. Paling, Mikhail slid his chair back, out of Bob's reach.

"He's asking good questions," Sam said. He wrapped a hand around Bob's arm to keep him from lunging across the table and killing the other vampire.

"Let's find them before we worry about them killing Mal; they're planning on doing that anyway," Bob said after a long look at Mikhail.

"Okay," Mikhail raised his hands, palms toward Bob. "I get it. Stay positive or get your throat ripped out. I can work within those guidelines."

Sam smiled at Mikhail. "We have to believe she'll make it. Besides they don't know what kind of vampire she is."

Bob frowned. "Let's hope she doesn't do anything foolish before we can get her."

"Anything she does to protect herself is deserved." Hope filled Sam. He had to remember his smart, pretty little girl could suck out someone's life force. She would do it too if she felt threatened. "Hopefully, they're keeping her awake."

Bob nodded beside him. They quickly finished eating before leaving the table and telling the others where they could be found in the case of an emergency.

Following his lover up the stairs, Sam felt off-kilter and uncertain. If those dark wizards did anything to Mal, his anger would be echoing in every world. "They better not hurt our daughter or they will feel my true power." Sam didn't like to hurt people, but he wouldn't let her kidnapping set a precedent to others as a way to get to him and Bob. He would protect his family no matter what the cost.

"I agree."

After multiple flights of stairs, when Sam thought his legs would fall off, they reached the top of the tower. "Why didn't you just pick me up and rush me up here?"

"I thought you needed the exertion to calm your mind," Bob said, no remorse on his face.

Sam wished he could argue, but it was probably a good move on his lover's part. The pain in his legs made him refuse to agree. Bob's smirk told him he didn't need to.

The stone tower had nothing but more stone at the top. Nothing was there to distinguish it from other parts of the castle except it was up high. Wind whipped around them with an ominous howl.

"Come stand over here Sam; I'll protect you from the elements while you concentrate."

Sam walked over and stood close to the edge. A small outcropping of stone rose to his waist, blocking him from toppling over the parapet. "I'm not sure about this."

"Don't worry love; I'd never let you fall. Do you trust me?"

Sam took in a long breath and banished his fear as he exhaled. Right at that moment, he couldn't let doubts and worries cross his mind. He had to find their daughter. "I'm ready."

Leaning against his strong lover, Sam released his magic.

# Chapter Eleven

ETTORE STOOD BEHIND TEDDY, HIS ARMS AROUND THE OTHER man, his head resting on Teddy's shoulder. He'd pulled his long hair into a tail of sorts, tied back with leather. Ettore rubbed his cheek against Teddy's soft hair, inhaling the scent of lemons. They'd gone back to their room, to view the tower from their east-facing window. The view only a little warped through the leaded glass. They could watch Bob and Sam from there in the safety of each other's arms.

He really hoped that his brother knew what he was doing. Sam was like a container of everything that had been shaken to the point where it was going to explode. The terrifying idea of letting Sam's magic out in one burst had him clutching Teddy tight. They couldn't be killed again, but that didn't mean they couldn't be injured.

Ettore had never met anyone as powerful as Sam, but somehow Sam remained human and in love with Bob. He wasn't allowing the power thrust upon him to change who he was.

"You think this is the right thing for them to do?" Teddy asked, his arms crossed over his chest.

"I have no idea," Ettore said, with a sigh.

They stood in silence. There was no sign of any magical explosions yet in the darkness.

"I don't want you to go back to Aset Ka," Teddy said, tension in every line of him.

"I don't have a choice," Ettore began.

Teddy turned in his arms and linked his hands behind Ettore's neck. "You can take me with you."

"Teddy—"

"I don't want this half-life anymore. I want to be with *you*."

Ettore's heart shattered. "Teddy, please, you know I only have a short time here. I have to go back when this is all done."

"I'll follow you," Teddy said, stubbornly. "I'll get Sam to use his magic somehow to destroy my connection here, and I'd be free, and we'd be together forever."

Ettore shoved Teddy away in horror. "No," he said. "You have an entire lifetime ahead of you."

"An eternity as a ghost, or an hour whole and able to love you? I know which one I'd pick."

Ettore began to pace. "I won't let you do it. I won't let Sam do it."

"And I won't live as a ghost anymore. I'm done." He raised his gaze to the ceiling. "You hear me, Aset Ka? I won't play your games anymore."

Ettore stopped pacing and sat on the edge of the bed. "Don't anger Aset Ka," he said, his tone soft. "Please don't make him hurt you." He sent up a silent prayer, and a promise that he would do anything for Aset Ka not to hurt Teddy.

But then Teddy was there, right next to him, standing between his legs, and cradling his face in warm hands.

"I love you," he murmured. "This is forever love, and I refuse to stay here alone."

"I will have to go back; you know that. Please promise me you won't hurt yourself, or let Sam hurt you, please, you have to live and stay safe."

"But I'm not safe, I'm only half a person, a ghost, my body is already gone why not take the rest of me?"

Ettore surged to his feet and gripped Teddy tightly. "Promise me you'll live."

Teddy looked right at him, his eyes bright with tears. "Ettore, I'm not living now. I don't even know how long this will last." He waved a hand to indicate his body.

"Promise me you won't give up." He shook Teddy.

"Ettore—"

"Teddy—"

"I promise, okay, I promise I won't hurt myself or ask Sam to help me. I can't make any promises to stay alive since technically I'm not." Teddy scowled.

Ettore sagged in relief. At least when he was back in Aset Ka's realm, he would know that Teddy was back with Sam and even as a ghost he would be living some kind of life. Even if only a half-life.

He pulled Teddy close, inhaling the citrus smell again, recalling the times they had lain in bed before Radim's hatred ripped them apart.

"I tried to find Radim you know," Ettore said.

Compassion flooded Teddy's expression, "It's okay, you don't need to tell me."

"I do. Teddy, listen to me, when I woke up, I knew you were gone, I didn't have to see your body to know that our connection had been severed. I cried and held you, and prayed to any god listening to bring you back to me. When the guards found me, I tried to fight them off. They told me I had to let you go," his voice cracked with the emotion. "You stood between me and the knife, and you died for me."

"I couldn't let him kill you," Teddy said the words simply as if he'd had no other choice.

Ettore wanted to shake Teddy until he realized what he'd done. Radim wanted him dead, and Teddy had taken his place. *It should have been me.*

"I took your body to the chapel; they tried to stop me, said it wasn't for humans, but I had a wizard place a magical guard around you. Then I left the castle to look for Radim. I searched everywhere for him. A century of searching, while being king. My absence allowed the council to gain power. I had to give up and come home."

"It's okay," Teddy was comforting him, but Ettore wasn't ready for that. Teddy had to be so angry over their long separation.

"Everyone told me Radim was dead. I had to believe that was true."

"We'll take him down this time," Teddy reassured. "We don't know what Sam can do, but this can be ended."

The ground shook beneath their feet, and the room flooded with light before the glow dimmed.

"It's started," Teddy said. They crossed to the window.

A swirl of rainbow colored lights bathed the tower, twisting and turning around the stones. From their distance, they couldn't spot Sam or Bob, but they could see the colors expanding outward from the tower, and Ettore imagined Sam up there with Bob at the center of the magic.

Part of him, a small tiny part that was hidden away, prayed that Sam could do it, locate his daughter, bring her home, and prove himself strong enough to take down a god.

Because that was the only hope he had of ever being with Teddy for eternity.

SAM CLENCHED his hands into fists and tried to concentrate on Bob's words.

"Imagine the power inside you," Bob said.

"It isn't in me," Sam defended, and shook his bracelet where the charms from all manner of paranormals were displayed. "It's here."

"Focus on that then."

Sam lifted his fist, and the bracelet slid a little on his arm. Each charm was backlit by an eerie glow. Green for the mark of the fae, orange for the dragons, blue for the nyad, along with red and purple and a silvery glow that seemed to encompass his hand.

"That's it, Sam," Bob said from behind him.

"Should you be here?" Sam asked. What he was doing terrified him. He was a human, and he didn't know how to control the magic he'd been told he had inside. What if the power lashed out and attacked Bob?

In answer to that Bob moved forward, standing to one side of Sam, their arms brushing.

"I'm right where I need to be," Bob announced. The wind blew back his long hair. Sam had never seen him look so sexy.

"I love you," he said, his voice a little louder over the wind that was picking up and nudging at his fist.

Bob laid a hand on Sam's arm. "Always," he said.

The orange behind the charm began to move, at first nothing more than a wisp of color, before it became more, circling his wrist, and floating up and away. Then the scarlet, the green, the blue… the silver joining and rising upwards, until a swirl of colors consumed the top of the tower, twisting in and around and forming a cloak of pigment around Sam and Bob.

"That's good," Bob said, in awe. "Try to imagine it wider."

Sam stared at the moving rainbow and imagined it larger than it was, but it expanded only to fall back on itself.

"I can't do this," he snapped, and the colors began to die around him.

Bob gripped Sam's other hand, "Yes you can. Focus."

Bob's touch grounded Sam, and he closed his eyes for a moment, imagining the castle built into the mountain, the solid stone, the tower climbing into the sky, and he felt a burning in his fist. He opened his eyes, and the rainbow cloud had grown; the distinct ribbons of colors danced around him and Bob, and the silvery glow was changing as well, becoming more defined. The burning moved from his fist up his arm to his elbow, and he winced because, hell, that hurt. But it didn't stop there, climbing his arm, and reaching his shoulder, darting across to his neck and down his spine.

He yelped at the burning, but Bob tightened his grip. "I love you, I love you," he repeated over and over, and Sam focused on the words even as the burning seemed to consume every part of him. He felt like there would be nothing left of him but a hollow husk at the end.

*As long as Mal is safe, I'm ready to die.*

He looked sideways at Bob who was staring at him with fear and sadness in his expression.

Then Bob's words echoed in his head.

*As long as Mal is safe, I'm ready to die with you.*

His heart beat loudly in his ears as the burning reached it, and abruptly Sam knew what he needed to do. He had to let the magic come from his heart, the place he held Bob, Mal, and his friends. That was where the magic was hiding.

He raised his fist a little higher and concentrated hard on

each color he could see, the silver sparking and hissing, growing bigger by the second. The light expanded away from the tower and into the darkness, illuminating the courtyard and the wall, then further out to the mountainside. Like it was daytime, Sam could see every detail of the rocks, and the night receded as the rainbow light moved away from him. He saw areas of darkness that refused to fill with brightness in the courtyard below and realized it was where the words from Radim had appeared.

It was working, his heart magic was showing where the darkness lay. To his left a dragon call had him looking. Jin rose from the courtyard, hovering in front of him, orange color connecting to him, and then the dragon bowed his head to Sam and wheeled up and out of sight, followed by a hundred more, an army of beasts flew away searching for the darkness where Mal could be.

"They will find her," Bob shouted over the noise of the wind. The breeze whipped his hair around his face and had Sam gripping his hand tight in case they were blown over. A fall from the tall tower would break every bone in their bodies.

The burning lessened, and Sam focused on what was left, the silver that swirled around them, and he pushed harder, forcing more of his light out into the darkness. Before his eyes the bangle began to disintegrate, chipping away and vanishing, and he pushed harder before all his magic left him. If the bracelet was gone, he would lose all the gifts bestowed upon him, and that wasn't happening until Mal was safely at home.

"Your skin!" Bob shouted.

Sam looked at Bob's horrified expression, then saw the silver was burning into his skin. It didn't hurt, even as blood dripped from his fist. He uncurled his fingers and watched in fascination. Bob reached for him, as the silver carved runes from his bracelet right into his skin.

Abruptly, the colors vanished from around him, the silver dancing just out of reach, and he fell to his knees, Bob still holding him.

"You did it," Bob said, "I love you."

"I didn't; it's all gone." Tears dripped from Sam's eyes. His chest felt hollow as if he had nothing left to give.

Bob helped him stand and gestured beyond the walls of the castle. All Sam could see was colors, and then he saw through them to the forests and fields outside. The colors were moving on their own, the light of them resting on every inch of the land.

"Jin or the others will find her and bring her home."

Sam looked down at his wrist, at the marks there, which healed as he watched. He may not have the bracelet anymore, but he had the permanent marks on his skin in a circle around his wrist. Was that because his magic was gone?

Was he now *just* a human?

Or had he become more?

## Chapter Twelve

EMPTY. SAM REMAINED KNEELING ON THE TOP OF THE TOWER. Fragile and burned like the aftermath of a forest fire. Would his magic ever be reborn in fresh unfurling leaves, or would he remain a gray, ashy stump?

"It will come back," Bob whispered, clutching Sam tight.

"The magic?" Sam checked. Sometimes they talked at cross-purposes. So he needed to make sure they were discussing the same thing.

"I can feel it rising up," Bob said.

"Yeah, that's not creepy." How could Bob feel something when Sam didn't recognize a twitch of power?

Bob laughed. "It's not creepy, I promise. I'm just attuned to you."

"Apparently more than I am." Sam closed his eyes and rested his forehead on Bob's shoulder. "Waiting is the hard part."

"Not burning yourself from the inside out?" Bob kissed Sam's head.

"No. If they find Mal it was worth it." Sam would set

himself on fire if it got their daughter back. A bit of magical backlash meant nothing in the scheme of things.

"I love you," Bob whispered.

His tone had Sam looking up. "I love you too."

Naked adoration lit Bob's eyes, and Sam knew no one would ever love him as much as the vampire wrapped around him. "I know."

Deep in his heart and infused in his bones he could feel Bob's love for him. Despite his sarcasm and self-doubts, the one certain thing in Sam's universe was Bob's love. "Let's get up. The stones are killing my knees."

Bob's huff of laughter made Sam smile. He gave Bob another squeeze before using his mate's shoulder to help him stand, then reached down and took Bob's hand to pull him up.

A dragon cry had them both turning toward the sound. "That didn't sound good," Sam said.

"No." Bob wrapped an arm around Sam's shoulders as they faced the direction the dragons had disappeared.

"Do you think the dark wizards have hurt them?" Worry wormed its way into Sam's stomach making it ache. Had he sent the dragons to their death?

"They might hurt them, but dragons are tough, it takes a lot to kill one," Bob's tone indicated he was trying to reassure Sam but didn't completely believe his own words.

"I hope so." If Jin died, Mikhail would skewer him. He might be fond of Mal, but Mikhail would die without his mate.

"Let's go down and see who's around. We're not going to get anything done until we hear about Mal." Bob began leading Sam to the stairs.

"Will they find us if we move? Jin saw us up here."

"They'll come to the throne room first. Let's wait for them there. It's too cold to wait out here all night."

Sam thought it over and had to agree. "All right."

They descended the stairs in silence; Sam was thinking over the events of the day and wondering what Bob thought of things. Were his vampires being difficult over finding Mal? Did their lack of interest in finding their daughter hurt Bob's faith in his people?

"Stop worrying about me Sam," Bob admonished.

"I can't help it. What if your people decide they want to keep you as their leader?" He couldn't compete against ruling a kingdom of vampires. If they chose Bob, he didn't think it would be easy to get them to change their mind.

"We'll worry about that when the time comes. We have bigger issues right now."

Sam nodded his agreement. "What do you want to do if the dragons don't come back?"

"Why wouldn't they come back?" A new harsh voice spoke.

"Mikhail!" Sam bit his thumbnail as he tried to come up with a good explanation.

"We heard a dragon scream," Bob said.

Mikhail's expression changed from questioning to grim. "He'll be back. He won't something evil end him."

The conviction in Mikhail's voice eased some of the tension between them.

"I'm sure you're right," Bob said.

"If the dragons don't come back, we are going there and rescuing them," Sam said. He wouldn't leave a friend behind.

"You aren't going anywhere," Bob said, scowling.

Sam crossed his arms across his chest. "And who's going to stop me." He kept his tone calm, but he knew his eyes must be blazing. The magic he thought had died sparked along his skin in a low golden flame.

"Wow," Mikhail said, eyeing Sam's arms.

Sam stretched his hands out before him. The circle around his wrist, where the bracelet had been glowed brighter than the flames on his skin. "What's happening?"

"I think your magic is now fused with your skin. When you poured out all that power, you brought your magic to the surface, literally."

"Huh," Sam watched the little flames. He poked his right index finger against the skin on his left arm. A small flicker of fire burst brighter. "That is very strange."

"It is."

If that kept up, there was no way he could interact with humans anymore. Being caught having flames flaring across his body wouldn't end well. "Maybe it will settle after a time," he said with more hope than sense.

"Sure, maybe." Bob agreed with even less confidence than Sam had used.

"Concentrate on pulling it in," Mikhail advised.

Sam stared at him.

"What, it's just an idea," Mikhail said.

Sam sighed. "Why can't my life be boring?"

"If it was boring you'd be anxious to do something interesting. You did become a private detective after all. Did you expect it all to be pencil pushing and stake outs?" Mikhail asked.

"No, I thought it would be pencil pushing and internet research. I thought the actual cases would be pretty tame. Even with the paranormal aspect, most cases are finding things or relationship issues. My cheating case was more complex than expected."

Bob half-smiled. "That's because you are a complicated man."

"That must be it," Sam said, his voice laden with sarcasm. "It's obviously me who's the problem."

"Must be," Bob agreed.

"How long should we give them?" Mikhail hadn't been distracted by their banter, not while his mate was out there.

"Until tomorrow. If we interfere too early, we might do more harm than good. Dragons will fall into a coma if hurt too deeply, and their scales will prevent the wizards from hurting them further. Even if he is injured, he will be fine. Can you feel if he's hurt? As his mate, you should be able to," Bob said.

Mikhail closed his eyes, no doubt to block outside interference. "He feels angry. More emotional, but I don't feel any pain coming from him."

"Then he's probably fine. If you feel he's in critical health let us know and we will send people out. Mal's location didn't seem to be more than a few miles away. Smudge can teleport us closer in an emergency," Bob said.

"Good." Relief crossed Mikhail's expression. "I know you wouldn't purposely do anything to harm Jin, but sometimes he's too heroic for his own good, and he really likes Mal. I'm hoping to have kids with him one day. He'd make a great father."

"Who's going to have the kids for you?" Sam asked. He needed to talk about the mundane and normal. Otherwise he was going to lose control. Mal was out there without him and Bob, and fear snaked inside him. Mikhail seemed to recognize the question for what it was and began to explain.

"The dragons have a whole surrogate system for any same-sex partners who want kids. Our child wouldn't be a vampire, but I'd be all right with a dragon shifter baby that took after Jin." Mikhail's warm smile made Sam optimistic about the couple.

"I'm sure he or she would be adorable," Sam agreed.

"As long as Jin doesn't get killed in the line of duty," Mikhail said, allowing the worry free for a moment.

"He won't." If something could be true from Sam willing it, he used all his energy to push happy vibes toward Jin and Mal. Not that he thought it would make any difference, but it couldn't hurt either. The slight pulse of power that left him must've been his imagination.

"What are you going to do while you wait?" Mikhail asked.

"I was just going to sit here and enjoy my mate, but we can plot the future of vampire kind if you wish," Bob's politely enquiring tone made Sam smile despite the worry inside him.

Mikhail sat down in a chair close to them. "I can do that."

Before any planning for world domination could commence, the outside doors slammed open.

One of the dragon shifters stumbled in, cuts covered his entire body, and he bled sluggishly from several wounds.

Mikhail ran over to him. "Freryn, what happened?"

"They figured out our weaknesses. They threw icicle spells and impaled our wings." He held up his left arm. A long gash went from elbow to wrist, jagged and ugly, it bled profusely as they watched.

"How did you escape?" Mikhail asked the question they were all wondering.

"Jin distracted them so I could make my getaway," he said, paling beneath Mikhail's fury.

"You left him!" Claws grew out of the tips of Mikhail's fingers, and the walls vibrated from his wrath.

"He told me to. He told me to come here and get help." Freryn cowered beneath Mikhail's anger. "He said that only Sam could help him."

"Then that is what we will do," Bob interrupted. "How far

away are they?"

Freryn winced when he moved too sharply when Bob addressed him. "They are three miles direct flight."

"Can you lead us?" Sam asked.

"Yes. I can show you the way." Freryn's confident answer reassured Sam.

"Good. Let's go." Sam stood ready to leave.

"He needs to be patched up by healers," Bob said, eyeing Freryn's extensive wounds.

"We don't have time." Sam glared at the dragon shifter. Desperate to get moving he focused energy into his hand until he could feel it pooling in his palm. "Heal." Sam flicked the ball of white light at Freryn.

The dragon shifter gasped as the gathered magic slammed into his chest. Before their eyes, his cuts healed and the bruise on his face vanished.

"Good, now let's go," Sam snapped.

Before anyone could offer any more excuses, Ettore and Teddy appeared in the doorway.

Ettore spoke first. "I hear we have my niece to rescue."

"You don't have to come. I know you are on a time limit," Bob said.

"There is nothing as important as making sure your daughter is found. Whatever Aset Ka wants of me, will have to wait. Especially since I haven't discovered what exactly I'm supposed to do. It would be better if I spent my time doing something useful."

"Let's go. Now that I'm healed I can fly you there," Freryn said.

Determined not to let his daughter spend another minute more than necessary in the company of her kidnappers, Sam grabbed Bob's hand and followed the dragon shifter out of the castle.

## Chapter Thirteen

BOB DIDN'T KNOW WHAT TO EXPECT.

They were flying deep into the mountains with Bob and Sam clinging to Freryn's back. "I don't like this," he said to Sam through their link.

Sam's only answer was to nod his head, the cold wind buffeting his face. His thoughts were nothing more than panic and the need to hurry and find Mal. Bob tried to keep his own thoughts under control, blocking the worst of them from Sam. What if they were too late? What if Radim had already killed Mal? What if this was one big trap that meant they were flying to a certain death? With one hand, he held on tighter to Sam in front of him, the other hooked under a leather rope that Freryn had asked them to use to keep their balance.

Battle ready he called it. A hark back to days when each dragon had a dragon rider to go into battle. They were no more, but that didn't mean that dragons weren't ready for battle.

Before he left to find the pockets of darkness Jin had breathed fire into the message that Radim had left in the courtyard and destroyed it all in one blaze of white hot heat.

He'd vowed that anyone who hurt Sam's family would be destroyed the same way. He was magnificent in his dragon form, and Bob didn't doubt for one minute that he would die for them if it came to it. Mikhail said as much to him, but there wasn't sorrow in his voice; resignation maybe, and also a fierce pride from him. Mikhail was there, astride a dragon Bob didn't know, Teddy clinging to him with his eyes shut. Seemed like ghosts-made-human didn't like to fly. Something passed between the two dragons and Bob gripped even tighter as Freryn wheeled left and, followed by the other dragon, skimmed the tops of dark trees.

The greenery was turning brown, darkening as they flew further, like whole swathes of the forest were dying. He spotted burned areas where nothing could surely survive. Had all that happened today? Or had Radim hidden himself so well that no one had seen what he was doing?

A commotion to his left had both him and Sam startled, but it was a core of three dragons swooping in on their flank, joining the steady flight, and then another four from behind. Nine dragons were fighting the battle with them, and Bob owed them everything. Ettore saluted Bob when their eyes met.

Ettore looked alive and was making the most of his time in human form. He seemed to think he was invincible with the fact he was actually dead. Although that made sense, it didn't make Bob any calmer over going up against their younger brother.

Sam's thoughts echoed in Bob's head, a mix of desperation, fear, and the intense will to fight whatever they came across.

*I could lose you*, Bob thought.

Sam stiffened against him.

*And I could lose you.*

*I love you.*

Sam's reply wasn't swift, but he snuggled back into Bob's hold and said one word that meant everything. *Forever.*

Freryn darted left and then smoothly wound down in circles through bare trees to the ground below until his claws hit the soil. Sam and Bob slid off, allowing him to shift. Each dragon followed the same path until all had shifted into their human form and the riders were gathered in the same group.

They spotted Jin leaning against a tree and rushed to his side. He looked in pain, but alive. Mikhail fell to his knees next to him.

"We're safe here," Jin said, wincing. "Dragon magic is shielding us for the time being."

Everyone looked expectantly at Sam, who stared back at them, his hand reaching for Bob.

"Tell us?" he asked Freryn, who dipped his head in acknowledgment.

"Through the trees," he announced and pointed to the north and upward from where they were standing.

"They know we're here," Sam announced, and Bob wondered how the hell he knew.

*Can't you feel that?* Sam asked him. *The dead feeling, loss, pain?*

Bob wanted nothing more than to say he could feel whatever was causing Sam to look so horrified. *I can't,* he finally admitted. *But I wish I could so you didn't have to bear it alone.*

Lambert stepped forward, right up into Sam's space, and Bob bristled. There was something about Lambert and his insistence that Sam was the mythical savior of everyone that hurt Bob's heart.

"The prophecies say that you'll fight a final battle alone," Lambert said.

"He's not going up there alone," Bob snapped and moved between Lambert and Sam.

"He's the only one that is strong enough to go up against Radim and his army of dark magic."

"Exactly, it's an army," Bob snapped.

"There is nothing written that says it is *Sam* who has to defeat Radim, but he is powerful."

Bob poked Lambert forcefully in the chest. "And nowhere does it say that Sam is this mythical savior you keep talking about, nor that Radim is the ultimate evil."

"Sam needs to do this alone," Lambert repeated.

"No."

"How—"

"He's not doing this—"

Sam sidestepped Bob and held up a hand to stop everyone talking, lifting his hands palm upward, silver sparks dancing on the skin. "It's me he wants to hurt, right? Me and the vampire kingdom in exchange for Mal."

"He just wants your magic." This was from Teddy who looked pale and unsteady and was worrying at a hangnail. "We should all go with you."

"Agreed," Ettore said.

"I'm not letting him go alone," Bob snapped. Nothing Lambert could say would change his mind. Mal was *their* daughter, and Sam was the other half of him; he wasn't letting Sam die without Bob being by his side.

The last thing Bob saw was Sam snapping his fingers and the flash of silver that went with it.


SAM REGRETTED NOTHING. He couldn't think with Bob's fears in his head, and he felt utterly clear about what he needed to do. Freezing his friends, his lover, was temporary, just for enough time to think.

A crack and flash and Smudge was at his side, sitting on the dark ground and looking up at him expectantly.

*It's time Sam,* Smudge thought.

"You knew this was going to happen?" Sam asked and crouched down in front of his familiar. "You knew from the start."

Smudge leaped from the ground and up to his shoulder, winding around his neck, purring.

*We need to go, Sam.*

*You'll be with me?*

*Always,* Smudge said and purred again, butting her head against his chin.

Sam turned to Bob, seeing the unmoving expression of sorrow and shock, his dark eyes staring. Gently Sam traced Bob's face from cheekbone to lips, and then kissed him gently.

"This won't keep you for long," Sam whispered to his lover, even though he wasn't sure Bob could hear a thing. "You'll be free in moments, but promise me you'll let me do what I'm supposed to do."

Of course, there was no answer, Bob's expression still frozen.

Then, because there was nothing else he had to do, Sam stepped close to the shimmery barrier that kept them hidden, and passed through, the chill of dark magic making him shiver. Past the barrier, the earth was scorched, the trees dead, some of them nothing but stumps, and nothing lived there, just the press of darkness that stole Sam's breath.

"I never wanted to work with paranormals," Sam murmured.

*I know,* Smudge answered.

"But this was all going to happen anyway, wasn't it?"

Smudge didn't answer as the path steepened past blackened rocks and finally they reached the top of the rise. Spread out before him was his battleground, and at the center of it, arms crossed over his chest, stood Radim. Ranged behind him Sam counted twenty figures in black, immobile with hands at their sides. From where he stood, awful gray tethers of magic from Radim to them were obvious. That was no mind control. Radim was sucking everything from them, making himself as powerful as twenty wizards.

"Twenty," Sam whispered. His wrist burned and he looked at the marks, the angel's mark was there, front and center, a gift from Zephariel, the Angel of Vengeance, and next to it, a tiny candy cane that he knew was the mark of the Klauson family. He had the fire of the dragon, the hell of a demon, the touch of fae and elf, he had every part of him hidden inside.

*And me,* Smudge said clearly, *you have me.*

"I can't see Mal," Sam said, searching the area for his daughter, and then abruptly he found her. Tethered to a pole to one side, she was wrapped in chains and looked unconscious. Fear had him walking toward her, and Radim did nothing to stop him. He didn't move, only watched as Sam made it to Mal's side, relief flooding him when he saw her chest rising and falling. Sam went to one knee next to her, touching the chains, thinking them as nothing more than mist, and watching as they vanished. Mal stirred, her eyes flickered open.

"Daddy," she said, her voice scratchy, and she coughed. Sam scooped her up and set her on her feet.

"Can you walk?" he asked urgently. He was facing Radim, who still hadn't moved. What kind of game was he playing?

"I can."

"Go back to Poppa. Run over that ridge and you'll find him where you can't see him, just keep walking, and you'll break through the charms there."

She opened her mouth to say something, but then shut it again, her lips pressed in a thin line of determination. Then she walked away from Sam, toward the edge of the devastation then over the ridge.

"I let her go," Radim announced, his voice curiously loud, echoing on the canyon walls. "I said I would." He chuckled then, a nasty, vindictive sound. "So, you'd better come over here."

"I'm okay here." Sam judged where each wizard stood; a single shot would break some of the tethers, but it would go from a weird standoff to a battle in seconds. His wrist burned to the point that he imagined his whole hand was on fire.

*Steady,* Smudge warned.

Radim tugged at the wizard closest, the gray tendril turning scarlet, and pulsed magic into Radim; the wizard fell to the ground, turning to ash at Radim's feet. Radim seemed to grow a few inches, his presence larger than the broken wizards around him.

"Let them go," Sam said. He didn't want any more deaths; they were puppets to the darkness that Radim had inside him.

"Kation needs feeding," Radim explained, yanking another to him and draining a wizard again.

*What does he mean? Kation?*

Smudge wriggled a little then jumped down to the ground by his side. *Kation is here.*

Sam looked around him. *Where?*

*That isn't Radim anymore*, Smudge explained, the

thoughts tinged with shock. *He He H He is carrying Kation in a human form.*

*But, Kation is a god, I'm only a human, I can't defeat a god.*

He heard raised voices at the ridge, and he knew the spell had done its work. With a flick of his wrist, he threw a barrier to stop any of his friends coming into the ravine. Bob called his name and cut him to the core. He sensed Mal was with Bob, and how the hell he did that he didn't know. Everything was out of control.

Sam moved forward, closer to Radim, fear pricking him, his skin tight, the energy snapping and cracking around him, and with every step, Smudge was there beside him.

*You were always meant to be here,* Smudge said. *Be brave, Sam.*

When only twenty feet or so separated them, Sam stopped, lifting his hand, the silver already there, coating his skin.

"Let them go," he demanded again, as another wizard vanished to dust and was carried away by the wind. Radim grew taller; broader, stronger.

"We all need our allies," Radim said, his lips curled back in a snarl.

Sam tasted blood in his mouth as his canines descended, and abruptly his heart felt lighter, his head clearer. He could even hear Bob in his head, encouraging, pleading for Sam to live.

"Don't make me hurt you, Kation. I won't give another warning." Sam said.

Radim's snarl disappeared. Then in a grotesque show, the skin began to peel away from Bob and Ettore's brother, his skull splitting, flesh and bone falling away. From the mess of vampire, a new form uncurled, a nightmare of claws, horns and exposed sinew, with skin stretched obscenely over veins that seemed to carry fire.

"You can't hurt me," the figure screamed, blood foaming at his mouth. Kation, Sam assumed. "You are nothing but a human with gifts, the magic you have is borrowed."

The wizards ranged around him were leaning close to the monster. Kation yanked at the closest wizard, lifting him bodily and sucking at the magic, the dust of the resulting body's decay falling on Kation's face.

Sam felt sick.

*What do I do?*

He thought he heard voices in his head. Jin telling him to throw the first shot aiming for the connections to the wizards, Bob telling him to win, and Mal's voice saying she loved her daddy.

Focusing everything inside him, he snapped a finger and energy pulsed from him, taking down half the wizards and severing the connections. Kation merely brushed them aside; like he was done with them, and they scrambled away with horror on their faces as they broke out of whatever fugue state they had been in. Another quick pulse to free the others was blocked by Kation holding up a hand, a haze of scarlet protecting them from the attack.

Had Sam used the only trick in his arsenal? Kation clenched his hands and created a ball of purple magic that he directed right at Sam. The wave of it knocked Sam to the ground, sending him backward another twenty feet. The breath was knocked from him, but he scrambled straight to his feet, raised his own shield then stalked toward Kation. Images were being thrown at him of Kation's vulnerabilities

His skull. Jin's words were as clear as day.

Sam ducked another barrage, the air thick with magic and dust, realizing he had lost sight of Smudge. He slid to his knees and forced the power in his hands outward and up from that angle, forcing Kation back a few steps, caught unawares by the energy directed at his neck. A few of the tethers snapped as the wizard backed away, and only five remained bound and immobile.

Sam spotted Smudge leaping at Kation's face, claws out, scraping at his eyes, and Kation ripped the cat away, throwing Smudge into the wizards. Sam saw Smudge fall on four paws, and then after a few seconds he vanished and reappeared next to Sam.

*Again.* Smudge's voice was clear in his head. *Free them all.*

Sam called up the power inside him and aimed it at the wizards, but Kation snarled and rebounded the magic in water form. The water cascaded over Sam and formed a bubble around him.

At first, Sam panicked, the water ran into his mouth, up his nose, and his eyes blurred from the iciness of it. But then he realized he could breathe in the water, and he thanked whatever part of his paranormal makeup meant he could do that.

The vampire side was already planning the next attack point. While the human in him had absolute conviction that good could overcome evil. He felt dragon's fire at his fingertips, and he threw shot after shot. With each one Kation backed away, looking more startled. He would rally and then be pushed back, yanking the remaining wizards with him. Kation defended the shots, returned some, fire burning into Sam, and weakness making him fall to his knees. Kation looked momentarily triumphant, even stepped closer, and in that instant, Sam rolled to his side. He threw bolts of energy to release the last tethers. A single bolt of pure light energy slammed under Kation's chin, carving through his neck, up into his skull. With a scream of pain Kation stumbled back, grasping at his neck, his eyes skyward, and Sam knew he had one last push, one last shot, and he took the chance, aiming for Kation's chest, channeling every supernatural power he had inside him, and forcing it all out.

Kation screamed as Sam's magic hit his body, engulfing him in the purest white, blue light, his body crumpling, and in a crack of power Kation was gone, and all that was left was a perfect circle of burned soil. The remaining wizards crawled away in fear, cowering together and looking at Sam, blinking at him like they were coming out of a long sleep and into a nightmare awakening.

And Sam?

He fell back to the ground, looking up at the darkening sky, his gaze fixed to the moon, with Smudge curling up on his chest.

Smudge's words filled his head. *And the prophecy is that the hero of the ages would defeat the evil that filled one vampire's heart, and the hero would find victory when he fought alone.*

Sam shook his head, difficult as he was stuck fast in the wet mud. He'd heard Jin, and Bob, Ettore, Lambert, demons, angels, fae, nyads….

"No," he said to the sky. "I was never alone."

## Chapter Fourteen

SAM BARELY CAUGHT HIS BREATH BEFORE BOB THUNDERED down the ridge and fell to his knees beside him.

"Sam, Sam. Are you all right? I'll kill you if you aren't," Bob snarled. "You almost gave me a heart attack."

"Sort of defeats the purpose, doesn't it?" Sam asked, barely able to get the words out. His mouth felt ashy. He frantically hoped he hadn't inhaled some wizard dust.

"Here, take a sip." Someone pushed a canteen into his hands and Sam gratefully chugged the tepid, metallic water. It tasted glorious.

"Thank you," Sam said, pushing the canteen back to the giver.

"What happened?" Jin asked.

"You kicked ass," Mal piped up, hopping up and down with glee.

"Language," Sam and Bob said together. Truthfully Sam didn't care what she said right then. She had almost been snuffed out by a psychotic god and some crazy wizards; he would give her a lot of leeway for the next few days.

Mal made a funny face at them but didn't complain about the scolding.

Bob helped Sam to his feet then wrapped an arm around him to keep him stable. "What happened?"

"Kation took over Radim's body and began sucking energy out of the wizards. They turned to ash." It was an oversimplification but still managed to include the horrifying truth of what happened.

Sam could still hear their screams and the vibration of magic beneath his skin had him trembling. What kind of monster had that much power?

"You're not a monster," Bob said.

Sam narrowed his eyes at his mate. "Were you in my thoughts again?'

"Of course." Bob didn't even have the courtesy of being ashamed.

"Stay out."

"Uh, huh. Let's get back to the castle," Bob said, making no promises.

It took a bit of arranging and a few trips, but soon they were flying back with the dragons.

They entered the castle and made their way to the dining hall. Sam's stomach growled aggressively. He rubbed it to try and soothe the angry sounds.

"I guess that's it then, you will have to be the new king," Sam said to Bob. Depression crushed him as he fiddled with his water glass. The servants were quickly bringing out food as if anticipating they would return hungry.

"Not necessarily," Lambert said.

"Why not?" Sam didn't completely trust Lambert, but he didn't think the vampire truly meant them harm.

"There might be a way to bring back our previous king."

Lambert tilted his head toward Ettore who watched him with a puzzled expression.

"How? I don't want to be caught in another soul trading scheme. You saw how the last one turned out." Gods were tricky, and Sam didn't want to be the one who made a bad deal with a god of the underworld, vampire god or not.

Sam smiled at the server as a bowl of soup was set before him. Damn, he was hungry. He took a sip while he waited to hear Lambert's crackpot scheme. Lambert might be a knowledgeable scholar, but he was also a bit odd. Maybe that was how he would turn out when he was as old as Lambert likely was.

"You will have to steal his soul from Aset Ka," Lambert said as if it was the easiest thing in the world to accomplish.

"Oh well, if that is all," Sam rolled his eyes before floating a saltine into his soup and crunching it with his spoon with deep satisfaction. He felt sick and hoped that the food would calm his stomach. Fire snapped from his finger and turned the spoon white hot.

*What is happening?*

"Focus Sam," Bob said. "Are you okay?"

Sam blinked a few times as he realized his vision had begun to go hazy. "I don't think I'm feeling so well after all."

Before he could say anything else, the world went black.


SAM WOKE up in a white room. Energy pulsed from the walls in a glowing tribute to power. Sitting up Sam found he had been lying on an altar. "Yeah, that's not ominous."

Nothing else occupied the room as Sam slid off the white marble slab to his feet. He shivered when his bare feet met the cold floor. Glancing down, he discovered he wore a T-shirt and cotton pants, all in white.

"This is the strangest dream ever," he mused, hoping it was truly a dream.

"I've been hoping to meet you, Samuel Enderson," a female voice spoke behind him.

Sam whirled around to face a woman with flowing blonde hair and vivid blue eyes. She wore a simple dress of pure white, and stared at him with such sorrow that Sam began to worry.

"Am I dead?" he blurted out.

Her light laughter didn't reassure him much. "Why does your mind automatically go there?"

"Let's just say it's been the trend lately." Sam could feel the magic coming off of the woman before him. "Who are you?"

She laughed. "A better question would be what am I?"

"Okay, what are you?" Sam tried to hide his irritation. He had a feeling if he didn't play along he would be waiting a while before she got to the point.

"I am your magic."

Sam didn't respond right away trying to think over the proper response but finally gave up. "Is there a reason my magic is a girl?"

She shook her head. "Magic doesn't have genders. I was trying to appear the least threatening to you."

"Okay." Sam floundered, not sure what to ask next. Questions cluttered his mind each vying to be asked first. "Why am I inside my mind talking to magic?"

"You need to center yourself. Until you fought Kation, you were still questioning your abilities and blocking a vast portion of your power. Now that you freed your magic, it will continue to overwhelm you until you learn how to burn it off properly."

Sam ruthlessly pushed away the memories of how he and

Bob generally liked to burn off energy. It didn't seem like the time or the place. "And how do I do that?"

"You must expend a great deal of the magic inside you," she said as if that was the most obvious thing in the world.

"Didn't I just do that with Kation? I figured I was here because I spent too much of it." Really, for an embodiment of himself, she didn't make much sense.

"What you did with Kation created a vacuum of sorts. It cleared out your blocks, so you are free to use your full potential. You now have the chance to settle your powers. If you don't do something soon, you will always be fighting within."

"Great," Sam muttered. If it wasn't one thing, it was another.

"I think you know what you have to do," she said.

"No. No, I don't." Sam's voice became louder with each word. "And I'll thank you to keep your cryptic comments to yourself. If I wanted vague, I would ask Lambert."

She nodded, not appearing insulted in the least. "He does give good advice."

"He doesn't give any advice, he just rambles," Sam said.

"You just need to listen deeper. Now go back and expend a lot of magic so that you will be stable and we won't need to have another chat," she scolded as if she were his mother.

Sam opened his mouth to ask how he was supposed to do that when everything went dark.

"SAM. SAM." Bob's soft voice pulled at him.

Forcing his eyelids up Sam carefully turned his head to see his lover. "Hey."

"Will you stop collapsing? It scares me every time," Bob said, his lower lip came out in a pout.

"Sorry. Hopefully, that will be the last time it happens for a while." Sam couldn't promise it would never happen, and he tried not to lie to Bob.

"We were talking about the kingdom, and then you just fell over. What caused it?"

"Apparently, I have magical buildup." Frankly, it sounded like a clogged drain and Sam had never been good at plumbing.

"Oh." Bob nodded as if what he said made complete sense. "You need to use it up then."

"That's what I was told." Bob seemed to understand much better than Sam. He tried not to sulk.

"Maybe you can do something about Ettore." Bob smiled.

"Like what?" Sam couldn't imagine he could do anything for a ghost vampire.

"Well, technically he wasn't killed. He agreed to give up his soul to Aset Ka in exchange for mine. If you could pull him back together, you might be able to give him life again."

Sam's jaw dropped. "Is that even possible?"

"With your magic, maybe."

"What about Teddy?" He wouldn't be doing Ettore any favors if he separated him from his soul mate.

"He was killed with an enchanted knife. You might be able to pull him through also. I'm not sure. If he's solid now, you might be able to keep him solid."

"We should talk to Ettore and Teddy before I try anything. I don't want to curse them for eternity or something. You never know what will happen with my powers."

"True." Bob brushed Sam's hair back from his face. "Get some more rest. Once you're ready, we can go talk to them."

"Okay." Sam closed his eyes, the headache pressing against his eyeballs made him ache. Magic crawled beneath his skin pushing at him to use some. "Let me rest for a bit then we'll see what I can do."

The urge to push magic out of him battled with the exhaustion deep in his bones. Before he could decide if it would be an effort, he fell into a dreamless sleep.

SAM JERKED AWAKE, his entire body convulsing beneath the pressure of his power.

"Sam? Bob said you needed me."

Ettore sat at his bedside and before Sam could speak, or do more than whimper he grabbed the vampire's wrist and pushed magic into him.

Ettore screamed as runes glowed across Sam's arms. Ancient signs of infinite power, shared only with the gods pulsed across his skin. Sam didn't know what he was saying, the words were gibberish on his tongue, but the more he spoke, the more Ettore glowed with vitality as if Sam was pouring Ettore's essence back into an empty shell.

A silent signal had Sam dropping his grip on Ettore and collapsing against the mattress. He took long slow breaths to try and get his pounding heart under control. On the positive side, the magic no longer burned at him from the inside out.

"What the hell did you just do?" Ettore asked, his voice barely above a whisper.

"I think I made you alive again, although I can't be entirely sure, and I make no promises of how long it will last. Bob thought it might be possible." He skipped the part where he wanted to talk to Ettore first. He refused to take responsibility for his pushy magic and hoped to hell Bob and Ettore had talked it out.

"What about Teddy?" Ettore asked, unknowingly repeating Sam's question from earlier. "Bob said you might be able to fix him as well? I don't know if I want to be alone...."

Sam's chest tightened. "Let's go find him and see what I can do. I make no promises."

"Fair enough," Ettore said, but the growl in his voice told Sam otherwise. Sam didn't think Ettore would take it well if his lover couldn't be alive also.

"Well, on the bright side, he could still haunt you." Sam grinned at the vampire and ducked the hand that jerked out to swipe at him. "Not nice."

"I don't have to be nice." Ettore straightened his stance. "I'm the king."

"Pfft, what if Bob has become all power-hungry and decided to keep the throne?" Sam teased.

Ettore gave one disbelieving glance at Sam before he began to laugh hysterically. "I dare you to tell him that."

Sam grinned. "I will."

He followed Ettore to a large, comfortable room with several couches and tables decorating it. All of their group were seated close to each other so they could talk.

"Sam!" Bob jumped up and rushed over to give him a hug.

"Bob, my power-hungry king," Sam cooed in false sweetness.

Bob jerked back so he could look Sam in the eyes. "Why am I worried?"

Sam chuckled. "I followed your advice and Ettore is solid again. I don't know if it will last or not."

Bob examined his brother. "It will. I can tell he is whole once more."

"How did you do it?" Teddy asked, eyeing Ettore with an excited expression.

"Magic." Sam didn't have any other explanation than

that.

"Can you do me?" Teddy asked.

"I don't know, but I'm willing to try."

"When?" Teddy's eyes brightened as he studied his lover then Sam in equal turns.

"No sense in waiting," Sam said. "Let's go sit down on the couch."

He had no wish to fall over and crack his head open while trying to do a good deed. He followed Teddy over to one of the longer couches. Bob and Ettore hovered behind him.

"Could you two go over there?" He pointed at a couch several yards from them. "I don't want you interfering with my magic." He didn't know if they could, but having them hover over his shoulder would make his power flare out from his irritation.

They nodded and walked far enough away that Sam didn't want to punch them anymore so he would have to be satisfied with that.

"Give me your hands."

Teddy placed his hands in Sam's. Luckily, they were still solid, or Sam didn't know how he would do this part. Going on instinct, the words began to flow from his lips and the magic from his hands. He just let the power flow from him and do what it wanted. After several minutes while Sam felt the last of his energy fade, a soft ringing sound filled the room and Sam fell asleep.

"I THOUGHT WE TALKED ABOUT THIS?" Bob said as soon as Sam opened his eyes.

He still lay on the couch he'd chosen, but his head was in Bob's lap, and the vampire didn't look as pleased to see him.

"Did it work?"

"Yes. Teddy appears to be the same as Ettore."

Sam smiled. "Good. I think that settled my magic."

Bob helped him sit up then kissed him, a soft brush of lips together. "Nice job."

"Thanks."

A loud boom reverberated through the castle. "Bring me Sam Enderson," a voice bellowed.

Sam frowned. "Who is that?"

"Can you not feel it?" Ettore said in a whisper. "That is the power of Aset Ka," Ettore said.

Sam groaned. Just what he needed, a psycho god on his case. He stood and headed to where the sound came from.

"What do you want?" Sam grumbled when Aset Ka came into view.

The god stood in the very center of the large inner hall, magic swirling around him, his face twisted in a snarl. "You think you can just take souls from my realm? My people?"

"You mean Ettore? Um, yes. You threw him out, so I get to keep him." It made perfect sense to Sam. He even gave the god a hopeful smile. Maybe Aset Ka would see the logic and not want to kill anyone, or at least maim. "Makes sense, right?"

"No!" Aset Ka shouted.

Sam rubbed his forehead. "I got rid of Kation for you which I assume was the whole point of this elaborate thing with Ettore." He waved at the castle, but he meant much more, the realm, the paranormal world, his friends.

Aset Ka stared at him, his tail twitching. "Taking souls was not our deal."

"I don't remember making a deal with you," Sam said.

The light around Aset Ka diminished a little. "The deal was with Ettore."

Sam sighed. "You sent Ettore back here with some half-assed theory of chaos, but we all know that was a cover up for pulling me into your petty god battles. I should get at least one soul as part of the deal." He didn't feel any fear; relatively invincible even though an angry god stood in front of him.

"You get nothing. I will kill you for this and drag you into my realm," Aset Ka said.

Something flared inside Sam. Aset Ka had used Sam, and Bob, he was the one who sent Ettore to them, the one who likely made Teddy call Sam back to the house in the very first place. It was all some kind of twisted plan, and to be honest, Sam was done with it all.

"How about I banish you to yours instead."

Aset Ka made a dismissive sound. "I am a powerful god; there is none more powerful now Kation is gone."

Sam held out his hand, palm out. He had confidence that swelled inside him, and he knew exactly what to say. "I, Samuel Enderson, banish Aset Ka back to his realm, back to the underworld."

"You can't do that." Aset Ka looked so confident. Then his expression changed, and he let out a terrible scream as a large ball of white light flashed from Sam's hand and slammed into him. Before the god's last scream ended, he had vanished.

"So much for him," Sam said, smiling. He felt like he should wipe his hands at the deed he'd accomplished, or be like one of those old cowboys who twirled a gun and blew the smoke after a shot. He did neither, of course. He didn't even have a gun, and his hands were buzzing with power, so he wasn't wiping them anywhere. Still, he felt good.

"What did you do?" Bob asked. "How did you do that?"

Sam shrugged; like the rest of his life, he had absolutely no idea.

"We are finally free from Aset Ka?" Teddy asked, cautiously.

"Yes. I think so."

Teddy looked concerned, and Sam knew he'd said that wrong. He had to channel that strong certain god-like type magic guy thing he had going on and convey confidence in his abilities. "I can't offer eternal life, but I think you have a second chance," he said finally.

He had no idea what would happen when they died the second time, but for now, they were together.

Teddy and Ettore embraced, and Bob was at his side. The dragons were arriving back, some weary from injury. He healed them all. The grand throne room was empty of light, but the ozone in the air reminded him of the calm after the storm.

"What now?" he asked Lambert who stood in the very place from where Aset Ka had vanished.

"The prophecy is fulfilled," he announced, rather grandly.

"Okay," Sam began. "Can someone tell me what this prophecy was, and I mean in detail."

Bob squeezed his hand. He seemed to be the only one who could touch Sam, everyone else kept a healthy distance from the random sparking power that swirled around him.

Bob cleared his throat and began. "One day the gods would fight for dominance, power, and control. The light god, Aset Ka, and the dark god, Kation."

"I still don't understand how Aset Ka was a light god," Sam murmured, then waved a hand for Bob to continue.

"There will be a man in the cloak of a human, the seventh son of the seventh son—"

"Yeah, I get that bit," Sam interrupted.

Bob looked affronted, "Do you want to hear this or not?"

Sam poked him in the chest, "Skip to the good bit."

"And a vampire from the royal line will find that man and be his guard and soul mate and that man will bring balance to the kingdom of vampires and all supernatural beings."

Sam pressed a kiss to Bob's lips. "So, you were my destiny?"

Bob smiled into the kiss and held him close. "I was."

Sam may not have liked paranormals before, he may have shied away from contact, but he'd always meant to be part of this story, alongside Bob.

"We need to rebuild the council," Lambert said and stopped right in front of Sam and Bob.

But Sam was tired, and all he wanted was to spend a short time with Bob and Mal.

"Later," he said, "I want time with my family."

Mal crossed to him and ignored the sparks of power, climbing him like a tree until he could hold her tight.

This was his family, and he was ready to start the rest of his life.

# Epilogue

## One year later

SAM HESITATED IN HIS OFFICE, RUNNING A HAND OVER THE battered desk, at the faint burn marks and scuffs from the gargoyle that used to sit on it.

But of course, the gargoyle turned out to be a cursed fae and was finally happy somewhere with his king.

Smudge jumped up on the desk and sat right in the spot he was staring at.

*Ready?*

*As I'll ever be,* Sam answered.

*She'll be here in five minutes.*

Sam nodded. Patricia was his third cousin twice removed, or something, through his adopted parents' line, not his real family that held giants, and wizards, and fae and all the other weirdness he had going on.

Patricia had been an easy sell; just out of college, she had an overwhelming need to be a private detective and had agreed to take over End Street. Whether she really wanted to do it, or whether Smudge had *encouraged* her, Sam didn't know, but she seemed nice enough on the phone.

"Did you get rid of the spiders?" he asked, recalling the mental list of things that needed doing.

"What spiders?" Bob said from behind him.

Sam spun to face Bob, and in a quick move, he was in Bob's arms. "The giant man-eating ones in the attic."

"Oh, those spiders. Yeah, they're gone, we moved them to the Vampire Castle up to the altar room."

"You moved them to the place we'll be living."

Bob smirked. "I know how much you like them."

Sam didn't know whether to believe Bob or not; sometimes his vampire was sneaky.

"What about the—"

Bob cut him off with a hard kiss, holding him tight. "I love you, Sam," he said.

Sam kissed him back. "I love you, too."

"And yes, the file room is empty, the leak in the bathroom is fixed, the attic is free of spiders, the goblin thing is cleared up—"

"Wait," Sam interrupted. "What goblin thing."

Teddy snorted a laugh from the hallway. "We weren't going to tell Sam about the goblins, Bob."

Sam pulled away from Bob and glanced around him to see Teddy, hand in Ettore's, grinning like a fool.

"What goblin thing?" he asked Ettore, who seemed to be the most sensible one there. The two of them looked good together. Teddy was wearing jeans, which seemed odd since he still preferred the fussy shirts with their layers, and his hair long.

Ettore side-eyed Teddy. "I know nothing about a goblin thing," he deadpanned, like he'd been forced to rehearse the line.

"We'll see you at the castle," Teddy said, and he and Ettore walked through the temporary vortex back to the vampire stronghold. They were key members of the new mixed paranormal council which, despite setbacks, was working well. The vortex closed behind them. Sam and Bob were physically driving the distance to Mal's school, picking her up and taking her on to her new home. It had been an entire year since Mal's kidnapping, and although she'd bounced back like nothing happened, Sam and Bob were even more protective. Not to mention her assorted Uncles.

*She's here,* Smudge said.

Sam straightened his shirt and opened the door on the knock. A slim woman stood there, a concerned look on her face.

"Hey, are you Sam?" she asked.

Sam stood to one side to let her in, and she jumped at the crackle of static between them.

"Sorry," Sam apologized, "carpets," he added, like that explained everything. He tugged his sleeve down to cover the marks on his arms. At the castle and with his friends he wore the marks proudly, but no sense in having to answer questions about where he had got tattoos that glowed.

"Hi, I'm Patricia," she said, holding out her hand to shake Sam's and then Bob's hands. Sam managed to avoid more of the crackles of power.

Smudge wound around Sam's legs, and Patricia immediately crouched to stroke the cat, managing not to fall over when Smudge jumped onto her shoulder and wrapped like a scarf around her neck. She laughed as Smudge nuzzled her.

"That's Smudge," Sam said.

"Is he yours?" Patricia asked, and smiled again as Smudge butted her cheek. "What a beautiful cat."

Sam and Smudge had already been over it. He thought Smudge would be going with him, but it turned out Smudge had another project, another person, and it was all tied to the house. *I'm staying here,* Smudge had announced, and although it made Sam sad, he tried to understand.

"No, Smudge lives here."

Patricia's smile turned into a grin. "So not only do I get this huge house and a detective agency, I get a cat too. That was some will our distant uncle drew up."

"I know," Sam said.

They chatted for a little while; she seemed happy, and at home, and Smudge purred.

"So, it's mostly human cases, right?" she asked as they were leaving.

Sam bit back his instant reply. Smudge was there, looking after her, and Sam had personally imbued the house with as much protection magic as he could.

"Mostly," he hedged.

"Good," she leaned in to whisper, "I'm not that fond of paranormals."

Sam nodded, a sudden overwhelming desire to laugh ending up in a weird half cough snort type thing.

He and Bob left the house and Sam waved at Smudge.

*Goodbye Smudge, speak to you soon, maybe? Hopefully?*

*Goodbye Samuel Enderson,* Smudge said. *Our paths will cross again.*

Patricia shut the door on them, and for a second Sam stared at it, lost as to what to do next.

Bob took his hand, kissed him, hugged him. They climbed into the car, and Sam realized he was in a daze.

"Let's go find our *new* home," Bob said, gently.

Sam took one last look at the house, hoping to hell that

there wasn't really a goblin thing going on in there, and started the engine.

"Yep," he said. "Time to start something new."

"Together," Bob said.

And all Sam could do was smile because he had the rest of his long life to start something new with the vampire he loved at his side.

"Always."

**THE END**

# Meet RJ Scott

RJ discovered romance in books at a very young age and realized that if there wasn't romance on the page, she could create it in her head. With over one hundred and fifty books published, she is a full time author of gay romance.

She lives and works out of her home in the beautiful English countryside, spends her spare time reading, watching films, and enjoying time with her family.

The last time she had a week's break from writing she didn't like it one little bit and has yet to meet a box of chocolates she couldn't defeat.

www.rjscott.co.uk | rj@rjscott.co.uk

**NEWSLETTER - rjscott.co.uk/rjnews**

instagram.com/rjscott_author
amazon.com/author/rj-scott
bookbub.com/authors/rj-scott
goodreads.com/rjscott
patreon.com/RJScott